"十三五"国家重点出版规划项目

李白诗歌全集英译

A Complete Edition of Pai Li's Poems in Chinese and English
With Annotations

赵彦春 译·注

Translated and Annotated by Yanchun Chao

第一卷

Volume Ⅰ

上海大学出版社
·上海·

图书在版编目(CIP)数据

李白诗歌全集英译/赵彦春译注.—上海：上海大学出版社,2020.10(2021.9重印)
ISBN 978-7-5671-3941-1

Ⅰ.①李… Ⅱ.①赵… Ⅲ.①唐诗—诗集—英文 Ⅳ.①I222.742

中国版本图书馆CIP数据核字(2020)第174582号

策　　划　许家骏
责任编辑　王悦生
助理编辑　陆仕超
封面设计　王兆琪
技术编辑　金　鑫　钱宇坤

李白诗歌全集英译

赵彦春　译·注

上海大学出版社出版发行
（上海市上大路99号　邮政编码200444）
（http://www.shupress.cn　发行热线 021-66135112）
出版人　戴骏豪

*

南京展望文化发展有限公司排版
江苏凤凰数码印务有限公司印刷　各地新华书店经销
开本710mm×1000mm　1/16　印张138.75　字数2271千字
2020年10月第1版　2021年9月第2次印刷
ISBN 978-7-5671-3941-1/I·603　定价　2300.00元（精装全8册）

版权所有　侵权必究
如发现本书有印装质量问题请与印刷厂质量科联系
联系电话：025-57718474

序　言

一

"千山鸟飞绝,万径人踪灭。孤舟蓑笠翁,独钓寒江雪。"这首在中国几乎家喻户晓的唐诗写的就是我的家乡——位于秀美的潇湘二水交汇处,以《永州八记》和"产异蛇"而闻名于世的永州。潇湘的两岸,四季青山绿水,常见白鹭齐飞,常闻渔舟唱晚。在这里我度过了梦幻般的童年和少年。

我们小时候学业不重,考试不多,没手机、电游可玩,甚至连电影电视也难得一见。可我并不寂寞,心灵也不空虚,因为唐朝文学家笔下的西山、愚溪、钴鉧潭、小石潭就在我的周边,唐诗就刻在河边的石壁上,有的历经数百年,有的历经千余年。我小时候读到的第一首唐诗不是在书上,而是在石壁上:"渔翁夜傍西岩宿,晓汲清湘燃楚竹。烟销日出不见人,欸乃一声山水绿。回看天际下中流,岩上无心云相逐。"这诗写的不仅是永州的山水,也是我们小时候的日常生活。我们是真正的"诗意地栖居"者。

也许是环境使然,我从小对唐诗就有亲近感,这感觉一直延续到今天。唐朝诗人群星灿烂,我最喜欢空灵不染的王维和豪迈不羁的李白。

二

李白诗才盖世,人称"诗仙"。他作诗,无意于工而无不工,"绣口一吐便是半个盛唐"。李诗风格豪迈,有驱遣风雷之势。读李白的诗,我们能明显感觉到它们的艺术冲击力。李诗个性鲜明,主观色彩强烈,想象飘逸玄妙,语言夸张雄奇,气势宏伟奔放。而且,许多诗有浓郁的中国文化色彩:道家、儒家、游侠、神仙、佛禅、神话,信手拈来,涵融万象。清代龚自珍认为,李诗并庄屈以为心,合儒仙侠以为气。如此神品,要用英语译出来,殊非易事。

赵教授迎难而上,心无旁骛,焚膏继晷,用心灵和才华将"诗仙"的整体神貌呈现给西方读者。赵译《李白诗歌全集英译》是世界上第一个李白诗歌全译本,是唐诗英译史上的一件大事。

最近半年多来,我与赵教授见面、交流较多,甚至还短时间共事,一起夜游。近距离接触,我深感赵教授是个有诗人气质和个性魅力的人。他言谈充满激情,常有玄思妙想;他在大会上演讲、主持或总结不用文稿,能出口成章,自然天成,还经常妙语连珠。2018年5月在北京召开的中国先秦史学会国学双语研究分会成立大会暨首届全国国学双语高端论坛上,赵教授的总结发言情理并茂,动人心弦。某媒体欲刊载此发言,向赵教授邀文稿。赵教授说是随性发言,没有文稿。赵之才情由此可见一斑。最近,我有幸多次聆听赵教授激情奔放的演讲。坐在下面,随着他文思起伏,我有时不禁遐想:如果放在唐代,赵教授一定是个很有魅力的大诗人。

虽然现在不是一个崇尚写诗、读诗的时代,赵教授无缘成为一个大诗人,但译诗给了他展现才华的巨大舞台。他译的《诗经》《三字经》《千字文》《弟子规》《英韵唐诗百首》《曹操诗全集》《曹植诗全集》《曹丕诗全集》等,形神俱佳,广获好评。李建波在《英韵唐诗百首(序)》中说"读赵译唐诗还真有读唐诗的感觉"。我细读此书,觉得李建波的评价并不过分。

三

收到赵教授的《李白诗歌全集英译》,我前后品读了三个多月,每次阅读都非常愉快。偶尔夜深人静时对照阅读,我似乎能感觉到赵教授的心与李白的心在同节奏律动,两人的诗情如双飞的蝴蝶随风起舞。赵译《李白诗歌全集》亮点多多,主要如下:

1. 以诗译诗,讲究诗的形式美

赵教授曾多次在演讲中强调,文学翻译,特别是诗歌翻译,形式非常重要,有时甚至比内容还重要。我深以为然。诗的形式美有多种表现,音韵和谐与诗句长短符合常规,是形式美的基本要求。赵译在以诗译诗,讲究诗的形式美方面,非常用心,非常出色。例如:

忆昔洛阳董糟丘,

为余天津桥南造酒楼。
黄金白璧买歌笑,
一醉累月轻王侯。
……

With Draffknoll in Loshine I spent each hour;
South of Kingford Bridge he built for me a wine tower.
For much gold and jade we bought songs and cheers;
For months, once drunk, we despised lords and peers.
…(Tr. Yanchun Chao)

原诗62行(篇幅所限,这里选前四行),既豪迈奔放,又含蓄深沉,情景交融,层次分明,手法多变,音韵和谐,诗句长短搭配,有很强的艺术冲击力。赵译创造性地再现了原诗几乎所有的特点,同样具有很强的艺术感染力。现在,我们重点看看赵译对形式美的传递:例中原诗1、2、4句押韵,第3句不押韵,韵式是aaba。赵译创造性地再现原韵,韵式是aabb,这符合英诗双行偶韵诗节(couplet)的韵体,如John Keats的名诗Endymion等。原诗1、3、4句每句7个字,第2句字数破格,多两个字。赵译1、3、4句每句都是10个音节,且基本是抑扬格五音步(iambic pentameter)的格律,第2句也破格,多两个音节,共12个音节。赵译对诗的形式的讲究给读者带来美的享受。

辜正坤说:"诗歌首先应该是一种精妙的语言艺术。同理,诗歌的翻译也就不得不首先表现为同类精妙的语言艺术。……何谓诗歌的语言艺术?无他,修辞造句、音韵格律一整套规矩而已。"(见辜正坤"皇家版《莎士比亚全集》翻译对策论"《翻译界》2016年第1期)。

2. 注重意象和文化的传递,注重锤词炼句

威利(Arthur Walcy)说:"意象是诗歌的灵魂"(见Arthur Waley. A Hundred and Seventy Chinese Poems. 1928: 29)。艾略特(T. S. Eliot)说:"抒情传意的唯一艺术模式,就是找到合适的'意之象'"(见T. S. Eliot. Selected Essays. 1932: 124-125)。意象是英诗的灵魂,更是汉诗的灵魂,因为"意象叠加"(juxtapositions of images)是汉诗最大的特点。Ezra Pound曾为之着迷,并提出"意象主义"(imagism)。赵教授深知意象对诗歌翻译的重要,在通过意象传神转义,营造

意境方面,反复推敲,几易其稿(赵教授数次发给我修改稿),真可谓"吟安一个字,捻断数茎须"。一千多首李白诗,每首都是如此。随举一例:

> 黄河西来决昆仑,
> 咆哮万里触龙门。
> 波滔天,尧咨嗟。
> ……

The Yellow River from Mt. Queen did pour,
Rushing down to Dragon Gate with a roar.
The sky-flushing waves Mound did loud deplore.
…(Tr. Yanchun Chao)

　　原诗 17 行,诗情纵横天地,穿越古今,意象和文化异常丰富。仅例中 3 行,便有"黄河""昆仑""龙门""(大禹治水时的)波滔天""尧"等文化意象。中国读者读到这些意象,会有珠联璧合的美感和文化感,还能感觉到诗的恢宏的气势。但如果将这些词语全部忠实地英译,原诗意象的珠联璧合便无从谈起,美感、文化感也消失殆尽。没有了这些文化意象,这首诗也就没有了灵魂。赵教授深悟此道,不仅创造性地传递了意象,还在脚注里解释了它们的文化含义。Mt. Queen, Dragon Gate, Mound 等在英语中第一次有了生命和神采。

　　再看词句推敲。赵译用 pour 译"决",用 rushing down 译"触",用 sky-flushing waves 译"波滔天",生动有力,与"黄河""昆仑""龙门"等宏大意象的气势十分吻合。这反映了赵教授锤词炼句的功夫和对诗的神韵的整体把握。以上翻译特色,我们可以从"蜀道难""梁甫吟""白头吟""古风"等意象丰富、文化浓厚的长篇名诗中进一步体会到。

　　3. 与西方汉学家的英译比,赵译最接近李白诗的神韵

　　译过《晚唐诗选》的英国著名汉学家葛瑞汉(A. C. Graham)认为,汉语文学作品,特别是古诗,不能让中国人英译,因为英语不是他们的母语("... we can hardly leave translation to the Chinese, since there are few exceptions to the rule that translation is done into, not out of, one's own language.")。在一定程度上,葛瑞汉是对的。但他似乎忽略了一点,汉语是意合语言(paratactic language),缺乏西方的语言形态,再加上不同的文化渊源,西方汉

学家常难领会其妙。汉语古诗更是如此。就李白诗英译而言,仔细对比赵译和西方汉学家的译文,我们发现李白诗的神韵在赵译中体现最好,而在汉学家们的翻译中常遭损害。例如:

访戴天山道士不遇

犬吠水声中,桃花带雨浓。
树深时见鹿,溪午不闻钟。
野竹分青霭,飞泉挂碧峰。
无人知所去,愁倚两三松。

全诗纯用白描,诗句平易自然,写景叙事,一目了然。可仔细品味,发现"水声""桃花""树深时见鹿""钟""青霭""飞泉""碧峰"等意象组合,围绕突访戴天山道士不遇这一主题,给全诗蒙上了浓浓的道教神韵,特别是最后两句"无人知所去,愁倚两三松",更是飘逸脱俗,透着仙风道气。如果全诗的神韵如此,那么,英译时该如何保持呢? 请比对原文和下面的译文:

译文1:
Where the dogs bark by roaring waters,
Whose spray darkens the petals' colors?
Deep in the woods deer at times are seen;
The valley noon: one can hear no bell,
But wild bamboos cut across bright clouds,
Flying cascades hang from jasper peaks;
No one here knows which way you have gone:
Two, now three pines I have leant against!
(Tr. Arthur Cooper)

译文2:
I hear the distant baying of the hound
Amid the waters murmuring around;
I see the peach-flowers bearing crystal rain,

The sportive deer around the forest fane.
The waving tops of bamboo groves aspire
In fleeting change the summer clouds to tire,
While from the emerald peaks of many hills
The sparking cascades fall in fairy rills.
Beneath the pines within this shady dell,
I list in vain to hear the noontide bell;
The temple's empty, and the priest has gone,
and I am left to mourn my grief alone.
(Tr. Charles Budd)

译文 3:

I hear the barking of the dogs amidst the water's sound.
The recent rain has washed each stain from all the peach bloom round.
At times amid the thickest copse a timid deer is seen.
And to the breeze in sparkling seas the bamboos roll in green.
From yonder verdant peak depends the sheeted waterfall.
At noon's full prime I hear no chime of bells from arboured hall.
Whither the wandering priest has gone is no one here can tell.
Against a pine I sad recline, and let my heart o'erswell.
(Tr. W. J. B. Fletcher)

译文 4:

A DOG,
A dog barking.
And the sound of rushing water
How dark and rich the peach-flowers after the rain.
Every now and then, between the trees, I see deer.
Twelve o'clock, but I hear no bell in the ravine.
Wild bamboos slit the blue-green of a cloudy sky.
The waterfall hangs against the jade-green peak.

There is no one to tell me where he has gone.
I lean against the pine-trees grieving.
（Tr. Amy Lowell）

译文 5：

The water mirrors a dog's bay;
The peach blossoms carry thick dew.
In the deep woods, deer pass or stay;
The stream at noon hears no toll due.
The wild bamboo divides the brume;
The waterfalls down the peak fly.
No one knows where he's gone to roam;
Against two or three pines I sigh.
（Tr. Yanchun Chao）

译文 1 较好地传递了主要意象，但细节上问题不少：用 roaring water 译"水声"，显得太吵；用 spray 译"雨"，意象不对；用 darken 译"浓"，色调不对；用 bright clouds 译"青霭"，色调、意象都不对。这些细节妨碍了原诗神韵的传递。

译文 2 颇有英语诗味，但增加了不少内容，渲染过多，与原诗的白描风格相去甚远。而且，译文多处用第一人称 I，显得主体介入太多，背离了汉诗意合、意会的特点。我们知道，人称对中文古诗英译，牵一发而动全身，在整体上影响译文的格局和意境。余光中说，中文古诗，"由于不拘人称且省略主词，任何读者都恍然有置身其间、躬逢其事之感"（见余光中. 望乡的牧神. 台北：纯文学出版社，1986：223）。此译多处用 I，有损原诗神韵。另外，我们发现 hound（猎狗）一词似有不妥，与戴道士居处（道观）的环境不太协调；sportive deer 与原句中"鹿"的道教意蕴也不太吻合，从上下文考虑，原句中的"鹿"应该是"白鹿"。我们知道，在中国文化里，白鹿常与仙人、道士、隐士等联系在一起。事实上，李白非常喜欢用"白鹿"这个意象来映衬仙人、道士、隐士、高士的风采，如"且放白鹿青崖间""清晓骑白鹿""身骑白鹿行飘飘""韩众骑白鹿""借予一白鹿""拜迎白鹿前""彤襟双白鹿"等。考虑到原诗的道教色彩，"树深时见鹿"中的"鹿"译为 white deer 也未尝不可。当然，译为 deer 也是好的。本例译成 sportive deer,译文 3 译为 timid deer,均属没有领会原诗的文化色彩和神韵。还有,用 mourn my grief 译"愁",语气过重,与原诗意境不符。

译文 3 也是多处用 I,主体介入多。而且,The recent rain has washed each stain from all the peach bloom round 与"桃花带雨浓"的意象、美感相差太大;"野竹分青霭"变成了"竹子绿浪滚滚"(the bamboos roll in green),"青霭"意象不见了。我们知道,在古诗中,"青霭"这个意象常被用来衬托神仙、道士、隐士的神秘、飘逸,如,李白诗句"云窗拂青霭""素手掬青霭,罗衣曳紫烟"等。丢了"青霭"这个意象,等于损了原诗的道教色彩和神韵。另外,用 recline 译"倚",意象不对,显得慵懒、散漫,缺乏原词的文化内涵和神采。在汉语古诗里,"倚栏""倚阑干""倚楼""倚松"等"倚"的意象常被用来衬托思考、思念等行为,如,"闻君亦多感,何处倚栏杆""沉香亭北倚阑干""明月高楼休独倚,酒入愁肠,化作相思泪""秋山春雨闲吟处,倚遍江南寺寺楼"等。recline 与"倚"相去甚远。

译文 4 简洁明了,与原诗白描风格相契合。但 dark 色调不对;"青霭"变成了"有云的青天"(the blue-green of a cloudy sky),有损原句的道教色彩。A DOG, / A dog barking 排成两行,第一个 DOG 大写,让"犬"和"犬吠"的意象特别醒目,这似乎与原诗的意境不太协调。

译文 5(赵译)最简洁精炼(读起来有点像唐诗),白描风格最明显,对原诗理解最到位,传递文化意象前后协调,最具原诗风采和神韵。具体点说,不使用 I,保持原诗意会特点;注意传递原诗的道教色彩;音韵和谐,韵式 abab cded,且每行 8 个音节。锤词炼句也可圈可点,例如,第一句 The water mirrors a dog's bay,用动词 mirror 连接"犬吠"和"水声",句子很有张力,给读者留下很多想象空间。第四句 The stream at noon hears no toll due,唐诗般干净利落,用 stream 作主语,景物有了灵性,意象灵动起来,诗句有了神韵。

南宋诗论家严羽说:"诗而入神至矣"(诗写出了神韵就是最高境界)。译诗何尝不是如此!诗译出了神韵也是最高境界。

4. 赵译的可读性和可接受性也很高

为了解上述五个译文的可读性和可接受性,我删去译者的姓名,向澳门理工学院的 7 位美国同事进行问卷调查。这 7 位同事是 Levi、Chloe、Mark、Emma、Clancy、Kelvin、Esther。问卷调查信的主要内容如下:

Please read the following 5 translations of a poem written by Li Bai (A.D. 701 - A.D. 762, the greatest poet in Chinese history) and give marks to each of them according to READABILITY (i.e. understandability, fluency, etc. Full Mark: 10 points) and ACCEPTABILITY (i.e. acceptable culturally, linguistically, etc. Full Mark: 10 points). And I'll be more grateful to you if I could have your comments on them or on either one of them. Thank you!

"可读性"和"可接受性"的调查结果的平均分(近似值)分别是:译文1: 5+5,译文2:8+9,译文3:7+6,译文4:5+6,译文5:8+8。值得补充的是,Mark老师懂一点中文,他大学时曾修读过英语诗歌,他的评论如下:

Version 1: it has some grammar issues (line 4) and lacks the emotional response to the "you" that has left.

Version 2: I like this version because it maintains a Western rhyme and rhythm poetic structure without losing meaning. It makes direct reference to the priest and temples that are lost in other versions. The language here is archaic and old but could be considered a stylistic choice by the translator due to the age of this poem.

Version 3: This version attempts to the same as version 2 with mixed results. Usage of "copse", "arboured hall", "I sad recline", and "heart o'erswell" are confusing.

Version 4: This version has lost the formal rhyme in the Chinese version in an attempt to keep meaning. There is a confusion to the emotional response (grief, sigh) with the imagery. This is because unlike other versions, there is no reference to "he" or the location as having religious significance.

Version 5: I also like this version because it has the brevity and flavor in the Chinese version.

从问卷调查的分值和Mark老师的评点可以看出,赵译的可读性和可接受性均很高。

四

李白诗歌英译有200多年的历史。很多著名汉学家都译过李白的诗,如,翟理斯（Herbert. A. Giles）在《古文选珍》（Gems of Chinese Literature）一书中选译李白诗 22 首，庞德（Ezra Pound）在《华夏集》（Cathay）中择其 13 首，库柏（Arthur Cooper）在《李白和杜甫诗选译》（Li Po and Tu Fu）中译 25 首，宇文所安（Stephen Owen）在《盛唐诗》（The Great Age of Chinese Poetry：The High T'ang）中译 32 首。第一个独立成册的李白诗歌英译本是小畑薰良（Shigeyoshi Obata）于 1922 年出版的《李白诗集》（The Works of Li Po, the Chinese Poet），小畑薰良选译了 124 首。第二个独立成册的英译本是艾黎（Rewi Alley）于 1981 年出版的《李白诗选 200 首》。赵译《李白诗歌全集》是第一个全译本，它在李白诗歌翻译史上具有划时代的意义。

五

余东说，品诗要有"三心二意"，所谓"三心"者，一曰诗心，二曰匠心，三曰童心；所谓"二意"者，一为意境，二为意味（见余东《中外诗人共灵犀》序）。我们说，译诗，特别是译李白的诗，除了这"三心二意"，还要有"三性二义"。所谓"三性"，一是悟性，译者能悟出原诗的意境和神韵；二是天性，译者有诗人的潜质和性情；三是痴性，译者能痴迷于此，能抗拒外在诱惑。所谓"二义"，一是义不容辞的责任感，《李白诗歌全集》此前尚无全译本，将"诗仙"全貌呈现给西方读者，既是光荣的使命，也是堪载翻译史册的大事；二是义无反顾、献身于翻译和文化传播事业的奉献精神。

仔细品读赵译《李白诗歌全集》，我们能读出赵教授的"三心二意"，也能感受到他的"三性二义"。赞诗曰：

语言不同神采同，追慕诗仙变诗翁。意走险峰见海日，笔驱风雷似真龙。
迷花倚石疑无路，破雾穿云响飞鸿。西人有幸窥仙貌，译坛无人与争雄。

蒋骁华

2019 年 12 月 26 日

于澳门理工学院致远楼

Introduction

"From hill to hill no bird in flight, /From path to path no man in sight. /A lonely fisherman afloat, /Is fishing snow in lonely boat." What this famous poem "River Snow" by Chungyüan Liu of the T'ang dynasty describes is my hometown, Yungchow, which is located at the junction of two beautiful rivers, the Hsiao River and the Hsiang River. In this God-kissed area, hills and waters are green and fresh all the year round; white egrets are often seen to fly along the rivers. And fishermen are often heard to sing some folk songs. Many famous poems of the T'ang dynasty are carved on the wall-like cliffs along the rivers, some of which have gone through hundreds of years. The first T'ang poem I read when I was a child was not in a book, but on a cliff: "By West Cliff a fisherman anchored for the night. /At dawn he boiled water with a bamboo fire. /When the sun rose he and the mist were out of sight. /A folk song came from waters green and hills higher. /Far down the river he looked back at the skyline. /Over the cliffs leisurely roamed the white clouds fine." What this poem depicts is not only a fisherman's life in the T'ang dynasty, but also part of the daily life that I was very familiar with when I was a child. It seems that the local people and I were "poetic dwellers". Perhaps because of the influence of my childhood environment, I've had a close feeling to T'ang poetry. And among the T'ang poet stars I like Pai Li most.

1. Pai Li's poetry and Chao's talents

In China Pai Li (A.D. 701 – A.D. 762) is known as *shixian* (a celestial poet, or a poet with God-given talent, or the Chinese Muse). He is so outstanding in poetry writing that there is no match for him among the T'ang poets. When reading Pai Li's poems, we can clearly feel their artistic impacts. Li's poems are characterized by his distinct personality, strong subjective colors, elegant and mysterious imaginations, exaggerative and magnificent language style. Moreover, many of his poems are full of Chinese cultural elements from Wordism, Buddhism, Confucianism, Immortals and so on. It is definitely no easy job to translate poems of this kind into English.

Professor Chao has overcome all the difficulties and translated Li's poems with his heart and talent. Chao's translation is the first complete English version of Li's poetry in the world, which is a great milestone event in the history of T'ang poetry translation.

Over the past six months, I was lucky enough to have several chances to listen to Professor Chao's passionate and thought-provoking lectures and speeches, and exchange ideas with him. Close contacts made me feel that Professor Chao is a charismatic scholar and translator with poet temperament. Sometimes I can't help but imagine: Chao would be a very successful poet if it were the T'ang Dynasty now.

Chao doesn't become a great poet, but a very successful poetry translator. His translations of Chinese classic poetry like *Book of Songs in English Rhyme*, *Three-word Primer in English Rhyme*, *One Thousand Words in English Rhyme*, *Tang Poems in English Rhyme*, *Song Lyrics in English Rhyme*, *Canons for Disciples in English Rhyme*, *Cao Cao's Poems*, *Cao Zhi's Poems*, *Cao Pi's Poems*, and so on, are so successful that they have won the hearts of hundreds and thousands of readers. Professor Chienpo Li says in his "preface" to Chao's *Tang Poems in English Rhyme* (2019), "reading Chao's translation gave me a feel that I was reading the original beautiful T'ang poems". After a close reading of the book, I agree with Professor Li's evaluation.

2. The characteristics of Chao's translation of Pai Li's poems

After receiving Professor Chao's manuscript of English translation of

Pai Li's poems, I read it off and on for more than three months. And it was an enjoyment to me every time I read it. Occasionally in the dead of the night, I could "see" the translator and the poet dancing harmoniously on the poetic beats; every now and then I could feel resonances between their poetic sentiments. Many strong merits can be found in Chao's translation, and they can be boiled down as follows:

2.1 Poem for poem and highlight on the beautifulness of poetic form

In his speeches, Professor Chao stressed several times that, in literary translation, especially poetry translation, the form is very important, sometimes even more important than the content. I can't agree more with him. There are many types of beautifulness in poetic forms. The harmony of rhymes and meters are the basic requirements for poetic form beautifulness. Chao did a great job in this aspect. For example:

忆昔洛阳董糟丘,
为余天津桥南造酒楼。
黄金白璧买歌笑,
一醉累月轻王侯。
……

With Draffknoll in Loshine I spent each hour;
South of Kingford Bridge he built for me a wine tower.
For much gold and jade we bought songs and cheers;
For months, once drunk, we despised lords and peers.
… (Tr. Yanchun Chao)

The original poem has 62 lines (because of the space limitation, only the first four lines are copied here). This poem conjures up a picture of bold and unrestrained images, it reflects to a certain extent Pai Li's distinct and unworldly personality. It is exaggerative and imaginative in style, but implicit and profound in meaning. The lines are well-organized, varied in techniques, harmonious in rhyme, and have a strong artistic impact on the reader. Chao's translation creatively reproduces almost all the characteristics of the original poem, and also has a strong artistic appeal. Now, let's focus on the transmission of the original poetic form beautifulness in Chao's Translation. The original first, second and fourth line are in the same rhyme, the third line is not. The rhyme pattern is aaba. Chao's translation is dynamically equivalent in rhyme with a pattern of aabb, which is in line with the rhyme style of "couplet" in English poetry, such as John Keats's famous poem "Endymion" and so on. In the original poem, line 1, 3 and 4 have the same length in "syllables" (or Chinese characters) while line 2 is unconventional with two more "syllables" (or characters). In Chao's translation, line 1, 3 and 4 also have the length in syllables, and line 2 is also unconventional with two more syllables. Chao's emphasis on poetic form beautifulness brings artistic enjoyment to the readers.

Chengk'un Ku, a famous scholar and poetry translator says in his essay "Translation strategies for *the Royal Edition of Complete Works of Shakespeare*" (2016), "first of all, a poem is an exquisite art of language. In the same way, the translation of poetry has to be an exquisite language art of the same kind. What is the language art of poetry? It's nothing but a whole set of rules for rhetoric, sentence making and rhyme and rhythm".

2.2 Highlighting the transmission of images and cultural elements

Arthur Waley says, "Images are the soul of poetry". According to T. S. Eliot, the only artistic mode of lyricism is to find the appropriate "image of meaning". Images are not only the soul of English poetry, but also the soul of Chinese poetry, because "juxtapositions of images" is the most striking feature of classic Chinese poetry. Ezra Pound was fascinated by this feature, and was enlightened to put forward the poetic theory of "imagism". Professor Chao is well aware of the importance of images in poetry translation. To create an appropriate poetic atmosphere with images, he revised his translation time and again before he sent it to me. He translated over 1,000 Li's poems with "image of meaning" in his heart. Here is a case in point:

<blockquote>
黄河西来决昆仑,
咆哮万里触龙门。
波滔天,尧咨嗟。
……
</blockquote>

<blockquote>
The Yellow River from Mt. Queen did pour,
Rushing down to Dragon Gate with a roar.
The sky-flushing waves Mound did loud deplore.
… (Tr. Yanchun Chao)
</blockquote>

The original poem consists of 17 lines. Here are the first three. The poet's brilliant imaginations fly over the worldly temporal and spatial restrictions, run through the ancient and "modern" times. Only in the above three lines can we find many cultural images, such as "*Huanghe* (the Yellow River)", "*Kunlun* (Mt. Queen)", "*Longmen* (Dragon Gate)", "*Yao* (King Mound)" and so on. When Chinese readers read these cultural images, they can get a sense of poetic beautifulness and feel the magnificence of the imaginations. However, if all these cultural terms (or images) are transliterated, there will be no combinations of images and senses in the translation, and the aesthetic feeling and cultural sense will disappear. Without these cultural images, the poem will definitely lose its soul. Chao's translation is a good combination of cultural images and poetic sentiments. To offer a reader-friendly version, Chao explains their cultural meanings in footnotes. It's worth pointing out that, because of Chao's efforts, Mt. Queen, Dragon Gate, King Mound, etc. have gained life and spirit in English.

Let's look at how the words and lines are weighed. Chao selects "pour" to translate "决", "rushing down to" to "触", and "sky-flushing waves" to "波滔天", which are vivid, powerful, and very consistent with the artistic momentum of such grand images as "the Yellow River", "Mt. Queen", "Dragon Gate". This reflects Chao's efforts in refining sentences and his overall grasp of the verve of the poem. The above translation features can be further proved in other image-and-culture-rich long poems like "The Shu Way Is Hard"(蜀道难), "Ode to Father Liang"(梁甫吟), "Ode to Gray Hair"(白头吟), "Old Airs" (古风)and so on.

2.3 Compared with Western Sinologists' translations, Chao's version is the closest to the original poetic verve and spirit

A.C. Graham, a famous British Sinologist, says in his "introduction" to his *Selected Poems of the Late Tang Dynasty*（1965）, "… we can hardly leave translation to the Chinese, since there are few exceptions to the rule that translation is done into, not out of, one's own language". To some extent, Graham is right. However, he seems to have overlooked one point that, different from western hypotactic language, Chinese is a kind of paratactic language with a different cultural origin, whose poetic beautifulness is sometimes really difficult for Western Sinologists to understand. It is especially true for Pai Li's poems. As far as the English translations of Pai Li's poems are concerned, we find that the verve and spirit of Pai Li's poems are best reflected in Chao's translation, but often bruised or spoiled in Sinologists' translations. Let's look at the following example：

访戴天山道士不遇

犬吠水声中，桃花带雨浓。
树深时见鹿，溪午不闻钟。
野竹分青霭，飞泉挂碧峰。
无人知所去，愁倚两三松。

In this poem, a writing technique called *Baimiao* (a straightforward and laconic Chinese writing style) is utilized. The whole poem seems to be simple and clear, but actually the description and narrative are culture-laden and suggestive. A combination of images such as "sound of water", "peach blossom", "deer at the depth of the tree", "fane bell", "green mist", "flying spring" and "jasper peaks", *etc.* is used to serve as a foil to create a mysterious and religious atmosphere for the scene where "Wordist priest Tienshan Tai is not met" (the title of the poem). The poem is endowed with a strong Wordist charm, especially the last two lines "No one knows where he's gone to roam, / Against two or three pines I sigh." give us a feel of supernatural and Wordistic air. If the charm of the poem is Wordistic, how to keep it in translation is a challenge. Let's compare the original poem with different English translations:

> TT1:
> Where the dogs bark by roaring waters,
> Whose spray darkens the petals' colors?
> Deep in the woods deer at times are seen;
> The valley noon; one can hear no bell,
> But wild bamboos cut across bright clouds,
> Flying cascades hang from jasper peaks;
> No one here knows which way you have gone:
> Two, now three pines I have leant against!
> (Tr. Arthur Cooper)
>
> TT2:
> I hear the distant baying of the hound
> Amid the waters murmuring around;
> I see the peach-flowers bearing crystal rain,
> The sportive deer around the forest fane.
> The waving tops of bamboo groves aspire
> In fleeting change the summer clouds to tire,

While from the emerald peaks of many hills
The sparking cascades fall in fairy rills.
Beneath the pines within this shady dell,
I list in vain to hear the noontide bell;
The temple's empty, and the priest has gone,
and I am left to mourn my grief alone.
(Tr. Charles Budd)

TT3:
I hear the barking of the dogs amidst the water's sound.
The recent rain has washed each stain from all the peach bloom round.
At times amid the thickest copse a timid deer is seen.
And to the breeze in sparkling seas the bamboos roll in green.
From yonder verdant peak depends the sheeted waterfall.
At noon's full prime I hear no chime of bells from arboured hall.
Whither the wandering priest has gone is no one here can tell.
Against a pine I sad recline, and let my heart o'erswell.
(Tr. W. J. B. Fletcher)

TT4:
A DOG,
A dog barking.
And the sound of rushing water.
How dark and rich the peach-flowers after the rain.
Every now and then, between the trees, I see deer.
Twelve o'clock, but I hear no bell in the ravine.
Wild bamboos slit the blue-green of a cloudy sky.
The waterfall hangs against the jade-green peak.
There is no one to tell me where he has gone.
I lean against the pine-trees grieving.
(Tr. Amy Lowell)

TT5:

The water mirrors a dog's bay;
The peach blossoms carry thick dew.
In the deep woods, deer pass or stay;
The stream at noon hears no toll due.
The wild bamboo divides the brume;
The waterfalls down the peak fly.
No one knows where he's gone to roam;
Against two or three pines I sigh.
(Tr. Yanchun Chao)

The first translation conveys the main images in general, but there are some problems in the details: it is too noisy to translate "水声" into "roaring water"; the image is wrong when "雨" is translated into "spray"; the color or hue is not correct when "浓" is rendered as "darken"; both the image and the color are misleading when "青霭" is translated into "bright clouds". These details hinder the transmission of the Wordistic and supernatural atmosphere of the original poem.

The second translation is quite flavorsome and full of English poetic sentiments, but it adds too many details and exaggerates too much, which is a far cry from the original *Baimiao* style. Moreover, so many subjects ("I") are used in the translation that it deviates from the original paratactic and suggestive characteristic. This characteristic is also a general feature of classic Chinese poetry. As we all know, a change of subject may greatly affect the associative meanings and poetic sentiments of a poem. Kuangchung Yü, a famous Chinese poet and translator, says in his book *Nostalgia* (望乡的牧神, 1986), "because the subjects are often omitted, classic Chinese poems give readers a feel of 'personal experience on the scene' when they are being read by Chinese readers". There are many subjects ("I") in this translation, which is harmful to the charm of the original poem. In addition, we find that the word "hound" is not a good choice as it is not in harmony with the environment of the temple where Wordist Tai lived; and it is inappropriate to translate "鹿" into "sportive deer". In terms of the context, the "deer" in the original should be "White Deer". Why? As we know, in Chinese culture, white deer is often associated with Immortals, Wordists and hermits. As a matter of fact, Pai Li likes to use the image of "White Deer" to set off the elegant demeanor of Immortals, Wordists, hermits and scholars with lofty ideas. Here are some examples from Pai Li's poems: "I just leave my white deer on the cliff now" (且放白鹿青崖间), "The morn sees me a white deer ride" ("清晓骑白鹿"), "Wearing it, riding a white deer, I'll go miles" ("身骑白鹿行飘飖"), "Mister Han, a white deer you ride" ("韩众骑白鹿"), "He lent me a deer purely white" ("借予一白鹿"), "And bow down before your white deer" ("拜迎白鹿前") and "Two white deer draw a red dray" ("彤襟双白鹿"). According to the Wordist atmosphere of the original poem, it's better to translate "鹿" into "White Deer". Of course, "deer" is an acceptable choice. If this analysis makes sense, "sportive deer" in this translation and "timid deer" in the third translation are inappropriate. Moreover, the choice "sorrow" for "愁" is a little too heavy in mood and does not well fit the artistic sentiments of the original.

The third translation has the same problem of using many subjects ("I"). In addition, the translation "The recent rain has washed each stain from all the peach bloom round" is much lower than the original "桃花带雨浓" in image beautifulness and aesthetic feeling. And when "野竹分青霭" is rendered into "the bamboos roll in green", the Wordism-related image "青霭" ("bluish brume" or "bluish haze") is lost. As we know, in classic Chinese poems, the image of "青霭" ("bluish haze") is often used to serve as a foil for the mysteriousness and elegance of Immortals, Wordists and hermits. In Pai Li's poems, "青霭" is also used in this way, for instance, "云窗拂青霭" ("To their cloud windows bluish haze did fall"), "素手掬青霭，罗衣曳紫烟" ("Your fair palms hold up bluish haze, Your silk robe tugs at purple rays."), and so on. The loss of the image "bluish haze" is, to a great extent, tantamount to spoiling the Wordist atmosphere and verve of the original poem.

In addition, the original "倚" poses a much more cultural and positive image than the translation "recline" that lacks the cultural associations and charm of the original. Here is why. In classic Chinese poems, images related to "倚" (literally "lean on something") like "倚阑干" ("lean on a balustrade"), "倚楼" ("leaning on a pillar of a building"), "倚松" ("leaning on a pine tree") etc. are often used to set off the demeanor of meditation, nostalgia or missing someone. For instance, "Hearing you are missing me, I wonder where you lean on a balustrade" ("闻君亦多感,何处倚栏杆"), "In Balm Pavilion they lean on the rail at ease" ("沉香亭北倚阑干"), "Don't lean alone on rails when the bright moon appears. Wine in sad bowels would turn to nostalgic tears" ("明月高楼休独倚,酒入愁肠,化作相思泪"), "Crooning poems in spring rain or an autumn mountain, I lean on pillars of all temples in the south of the Yangtze River" ("秋山春雨闲吟处,倚遍江南寺寺楼"), and so on and so forth. From the above examples we can see that "倚" in classic Chinese poems is culturally and poetically different from "recline".

The fourth translation is concise and clear, which is consistent with the *Baimiao* style of the original poem. But the word "dark" is not the right hue for "the peach-flowers after the rain"; The Wordistic image "青霭" ("bluish haze") becomes "the blue-green of a cloud sky", which seems to be inconsistent with the original Wordistic atmosphere. Besides, "A DOG,/A dog barking" are arranged in two lines with the first "DOG" capitalized, which makes the images of "dog" and "dog barking" particularly eye-catching. This seems to be inappropriate to the artistic sentiments of the original poem.

Chao's translation, the fifth one, is so laconic, refined and rhymed that it sounds like a T'ang poem. Chao's version outperforms most of its rivals in many aspects. To be specific, the original *Baimiao* style is well kept; the cultural and religious images are transmitted in harmony; no "I" is used to keep the original feel of "on the scene"; the rhymes "ababcded" is harmonious, with 8 syllables in each line. What's more, his word choices are also noteworthy. For example, in the first line "the water mirrors a dog's bay", verb "mirror" is used to connect "犬吠" (a dog's bay) and "水声" (the water sounds). Here "mirror" has a good artistic tension and gives readers a wider space for imagination. In the fourth line "The stream at noon hears no toll due", "stream" is used as the subject, which revitalizes the scenery, vivifies the images concerned, and strengthens the poetic verve.

Yü Yan (严羽), a literary critic in the Southern Sung Dynasty, says, "The best poem is the one with the best poetic verve and spirit", which is also true in the case of poetry translation. If a translated poem boasts of the best poetic verve and spirit, it is the best.

3. Readability and acceptability of Chao's translation

In order to compare the readability and acceptability of the above five translations, I deleted the translators' names and conducted a questionnaire survey with seven of my American colleagues in Macao Polytechnic Institute. They are Levi, Chloe, Mark, Emma, Clancy, Kelvin and Esther. The questionnaire and responses are as follows:

Please read the following 5 translations of a poem written by Pai Li (A.D. 701-A.D. 762, the greatest poet in Chinese history) and give marks to each of them according to READABILITY (i.e. understandability, fluency, etc. Full Mark: 10 points) and ACCEPTABILITY (i.e. acceptable culturally, linguistically, etc. Full Mark: 10 points). And I'll be more grateful to you if I could have your comments on them or on either one of them. Thank you!

The scores for "readability" and "acceptability" are as follows: the first translation: 5 + 5, the second translation: 8 + 9, the third translation: 7 + 6, the fourth translation: 5 + 6, the fifth translation:

8 + 8. Besides, it's worth mentioning that my colleague Mr. Mark can speak survival Chinese and majored in English poetry when he was a college student. His comments are as follows:

Version 1: It has some grammar issues (line 4) and lacks the emotional response to the "you" that has left.

Version 2: I like this version because it maintains a Western rhyme and rhythm poetic structure without losing meaning. It makes direct reference to the priest and temples that are lost in other versions. The language here is archaic and old but could be considered a stylistic choice by the translator due to the age of this poem.

Version 3: This version attempts to the same as version 2 with mixed results. Usage of "copse", "arboured hall", "I sad recline", and "heart o'erswell" are confusing.

Version 4: This version has lost the formal rhyme in the Chinese version in an attempt to keep meaning. There is a confusion to the emotional response (grief, sigh) with the imagery. This is because unlike other versions, there is no reference to "he" or the location as having religious significance.

Version 5: I also like this version because it has the brevity and flavor in the Chinese version.

As the above scores and Mr. Mark's comments demonstrate, Chao's version is praiseworthy both in readability and acceptability.

4. Significance of Chao's translation

The English translation of Pai Li's poetry has a history of more than 200 years. Many famous Sinologists have made important contributions in this field. For example, Herbert. A. Giles translated 22 of Pai Li's poems in his *Gems of Chinese Literature* (1923), Ezra Pound translated 13 in his *Cathay* (1965), Arthur Cooper translated 25 in his *Li Po and Tu Fu* (1973), and Stephen Owen translated 32 in his *The Great Age of Chinese*

Poetry: The High T'ang (2013).

The first exclusive English translation of Pai Li's poems is Shigeyoshi Obata's *The Works of Li Po, the Chinese Poet* (1922), in which he translated 124 of Pai Li's poems; the second exclusive English translation is Rewi Alley's *200 Li Bai's Poems Selected* (1981). Professor Chao's translation *A Complete Edition of Pai Li's Poems in Chinese and English* is special as it is the first complete English version of Li's poems, which is an epoch-making milestone in the history of Pai Li's poetry translation.

5. Concluding remarks

Tung Yü, a famous scholar of translation studies, says in his "preface" to Paohung Chang's *Poetic Minds Think Alike* （中外诗人共灵犀，2012） that, in appreciating poems, a person should have "three hearts and two minds": The "three hearts" are a poet's heart, a craftsman's heart and a child's heart; the "two minds" are a scholar's mind and an artist's mind. We believe that, in translating poems, especially the poems of Chinese Muse Pai Li, besides the "three hearts and two minds", a translator should have "three 'i's and two senses": the "three 'i's" are a) insight (a philosopher's insight into the deep and implied meaning of a poem), b) instinct (a poet's artistic instinct), and c) infatuation (a lover's infatuation with his or her love); the "two senses" are a) a sense of obligation, that is, feeling it is a matter of obligation to present to the world a complete English version of Pai Li's poems since there hasn't been such a version so far, and b) a sense of dedication, i.e. having a strong sense of dedication to the cause of translation and cultural dissemination.

If we have a close reading of Professor Chao's *A Complete Edition of Pai Li's Poems in Chinese and English* With Annotations, we can detect his "three hearts and two minds" and feel his "three 'i's and two senses". Here is my poem to serve as a summary:

The charm is one though the languages are two;
Chanting the muse, he becomes a muse true.
His spirit soars o'ver the peaks and the brine;
His pen drives thunders like Dragon benign.
In dazzling flowers and rocks is a dead lane;
The swans sing up, piercing the sky amain.
Westerners can see Chinese Muse so fair;
Which translator can challenge him, who dare?

Hsiaohua Chiang
December 26, 2019
Macao Polytechnic Institute

译者自序

问你：哪个朝代的诗歌最伟大？你可能毫不犹豫：唐朝。要问你谁是唐朝最伟大的诗人，你可能不好回答，因为有好几位难以取舍。如果不选冠亚军而推举几位出类拔萃者便容易得多。王维、李白、杜甫、白居易无疑是最优秀的，他们造就了唐诗的高峰。

这一高峰地球人应该有足够的认识，然而翻译绝非易事，而且误区颇多。最核心的是"道"的缺失。

"形而上者谓之道，形而下者谓之器。"这是《易经》对人类一切知识体系的高度而精准的概括，是人类知识的坐标系，是人类智慧的坐标系。然而，西方启蒙时代打开了思想的"潘多拉魔盒"，将"道"瓦解于无形——诚如《论语》所言："天下之无道也久矣。"在西方学术出现了多次转向之后，中华传统文化的复兴已然发生——集结号已经吹响，"道"的光辉已出现于东方的地平线上。

人类思想的大变革、大繁荣大多肇始于翻译——比如东方的佛经翻译、西方的《圣经》翻译，以及近代以来的西学东渐所带动的种种翻译。中华经典外译始于明朝末年，译者多是西方汉学家、外交家和教会人士。清朝末年以后出现了一些华人译者。

但我们遗憾地发现，诗性的中国经典和诗本身的神采在很大程度上被遮蔽了，正应了罗伯特·弗罗斯特那句话：诗就是翻译中丢掉的东西。

在诸多类别的翻译实践中，文学翻译是最复杂、最难以应对的一种类型，而诗歌翻译又是文学翻译中最值得关注的对象。

人是诗性的存在；诗是人类的家园；诗是人类的表征。作诗与译诗都是以诗来表征我们自身，来表征我们的世界。诗的文学特性在于以有形的文字铺排映现无形的灵魂的跃动，"有形"表现为诗的文字载体或织体特征以及押韵、节奏构成的格律，"无形"即意外之意。诗应和着宇宙的递归性，可表现为符号之符号，它表达意义，又表达意义之意义，言有尽而意无穷。

中国是诗的国度。历史的遗存可以追溯到黄帝时代的《弹歌》。《弹歌》是二字格，是四言体的先驱。四言体古诗在公元前六世纪盛行，随之骚体诗、五言体古诗、七言体古诗和杂言古诗等相继成型；进入唐朝，中华民族迎来了诗歌大繁荣，出现五言律体诗、七言律体诗和六言律体诗。

唐朝（公元618—907年）是盛世中的盛世，文学艺术在唐朝达到鼎盛，尤其是在诗歌方面达到了中国文学的巅峰。关于唐朝有多少诗人以及他们写了多少首诗，今人已无法统计，清朝编纂的《全唐诗》共收录四万九千四百零三首，所涉作者共有二千八百七十三人。仅从这些遗存，我们也可以看到唐代文人以体量巨大的诗歌记录了文人风骨和浩荡的盛唐气象。王维、李白、杜甫、白居易无疑是唐朝灿如明珠的诗人中最为耀眼的四人。闲逸如"诗佛"王维，寄情山水，禅意尽见于遣词造句中。浪漫如"诗仙"李白，才情恣意挥洒于诗行间；深刻、沉郁如现实主义诗人杜甫，忧国忧民之思倾注在一字一句中；真诚、清醒如白居易，所思所感皆可见于诗行。四人所作唐诗传世甚多，各领风骚，向后人展示了大唐气象和时代特征。这四位诗人能够代表中国诗歌的高度，在世界文学中也享有崇高的地位。为此，我觉得很有必要把他们留下的六千首诗完整地译成英诗。

西方最早大力进行唐诗英译的是18世纪英国汉学家、诗人詹尼斯（S. Jenyns），译作有《唐诗三百首选读》（*Selections from the 300 Poems of the Tang Dynasty*）和《唐诗三百首选读续集》（*A Further Selections from the 300 Poems of the Tang Dynasty*）。小烟薰良（S. Obata）最早英译了唐代诗人专集，比如1922年在纽约出版的《李白诗集》（*The Works of Li Po, the Chinese Poet*）。其他为唐诗英译做出贡献的英译家还有戴维斯爵士、翟理斯、理雅各、韦利、柳无忌、欧文等等。反观国内，自二十世纪八十年代以来，我国学者、翻译家翻译的唐诗译本有杨宪益与戴乃迭（Gladys）合译的《唐宋诗文选译》（*Poetry and Prose of the Tang and Song*）、徐忠杰翻译的《唐诗二百首新译》（*200 Chinese Tang Poems in English Verse*）、王守义与诺弗尔（J. Neville）合译的《唐宋诗词英译》（*Poems from Tang and Song Dynasties*）、吴钧陶翻译的《杜甫诗英译（一百五十首）》（*Tu Fu One Hundred and Fifty Poems*）、许渊冲翻译的《唐诗三百首新译》（*English-Chinese 300 Tang Poems A New Translation*）、《李白诗选译》（*Selected Poems of Li Bai*）、《唐诗一百五十首英译》（*150 Tang Poems*）等。可见，唐诗的英译版本虽然相对较多，然文言文的晦涩和唐诗独有的文学性为唐诗英译设置了重重障碍，回顾现有的翻译作品，唐诗英译成果并不成系统,译本多零散且译文质量参差不齐,偏离原文甚远,自然传播效果也不甚理想。本该灿如明星的唐诗反而由于翻译的精准程度不匹配而被拉下神坛,中华文化的神采在译文中被遮蔽、被消解。远游的诗神是一个蒙灰的形象,哲学内涵也被误解、被埋没。在当代文明大潮交汇的新形势下,唐诗英译亟待寻求新的翻译方法论作为指导,亟需开辟新思路以走出困局。

翻译虽然基本上表现于文字转换,实质上却蕴含着大学之道。翻译始终以言语系统之间的"易"即言语单位的切换与调变来传情达意,同时也以其与宇宙之间的全息律(holographics)表征着"davar""Brahma""道"。翻译是不乏理论的,但纵观形形色色的西方翻译理论,由于没有形而上的统领和关照,其认识是庞杂的、肤浅的、碎片化的,甚至有的理论竟是颠覆本原、本质以借翻译理论之名行解构翻译理论之实,而传统的准则,比如忠实、对等,乃至文本本身都成了负面的模因而被解构了,翻译成了是其所非的荒谬和无所不是的弥散。

笔者2005年著《翻译学归结论》一书,逆西方潮流而动,以《周易》指向,从众说纷纭的混沌中祭出一个明确的范式,这是摆脱混乱和无定的一个企图。它说:翻译是一个由原则统领的、译者藉此进行参数调变与否决的动态系统。由此,译/易的本质是类比的、可拓逻辑的,即化矛盾为不矛盾,变不可译为可译。正如唐朝的贾公彦云:"译即易。谓换易言语使相解也。"语言符号是对抽象语义的表征,无论采取何种表征方式,只要能达到对等的目的即可。翻译的最根本的目的是要传递原汁原味的原文精髓,这绝不是改写,不是操控,更不是通过直译、意译或零翻译就能解决的。它需要译者设身处地,体会原作作者的审美情调和意图,通过合理有效的调控,使译文最大限度地贴近原文,最大限度地实现形美、音美和意美的有机统一,即实现译文中各个变量间的平衡与相互制约,使译文自给自足,达致善译。译文虽然在语形和语义上与原文有所差别,但在意旨上又和原文保持高度一致。

自提出翻译学归结论后,笔者在典籍外译实践中就始终以翻译学归结论为理论指导,坚守悬置法则(ceteris paribus rule)即其他条件等同(other things being equal)下的语码转换。大道至简,这是最高效的方法论的起点。在其外围便是翻译生态——翻译伴随翻译生态环境而生。翻译与生态环境,犹如阴阳两种力量,相摩相荡,相生相克,交感成和,生生不息。

具体到诗歌翻译而言，诗的"有形"与"无形"为诗歌翻译带来了避无可避的翻译困境。在中西方诗歌体裁中，诗可以分为散体诗和格律诗两大类：散体诗强调自然、不拘束；格律诗是一种编排，照应生命的律动，在严谨中书写诗意，天各一方的民族还不约而同地造就了格律。世界范围内，英汉诗歌又占据世界诗歌的大半。英诗的格律由四种基调格（抑扬格、扬抑格、抑抑扬格和扬抑抑格）、两种变格（抑抑格和扬扬格）和不同音步数组合而成，再辅以交替韵、搂抱韵和重叠韵构成多种经典诗体。汉语古诗则以极富乐感的方块字写成，它的格律主要涉及四个方面，即押韵、节奏、平仄和歌唱或吟诵行为，通过押韵和平仄实现古诗的表情达意，或热烈欢快，或文静雅致。格律诗的诗体特征之鲜明，直接造成格律诗翻译的壁障。即使诗歌翻译艰难如此，就格律诗的翻译而言，我也是绝不含糊的——这样的诗不允许含糊，此乃格律之谓也。

虽说诗无达诂、译无定法，译者在翻译诗歌时也不可过度夸大主观能动性，更不可任意妄为、随意解构，诗人的思想性和诗的文学性需得到足够的重视，译诗必须须为诗。诗歌翻译首先要受到押韵、节奏这一形式因素的制约，甚至说还要满足演唱并可以适当发挥的需要。当然，这只是一个显性的要求。为保证作品的品位，语言、美学、哲学等层面的隐性因素都需要全盘考虑。笔者近年来着力进行典籍英译，其中一大类别就是中国古代诗歌英译。在翻译时，我始终践行的翻译原则就是"以诗译诗，译经如经，是其所是"。

译诗是高度辩证的制衡机制与审美行为。关于翻译标准，我认为：所谓辩证，它是不忠而忠、不等而等的调配；所谓制衡，它是依权重而逐层否决的仲裁；所谓审美，它是以可视、可感、可唱、可听的意象营造而直入心境。翻译必须被赋予一定的自由度。译者可以根据目的或意图的需要，在不影响大体的前提下增加译文的可读性或可唱性，甚至必要时可以做些许改动或牺牲，这样反而能使译文符合原文的初衷。翻译虽然多变，但决不是没有标准，只是它的标准不是机械的、僵死的、一成不变的，它的最高标准其实就一个字：美。

译好一首诗或一部作品首先要统摄原文要旨和神采，然后用另一种文字恰如其分地再现。何谓再现？再现不是字词的简单对应而是语篇的功能对等——译文与原文在逻辑关系、审美构成和语用意图等各个层面的对应。可见，在诗歌翻译中，逼近原则是首要的——这是翻译及评判的起点和根据；逼近的同时也为达到最佳效果进行灵活调变，以直译尽其可能，意译按其所需的辩证性为旨归。

翻译中国古代诗歌尤其是格律诗时,秉承着"以诗译诗"的翻译原则,笔者首先就要"保留"格律,绝不能以"自由"为托词对其格律任意阉割而损伤诗美。当然,我也不提倡因声损义的凑韵,或为了押韵而把句子搞得怪里怪气,这比平庸还低廉。韵律来自语义或语境,它是构成织综的重要成分,与之不可分割——分割了就不是这首诗了。它服务于整体效果,牵一发而动全身。具体来说,"译诗如诗"即译者在认识到诗的形式是诗的格式或模板的基础上,首先有必要对译文在形式上进行限定。译为无韵的散文体或有韵的参差不一的诗行不符合我的审美取向。译诗虽然无强制性的要求,但在实践中也能提取出便于操作和评估的一般准则。比如英语的一个音步一般为两个音节,而五个音步一般为十个音节,与汉语的七言在形式和内容上可以达到最佳匹配。所以为了便于操作我做了类比性的设定:将汉语三言类比为五音节;将汉语四言类比为六音节;将汉语五言类比为八音节;将汉语六言类比为九音节;将汉语七言类比为十音节;将汉语八言类比为十二音节;将汉语九言类比为十四音节。

其次,由于英汉诗歌中韵诗又占绝大比例,在译汉语韵诗时,译诗也必须押韵且有节奏,"以诗译诗,是其所是"在翻译韵诗时就包括"以韵译韵",这一点不能妥协,但如何押韵以及采用何种韵式则可以由译者自己调整。由于韵或韵式都是类比的,除了特殊的诗体,译诗中的韵式可以相对灵活。我多用偶韵和交叉韵或隔行韵;英诗绝大部分都是抑扬格,也会根据表意的需要夹杂扬抑格、抑抑扬格、扬抑抑格等,译诗也会求诸此类格律。在英译过程中,始终注重翻译的形意张力,避免因韵害义,同时又保证原诗风格的完整再现及诗歌情感、意境、意象等内涵的高度传达,最大化地实现翻译的效度与信度。英诗的格律不像中国的格律诗那样严格,总的原则是音韵和谐。好的译诗必须是不蔓不枝,自然天成的。

再者,除了对诗体、诗韵的保留与再现手段,中国古代诗歌翻译的另一重难点在于对文化名词的翻译处理。中华文化是一个复杂的大系统,内涵深厚,博大精深,可分为形形色色的模块,比如梅兰竹菊、琴棋书画、三皇五帝、三纲五常都是特定文化的产物。并且同一名词在不同文化语境中能够呈现不一样的内涵,中华风物可被赋予不同的内容。在中国古代诗歌英译实践中,一个负责任的译者不可忽视对这类名词的内涵和意义的解释和传达,因为翻译的目的就是不同文明之间的理解互通。对文化名词的妙用往往能体现并塑造文人的个人风格,李白的浪漫主义诗风瑰丽绚烂,白居易、杜甫等诗人的现实主义诗风发人深省,王维的田园山水诗风清新脱俗。译诗也重在译味(translating the taste)。如果仅是简单地释义,这便不是文学翻译而是文字翻译。因此,好的译诗也当一如原诗,文本自足,同时与原文的文学风格最大程度地映现。

对于在英语中无法完全找到对等表达的汉语文化名词时,笔者选择了以注释的形式扩展相关知识。不过,对于译文而言,注释属于副文本(paratext)即独立于译文的另一个文本,背景知识就语篇而言是缺省值(default value),尽管在一定程度上也会影响读者对文本的认知,但对于正文而言不是文本的必要成分,它只是揭示本族语者可能具有的默认知识。而对于英语读者而言,注释却可以在不影响译诗结构和表达的条件下,成为可辅助英语读者理解译文的、有效且必要的文本。作注和译诗是不同的路径,译者不需要想象,不需要发挥,不需要浪漫,但需要查阅、考证、取舍和提炼;同时译者还要借鉴最近的考古发现,如此才能做到用最简练的语言来概括某一注释所需的完整历史文化要素。对译者而言,作注还能再次验证译文的准确程度,起到查漏、勘误作用,反过来提高翻译质量。

在翻译和作注的过程中,译者对于专有名词必然有很多纠结,担心信息会有所遗漏、扭曲或冗余。笔者认为:为了保全原文信息和可读性,译者在翻译中应尽量避免音译;即便音译,也要照顾西方的阅读习惯,可采用西方读者和海外华人熟悉的威氏拼音;更重要的是翻译要避免编码的夹生,比如中国文化的层级体系的编码是从大到小,而英语则是从小至大,比如"蓝田山石门精舍"译成英语则应该把"蓝天山"的译文置后,如 Stonegate Vihara at Mt. Blue Field,而译作 at Mt. Blue Field Stonegate Vihara 则怪异。同理,"李白"姓李名白,译作"Li Pai"就违反了英语的编码规律,正如把"卡尔·马克思"译作"马克思·卡尔"那样悖谬,而译作"Pai Li"才符合英语的规范。

对于有些特有的中华文化概念如精卫、后羿、颛顼、秀才等,如果音译便过滤掉了中国文化的特有意义。译者还需要基于汉语词源和英语构词法在译文中进行合理创译,仿拟汉语的构词法,尽力把词素所表达的意义译出来,这等于向英语输入词汇,利用词汇在文化系统中的互文性,从而帮助英语读者通过上下文推断该词的意义所指。比如"秀才"译作"xiu cai"或"hsiu ts'ai"对于英文读者而言是毫无意义的,而重新编码为"showcharm",读者则可以产生相应的联想,而随着认知语境的增强,则可以达到等同于原文的认知效果。通过以上翻译策略,译诗可以尽可能保留原诗用典情况,并用脚注形式注释其中出现的历史典故、神话传说、文化习俗等,使读者能够迅速了解诗歌中的典故及文化内涵。可见,注释文本为达成文化互通这一翻译的最终目的也起到了积极的推手作用,一定程度上弥补了语言系统客观差异所带来的文化缺省的难解现象。

言而总之,译者如若在中国古代诗歌英译实践中,贯彻"以诗译诗,是其所是"和逼近原则,尽可能在诗体、诗韵上做到还原和再现,且以注释辅助文化名词的翻译,译诗才能一如原文,做到浅而不白、质而不俗,达成形美、意美、音美的辩证统一,这便逼近等值、等效了。如此说来,在诗歌翻译实践中,译文比肩乃至超越原文是可能的——这取决于如何操控"言尽意"与"言不尽意"的悖论和如何破解翻译的斯芬克斯之谜。

目前放眼译界,译者由于欠缺形而上的元理论意识,对翻译本体论以及语言本体论认识不足,同时欠缺语言各分相学科的系统知识,大多还拘泥于话语层次的静态的语码转换,其译文难免失真、异化。纵观典籍外译,翻译之敝不仅遮蔽了中华文化的神采而且还割裂了中西文化一体性,不仅没能促进文明互通,反而还弄巧成拙,造成更大的"隔阂"。

笔者基于对翻译本体论和语言本体论的深刻认识,以扎实的中华文化经典英译实践为佐证,提出:典籍外译新局面的突破口在于方法论的革新。译者须从翻译本体论出发,将词源学、句法学、语义学乃至哲学、神学等领域融会贯通,突破机械的二元论,以整全的、全息的眼光审察翻译这一悖论性的辩证系统,系统调和可译/不可译等矛盾,在形意张力逼近与趋同当中追求文化、文本的自恰,以期翻译理论的涅槃,使经典外译焕发勃勃生机。

受惠于中华文化复兴这个伟大时代所提供的机遇,我们拥有了便于利用的知识宝库,而国学双语研究也进入了新境界,促进了经典文化翻译的创新。在此背景下,笔者多年来一直思考翻译理论的创新并付诸翻译实践。笔者希望王维、李白、杜甫、白居易的英译可以展示唐诗的面貌,也希望与笔者已出版的其他中华文化典籍尤其是诗歌的英译作品形成呼应,继续提供经得起海内外读者检验、品读的系列译作,为中华文化"走出去"尽一份绵薄之力。

赵彦春

2020 年 9 月 1 日

于上海大学

Introduction by the Translator

If asked which dynasty is the greatest in poetry, you may reply without hesitation: the T'ang dynasty; if further asked who is the greatest poet in the T'ang dynasty, you may feel it uneasy to answer, because there are several poets too hard to rank. If not required to list the first or second but the best ones, it is much easier. Wei Wang, Pai Li, Fu Tu and Chü-e Pai, no doubt, are among the best. It is they who made the pinnacle of T'ang poetry.

This pinnacle should be well known to all earthlings. But translation is never an easy task and not without traps and fallacies. The most crucial of all is the loss of the Word.

"What is high above is the Word; what is down below is the vessel." This is a detached and exact recapitulation by *The Book of Changes* of the whole system of human knowledge, a coordinate of human knowledge and a coordinate of human wisdom. However, the Enlightenment in the West opened the Pandora's Box of thought and disintegrated the Word into dirt, as is said in *Analects*, "The world has gone astray from the Word for long." While after many turns in the West's academics, the renaissance of traditional Chinese culture has started off. The call to action has been tooted and the dawning of the Word has touched the horizon with a streak of red.

In a large sense, the great revolution or great prosperity of human thought began with translation, for example, the translation of Buddhist scriptures in the East, the translation of the Bible in the West and other kinds of translation brought about by the Eastward Spread of Western Culture in the modern era. The translation of Chinese classics started in the late Ming dynasty and translators at that time were mainly sinologists, diplomats and missionaries, and in the late Ching dynasty, some Chinese translators joined in this undertaking.

Unfortunately, we have come to find that the charm of poetic Chinese classics and poetry itself have been eclipsed to a very large extent, which happens to correspond to Robert Frost's dictum, "Poetry is what gets lost in translation."

Of all kinds of translation practice, literary translation is the trickiest and most complicated, and poetry translation is the most noteworthy kind of translation of all literary genres.

Humans are poetic beings, and poetry is the homeland of humans as well as a representation of humans. Poetry creation and poetry translation are both means of representing ourselves and representing our world. The literariness of poetry is a matter of mapping between the arrangement of visible words and the movement of invisible human souls: its visibility is manifested in what we can see, like words, texture and prosody formed by rhythm and rhyme; its invisibility refers to the meaning out of meaning. Poetry is in correspondence with the recursion of the universe and is embodied as a chain of signs or a sign of signs; it expresses meaning, and even expresses the meaning of meaning. As an old saying goes, words are finite but the meaning beyond words is infinite.

China is a nation of poetry. Its history of poetry can date back to *Song of the Catapult* in the age of Lord Yellow. *Song of the Catapult*, two characters or two syllables a line, is a forerunner of the four-character verse, i.e., verse of four characters or four syllables a line. The four-character verse flourished in the sixth century B.C., and then more types of verse came into being, such as the Woebegone form, the five-character old verse, the seven-character old verse and the varying-character old verse. The T'ang dynasty ushered in a golden age of poetry, when there appeared metrical poems with five characters a line, six characters a line and seven characters a line.

The T'ang dynasty (A.D. 618 – A.D. 907) is the most golden period among all golden times, the pinnacle of achievements in Chinese literature and arts, especially in poetry. In regard of the quantity of poets and poems in T'ang, there is no exact number yet. While it can be seen from *A Complete Collections of T'ang Poems*, a book compiled in the Ching dynasty, there are 49,403 poems produced by 2,873 poets in the T'ang dynasty. From these remains, we can also see that litterateurs then showed their charm and recorded the magnificence of that great age in a great multitude of poems. Wei Wang, Pai Li, Fu Tu and Chü-e Pai are, no doubt, the brightest representative figures of all pearl-like poets in the T'ang dynasty. Detached and delighted in nature, Wei Wang pursued the great Word through wording line by line; romantic and unrestrained, Pai Li implanted his sentiments and talents into poetic lines; incisive and realistic, Fu Tu showed his worries over the nation and people in his poems; sober and percipient, Chü-e Pai expressed his great concerns over his kin, friends and homeland. Their abounding poems, though distinctive in style, altogether mirror the history in different stages of that age. These four poets can represent the pinnacle of Chinese poetry and should have been given a stature in world literature. For this reason, I think it necessary to render their poems, 6,000 in total, into English.

The first sinologist who took pains to translate T'ang poetry is S. Jenyns, a British poet in the eighteenth century, with the fruition of *Selections from the 300 Poems of the Tang Dynasty* and *A Further Selections from the 300 Poems of the Tang Dynasty*. The first one to translate the collected works of a T'ang poet is S. Obata, renowned for *The Works of Li Po, the Chinese Poet* published in New York in 1922. Other pioneers are Sir Davis, H. Giles, J. Legge, A. Waley, Wu-chi Liu, Owen and so on. Chinese translators began to translate T'ang poetry in the 1980s, and representative translated works include *Poetry and Prose of the Tang and Song* by Hsien-e Yang and Gladys Yang, *200 Chinese Tang Poems in English Verse* by Chungchieh Hsu, *Poems from Tang and Song Dynasties* by Shou-e

Wang and J. Neville, *Tu Fu One Hundred and Fifty Poems* by Chunt'aoWu, *English-Chinese 300 Tang Poems: A New Translation* by Yüanch'ung Hsu, *Selected Poems of Li Bai* by Yüanch'ung Hsu, and *150 Tang Poems* by Yüanch'ung Hsu. As it can be seen, the obscurity of classical Chinese writings and the unique literariness of T'ang Poems set many obstacles for the translation of T'ang poetry, existing translated works, though in a relatively large quantity, are far from ideal in quality and are fragmented rather than systematic in scale. So, these translations, too far away from their originals in form and meaning, have resulted in an obviously poor communication effect worldwide by now. T'ang poetry that should have been as luminous as bright stars is now being pulled down from its summit by bad translations, and the glory of Chinese civilization gets dimmed and diminished by bad translations. It also means that the images of Chinese Muses travelling afar are covered with a veil of dust, and that Chinese philosophy has been misunderstood and undermined. Against the background of cultural exchanges, a new methodology is in dire need to guide the rendering of T'ang poetry into English, so that translators can find a way out of the current plight.

Translation, a process of text transformation by and large, has an implication in the Word of the universe. It always includes the transformation between two linguistic systems to convey meanings and express emotions, and also mirrors the universal holographics to represent "davar", "Brahma" or the Word. Though there is no lack of translation theories, we can find no directions from metaphysics for translation studies in Western translation theories. The viewpoints expressed in the so-called theories can be judged as sprawling, shallow and fragmented. Some of them have even overthrown the thing-in-itself of translation and have actually deconstructed the basics of translation. Classic norms such as fidelity, equivalence and the text itself are regarded as negative memes and are deconstructed. Translation has run into a state of what it is not, with the dispersion of its essence into being anything but itself.

In 2005, I published a book *A Reductionist Approach to Translatology*, a book that goes in the opposite direction of Western translation theories. With the guidance of *The Book of Changes*, the book aims to set a clear paradigm out of all current chaos and melee, trying to lead translation studies out of disorder. As it proposes, translation is a dynamical system guided by principles, and translators can take advantage of the mechanism of checks and balances to modulate and veto parameters in the process. Hence, the essence of "trans" conforms to analogy and extenic logic, which means converting contradictoriness into compatibility and untranslatability into translatability. Just as the T'ang Confucian Scholar Kungyen Chia put it, "'yi' (falling tone, meaning trans) is equal to 'yi' (falling tone, meaning changing), namely changing from one parole into another to ensure mutual understanding". Linguistic symbols are just representations of abstract semantic meanings, and all representations can reach the same goal, different they may be. The fundamental purpose of translation is to convey the quintessence of the source text in an original way; and definitely, it is not merely what rewriting or manipulation can achieve, and even far beyond the scope of what is called literal translation, free translation or zero translation. According to *A Reductionist Approach to Translatology*, translators are required to be empathetic enough to comprehend the original's aesthetic perception and intention, and then to reasonably modulate parameters to make the translations approximate to the original as much as possible, so that the beauty in form, sound and meaning can be achieved to the largest extent, that is to say, checks and balances among all variables can be realized, and self-consistent as well as high-quality translations can be produced. Translations, though still different from the original in linguistic symbols, are very likely to be highly consistent with it in semantic meaning and motif.

Since the establishment of the reductionist approach to translatology, it has been the theoretical guide throughout my translation practice, especially that of Chinese classics, abiding by the ceteris paribus rule, namely, transcoding in the condition of other things being equal, and insisting that the great Word is the simplest and is the starting point of a methodology of the highest efficiency. Besides, translation also concerns outer communicative environment, in other words, translation exists, concurrent with it. Translation and the communicative environment, just like the two forces Shine and Shade, which endlessly collide with each other, reinforce each other and counteract each other, two in one and united in one.

In terms of poetry, its visible and invisible poetic features bring inevitable obstacles to translation. Chinese poetry and Western poetry can be generally classified into free verse and rhythmic verse. The former highlights naturalness and freedom in verse, while the latter is a fruit of many nations though far apart, featuring rhythmic rules to represent the rhythm of life itself and the poetic atmosphere behind this restriction of rhythmic rules. Chinese poetry and Western poetry can boast of more than half of all poems ever produced. In respect of Western poetry, there are basic meter patterns including four basic meter patterns (Iambus, Trochee, Anapaest and Dactyl) and two variant meter patterns (Pyrrhic pattern and Spondee), metrical foot patterns and three common rhyming schemes (alternate rhyme as abab, enclosing rhyme as abba and distich as aa), which are the most adopted classical patterns. As for Chinese poetry, it is written in Chinese characters characterized by musicality, and the rhythmic verse features in four aspects, that is, rhyming, rhythm, tone pattern (piânn-tseh) and its chanting style for poets to convey meanings and express emotions, ardent or refined. These clear-cut poetic features of metrical verses directly challenge translators. Despite the difficulty and complexity, I show no perfunctoriness, and perfunctoriness is not allowed in metrical verses.

Admitting that "no final interpretation for literary texts, no definite translation of them either", while translating poetry, translators should not over-exaggerate their initiative, let alone wantonly interpreting and deconstructing original texts. An author's ideology and the literariness of a poem should be given enough emphasis, and its translation should still be a poem in itself. Poetry translation is firstly subject to the need of representing the original's poetic forms like rhyming and rhythm, and then to the needs of chanting or other purposes. Certainly, the requirements above are just overtones, and for ensuring the literariness of the original in the translation, invisible connotations of language, aesthetics and philosophy beyond words should all be considered. For years I have been devoted to English translation of Chinese classics, ancient poetry in particular. The ultimate translation principle I have long implemented is "translating poesie into poesie and classic into classic, translating it as it is".

Poetry translation is a highly dialectical system of checks and balances and an aesthetic activity. Speaking of translation criteria, as I see it, being dialectical lies in the modulation of parameters for dynamic fidelity and equivalence through seeming infidelity and in equivalence; checks and balances requires translators to decide whether an element should be preferred or sacrificed layer by layer based on its right weight; in aesthetic terms, poetry translation is expected to create visual and acoustical poetic imagery to impress readers. Translators should be given some independence, hence enabled to enhance the readability of a translated text according to pragmatic purposes without affecting the overall arrangements, and even to change or sacrifice some elements, if necessary, to better represent the original's intention. Translation, though ever-changing in the process, can never do without criteria, and criteria should not be mechanical, rigid or immutable. Its highest standard actually is just one word: beauty.

To produce a quality translation of poetry or literature in general, translators firstly need to fully comprehend the original's motif and style, and then appropriately represent it in another language. What is representation? It is not simple word-to-word equivalence but functional or dynamic equivalence in terms of discourse, namely, the equivalence of the original and the translated text in layers such as logical relationship, aesthetic component and pragmatic intention. This shows that in poetry translation, the principle of proximity is primary, which is the starting point and the basis for translation practice and translation criticism. Translators can flexibly modulate elements to achieve the best possible effect, aiming at the maxim "as literal as is possible, as free as necessary".

When translating ancient Chinese poetry, especially Chinese metrical poems, abiding by the principle of "translating poesie into poesie", I firstly retain the original's metrical features and never misuse a translator's freedom to arbitrarily abandon the original's metrical features at the expense of damaging its poetic beauty. Also, I don't advocate translators to unnaturally pile up rhymes at the cost of damaging meanings and twisting poetic structures. After all, going beyond the limit is as bad as falling short. Rhyme and rhythm are rooted in meaning or context, and as a significant part of poetic structure, they should not be sacrificed. They contribute to the overall poetic effect and will affect the whole body if ignored. Specifically speaking, "translating poesie into poesie" is in the condition that translators have realized the role of poetic form as a poem's base or template, at first fixing the translation's form as a poem. Translating a Chinese poem into an English blank verse or an English rhymed poem uneven in length does not conform to my aesthetic orientation. Though there is no compulsory limit for poetry translation, general translation techniques that are useful for specific performance and evaluation can be summarized from translation practice. For instance, in English, one foot generally consists of two syllables, and accordingly five feet equals ten syllables in English, which can tentatively match seven Chinese characters both in form and content. By analogy, I have set a set of rules below: translating a Chinese three-character line into a pentasyllabic line in English, a Chinese four-character line into a hexasyllabic line, a Chinese five-character line into an octosyllabic line, a Chinese six-character line into an enneasyllabic line, a Chinese seven-character line into a decasyllabic line, a Chinese eight-character line into a twelve-syllable line, and a Chinese nine-character line into a fourteen-syllable line and so on.

In the second place, as rhymed poems account for the largest part of poems, when translating rhymed Chinese poems, the translations must be in rhyme, as the principle of "translating poesie into poesie, translating it as it is" entails "translating rhyme into rhyme". It is something that a translator should never make a concession to. Of course, a translator can decide which rhyme or which rhyming scheme to use. Since rhymes are something of analogy, except some unique poetic styles or subgenres, the rhyming schemes applied in a translation can be relatively flexible. The commonly used rhyming schemes in my translations include couplets (aa), alternate rhymes (abab) or interlacing rhymes (abcb). Most English poems use Iambus as the meter pattern along with auxiliaries such as Trochee, Anapaest and Dactyl, relevant to the requirement of meaning. A translation can do likewise. During the process, a translator should constantly focus on form-meaning tension, avoid the misuse of rhymes at the cost of damaging meaning, and ensure that the translated poem can possibly represent the original's style, emotion and imagery and then can achieve the validity of, and fidelity to, the original to the largest extent. Metrical patterns of English poetry, unlike those of Chinese metrical poems, are less strict. And the general principle is being harmonious in rhyme. A high-quality translation of a poem should be pithy, smooth and natural.

In the third place, apart from the representation of the original's poetic forms and metrical patterns, one more difficulty for translation is how to translate culture-loaded words. Chinese culture is an ancient civilization of great complexity, incomparable in profoundness and exclusively rich in dimension. It consists of diverse motifs such as plant images and art images, such as "wintersweets, orchids, bamboos and chrysanthemums", "zither, go, calligraphy and painting", "Three Kings and Five Lords", and "Three Canons and Five Constants", all of which are outcomes of Chinese culture, and a single image can convey different meanings in different contexts and can be given a new content according to a certain language use. In the English translation of practice of Chinese ancient poetry, a responsible translator must never escape from interpreting these images and conveying their connotations in translation, for the reason that the purpose of translation is exactly to promote mutual understanding among all civilizations rather than a dialogue of the deaf. The use of culture-loaded words frequently manifests and shapes a poet's unique style, such as Pai Li's style of romanticism, Chü-e Pai's and Fu Tu's style of realism and Wei Wang's style of naturalism. Poetry translation also centers on the aesthetics of taste. Simple literal translation is none but translation of words, not translation of literature. In this sense, excellent translations of poems should be as self-consistent as the original as well, and should mirror the original's literary style.

When faced with the occasions of culture default in the English translation of Chinese ancient poems, I choose the way of annotation to provide additional information outside the translated poems. However, in regard of translation, annotations belong to the type of paratext, namely, another text independent of the main body. For Chinese readers, background information of a Chinese ancient poem is a default value, and is not an essential part for the original though it affects Chinese readers' comprehension to some extent. Annotations in Chinese contexts can only reveal hidden knowledge some Chinese readers may need to know while reading, while for English readers, annotations in a translated text can be of great use and significance for them to comprehend the translation, which is an integral whole. Annotating is different from translating in the operational method. While providing annotations, a translator does not need to be imaginative, creative or sensitive, and instead he needs to investigate and verify messages, to select those useful out of all and finally to summarize them into definitions. Meanwhile, a translator needs to refer to most recent archaeological findings to ensure that an annotation is able to contain complete and required historic and cultural elements with most precise expressions. In turn, annotations can verify the degree of accuracy of translations, help translators to check and correct errors, and enhance the quality.

During the process of translation and annotation, translators must be concerned about culture-loaded words, lest some information be lost, distorted or redundant. As far as I can see, to ensure the fidelity to the original's information and readability of its translation, transliteration should be avoided as much as possible; if there is no better method than transliteration, translators should fully attend to westerners' reading habits, for example, I adopt the Wade-Giles romanization, for it has been popular with westerners and overseas Chinese. What is crucial is to avoid the hybridity of recodification, for example, the encoding of the hierarchy of Chinese culture is top-down while in English it is a bottom-up direction, just the opposite, for example, "Stonegate Vihara at Mt. Blue Field", which shows a bottom-up arrangement, is good English while "at Mt. Blue Field Stonegate Vihara" is absurd. Similarly, in "Pai Li", "Pai" is first name while "Li" is family name or surname, it is good English, while "Li Pai" violates the rule of English, just like the case we call Karl Marks "Marks Karl", so preposterous. So, "Pai Li" is the right address.

As for those salient and peculiar words in Chinese culture like Ching Wei, Hou E, Chuan Hsü and hsiuts'ai, considering that their cultural connotations will vanish in translations if transliteration is applied, I suggest that translators coin English words based on Chinese etymology and English word-formation, so as to reveal the original's word origin and introduce new eastern cultural connotations to the English world. This use of lexicon's intertextuality in cultural systems can assist English readers to deduce the signified of a culture-loaded word from the translated context. For example, the word "xiu cai" or "hsiu ts'ai" makes no sense to English readers, while there codification, like "showcharm" can trigger off similar associations, and as the target reader's cognitive environment is improved, he may have the same cognitive effect as source text readers. Through translation strategies mentioned above, a translator will be able to retain the original's allusions in the translated text to the largest extent, and provide annotations via footnotes to explain historical stories, myths, legends, and customs in the original and to delve into their connotations. So to speak, annotations play a positive role in achieving the goal of mutual understanding and compensating for the unintelligibility of cultural default brought about by the facsimiles of translation.

All in all, if a translator abides by the principle of "translating poesie into poesie, translating it as it is" and the principle of proximity while rendering Chinese ancient poetry into English, attempts to represent the original's poetic form and rhyming patterns, and provides annotations to assist translations of culture-loaded words, a translated poem can be concise and insightful, well-worded and refined, achieving the dialectical unity of beauty in form, meaning and musicality, just like the original. In this way, a translated poem can be approximate and equal to the original. Hence, in poetry translation, translations are likely to match and even exceed the original, and it depends on how a translator solves the explicability-unexplicability paradox and how he solves the riddle of Sphinx in translation.

Throughout the current translation studies and practices, it can be seen that most translators are still trapped in the static transformation of language codes at discourse level, due to the lack of a metaphysical metatheory, the ontology of translation and the ontology of language. Inevitably, their translations are unfaithful and distorted. Looking back at the course of translation of Chinese classics, translations at present have overshadowed the glory of Chinese civilization, split the oneness of the East and the West, failed to promote cultural exchanges and ironically turned out to be a barrier for cultural communication.

On the basis of a deep understanding of the ontology of translation and the ontology of language and taking substantial English translation of Chinese classics as solid evidences, I call for the innovation in translation methodology for finding a way out of the *status quo*. I suggest that translators start from the ontology of translation, synthetically apply etymology, syntax, semantics, philosophy and even theology in translation practice, and thus break through mechanical dualism. They are also expected to look upon translation as a dialectical system full of paradoxes from a holistic and holographic viewpoint. In this way, they may systematically reconcile contradictions like the translatability-untranslatability paradox; and they may pursue self-consistence of cultures as well as texts during the process of approximation and convergence in form and meaning. We look forward to the nirvana of translation theories and a refreshed look of translation of Chinese classics.

Thanks to the encouragement of the age, an age of the renaissance of traditional Chinese culture, we have access to the great treasures of knowledge. Along with bilingual studies of Chinese classics stepping into a new stage, we are experiencing the renewal of translation of Chinese classics. In this context, I have been committing myself to academic researches and translation practices for many years. I hope that the translated works of Wei Wang, Pai Li, Fu Tu and Chü-e Pai will give a true picture of what T'ang poetry is like, and that along with my other translated works of Chinese classics, these translations will keep on offering reliable resources for readers in China and overseas and will help Chinese culture to "go global" in a way.

Yanchun Chao
September 1, 2020
Shanghai University

卷 一

目　录
Contents

1	序言	
	Introduction	
1	译者自序	
	Introduction by the Translator	
1	古风五十九首	
	Old Airs, 59 Poems	
115	乐府三十首	
	Conservatoire, 30 Poems	
117	远别离	
	Apart from Their Man	
120	公无渡河	
	A Mad Man Drowned	
122	蜀道难	
	The Shu Way Is Hard	
126	梁甫吟	
	Ode to Father Liang	
131	乌夜啼	
	Crows Cawing at Dusk	
132	乌栖曲	
	Crows Perching	
134	战城南	
	A Battle South of the Town	

137	将进酒	
	Do Drink Wine	
140	行行且游猎篇	
	The Young Hunters	
142	飞龙引二首	
	Riding a Dragon, Two Poems	
146	天马歌	
	The Sky Horse	
150	行路难三首	
	It's a Hard Go, Three Poems	
157	长相思	
	Long Longing	
159	上留田行	
	Upper Reclaimed Farm	
162	春日行	
	A Spring	
164	前有一樽酒行二首	
	A Golden Cup Ahead, Two Poems	
168	夜坐吟	
	A Night Croon	
170	野田黄雀行	
	Siskins in the Field	
171	箜篌谣	
	Ballad of the Harp	
174	雉朝飞	
	A Pheasant Flies	
176	上云乐	
	Wen K'ang, a Hun	
182	夷则格上白鸠拂舞辞	
	Turtledove White and a Stroke Dance Light	
185	日出入行	
	The Sun Rises	

187	胡无人	
	Hun, There Will Be None	
189	北风行	
	North Wind	
192	侠客行	
	The Knights	

195　乐府三十七首
Conservatoire, 37 Poems

197	关山月	
	The Moon over Mt. Pass	
199	独漉篇	
	Someone Wades	
202	登高丘而望远	
	Climbing High to Gaze Afar	
205	阳春歌	
	Song of a Sunny Spring	
207	杨叛儿	
	Traitor Young	
209	双燕离	
	The Swallows' Disaster	
211	山人劝酒	
	The Hermits Toasting	
214	于阗采花	
	The Bloom Picker in Khotan	
216	鞠歌行	
	A Football Song	
219	幽涧泉	
	A Creek Flows	
221	王昭君二首	
	Lady Glare, Two Poems	

224	中山孺子妾歌	
	King of Hilltown's Concubine	
226	荆州歌	
	A Song of Chaste	
227	设辟邪伎鼓吹雉子斑曲辞	
	Exorcising Priests Play Pheasants Bright	
229	相逢行	
	An Encounter	
230	古有所思	
	Missing Her	
232	久别离	
	Apart for Long	
234	白头吟二首	
	Ode to Gray Hair, Two Poems	
242	采莲曲	
	Lotus Picking	
244	临江王节士歌	
	The Song of Wang, the Worthy, from Riverside	
246	司马将军歌	
	The Song of General Ssuma	
249	君道曲	
	Lord's Worth	
251	结袜子	
	Knitting Socks	
252	结客少年场行	
	The Gallants Gather at East Gate	
254	长干行二首	
	Long Vale Lane, Two Poems	
260	古朗月行	
	The Bright Moon	
262	上之回	
	Coming Back	

264	独不见 He's Away	
266	白纻辞三首 White Hemp, Three Poems	
269	鸣雁行 Wild Geese in Flight	
271	妾薄命 Me Alone	
273	幽州胡马客歌 The Hun Man on His Horse Astride	

古风五十九首
Old Airs, 59 Poems

其 一

大雅久不作,
吾衰竟谁陈?
王风委蔓草,
战国多荆榛。
龙虎相啖食,
兵戈逮狂秦。
正声何微茫,
哀怨起骚人。
扬马激颓波,
开流荡无垠。
废兴虽万变,
宪章亦已沦。
自从建安来,
绮丽不足珍。
圣代复元古,
垂衣贵清真。
群才属休明,
乘运共跃鳞。
文质相炳焕,
众星罗秋旻。
我志在删述,
垂辉映千春。
希圣如有立,
绝笔于获麟。

No. 1

Psalms Major in disuse for long,

To whom can I complain, now old?
Airs of Kings thrown into grass,
The Warring States vied, sly or bold.
Dragons and tigers fought so hard
Until Ch'in arose, fierce and mad.
All verses and songs were subdued
Except one poet chanting, how sad!
Yang and Ssuma stood up to change,
And would spread vigor without bound.
But the system had greatly changed,
All rules and regulations drowned.
E'er since the age of Making Peace,
The style's been gaudy, so amiss.
His Majesty strives for Rebirth:
Returning to Truth, what a bliss!
All talents now have their best day,
And will chase the tide as they vie.
Their refinements shine each to each,
Like the twinkling stars in the sky.
My will is to uphold the good
To glorify the virtues of the age.
Like Confucius I wish to write
Till there dies the unicorn sage.

* *Psalms Major*: *The Book of Songs* consists of *Airs of the States*, *Psalms*, and *Odes*, and *Psalms* consists of *Psalms Major* and *Psalms Minor*. Most poems of *Psalms Major* eulogize the merits and virtues of the House of Chough.
* *Airs of Kings*: *Airs of the States*, the first part of *The Book of Songs*, contains ten poems, a decade called *Airs of Kings*, which was composed to reflect the degradation of the House of Chough after the capital was moved.
* the Warring States: referring to the seven most powerful states existing from 475 B.C. to 221 B.C., including Ch'i, Ch'u, Yan, Han, Chao, Way, and Ch'in. The Warring

States period ended in 221 B.C. when Ch'in wiped out the other six states and established the first unified empire in China's history.
* dragons and tigers: a metaphor for ferocious, cruel and bloodthirsty fighters in this context.
* Ch'in: the Ch'in State or the State of Ch'in (905 B.C.- 206 B.C.), enfeoffed as a dependency of Chough by King Piety of Chough in 905 B.C and enfeoffed as a vassal state by King Peace of Chough in 770 B.C. In the ten years from 230 B.C. to 221 B.C., Ch'in wiped out the other six powers and became the first unified regime of China, i.e., the Ch'in Empire.
* one poet chanting: referring to Yüan Ch'ü (430 B.C.- 278 B.C.), a great patriotic poet and the founder of Chinese romantic literature. Yüan Ch'ü drowned himself, so aggrieved at his broken state. His works signify a new era for Chinese poetry from collective authorship to individual ones.
* Yang and Ssuma: referring to Man Yang (Hsiung Yang) and Hsiangju Ssuma, famous men of letters in the Western Han dynasty.
* Making Peace: the third reign title of Emperor Hsien (A.D. 181 - A.D. 234) of the Eastern Han, when literature flourished.
* Confucius: Confucius (551 B.C.- 479 B.C.), a renowned thinker, educator and statesman in the Spring and Autumn period, born in the State of Lu, who was the founder of Confucianism and whose doctrine of the golden mean and adherence to the rite and music system has exerted profound influence on Chinese culture. Confucius is one of the few leaders who based their philosophy on the virtues that are required for the day-to-day living. His philosophy centered on personal and governmental morality, correctness of social relationships, justice and sincerity.
* the unicorn: the symbol of saintliness in Chinese culture. Confucius lamented the death of a unicorn captured and hence stopped compiling the *Spring and Autumn Annals* and died before long.

其 二

蟾蜍薄太清,
蚀此瑶台月。
圆光亏中天,
金魄遂沦没。
蝃蝀入紫微,
大明夷朝晖。
浮云隔两曜,
万象昏阴霏。
萧萧长门宫,
昔是今已非。
桂蠹花不实,
天霜下严威。
沉叹终永夕,
感我涕沾衣。

No. 2

The toad does great Luna invade
And eat her glamour as she shines.
From Heaven her bright light does fade
And her golden halo declines.
A rainbow tinges the palace there,
And hence the sun loses its grace.
Clouds floating can eclipse all glare,
And everything's covered with haze.
Longgate Palace rampant with weeds
Has lost all its grandeur, behold.
The laurel no longer bears seeds;

Hoarfrost falls from above, so cold.
Therein sad sighs all day one hears,
And I, so moved, feel warm with tears.

* the toad: referring to the shade when an eclipse of the moon happens. According to legend, when this happens, there will fall a disaster. As is believed by ancient Chinese, a lunar eclipse is caused by the toad that nibbles a piece of the moon away.
* Luna: the goddess of the moon and of months in Roman mythology, and in Chinese culture the imperial concubine of Lord Alarm (2480 B.C.- 2345 B.C.), one of five mythical emperors in prehistorical China. It has an important position in Chinese literature, the most frequent image of coolness, purity, loneliness, and hope for a happy reunion.
* Longgate Palace: the harem where Empress Ch'en of Han lived after being deposed (130 B.C.). Since then, Longgate Palace has become a symbol of an estranged queen.
* laurel: an evergreen shrub with aromatic, lance-shaped leaves, yellowish flowers, and succulent, cherry-like fruit, a symbol of glory usually in the form of a crown or wreath of laurel to indicate honor or high merit, especially when one had passed Grand Test, i.e. Civil Service Examinations for selecting government officials, in ancient China. In Chinese mythology, there is a laurel tree on the moon, and it would never fall even though Kang Wu has kept cutting it.

其 三

秦王扫六合，
虎视何雄哉。
挥剑决浮云，
诸侯尽西来。
明断自天启，
大略驾群才。
收兵铸金人，
函谷正东开。
铭功会稽岭，
骋望琅琊台。
刑徒七十万，
起土骊山隈。
尚采不死药，
茫然使心哀。
连弩射海鱼，
长鲸正崔嵬。
额鼻象五岳，
扬波喷云雷。
鬐鬣蔽青天，
何由睹蓬莱。
徐市载秦女，
楼船几时回。
但见三泉下，
金棺葬寒灰。

No. 3

The king of Ch'in swept off Six States;

How coldly the tiger did glower!
He swayed his sword to cut the clouds;
All vassals gave way to his power.
His acumen came from Heaven;
His gift against all did prevail.
He fused weapons into gold men
And could loiter east thru Case Dale.
His merits carved on Mt. Summit,
On Ivory Mound He would stand.
Seventy thousand criminals
At Mt. Black Steed built Palace Grand.
His alchemists failed, all in vain;
In disappointment he was drowned.
Arrows were shot to kill sea fish,
But a long whale rose like a mound.
Splashing water with a loud noise,
Its forehead and nose like a peak.
Its fins spreading to shade the sky,
Where can He Mt. Fairyland seek?
Bliss Hsu shipped the Ch'in girls away;
His tower ship ne'er returned, as told.
Lo, below Three Springs over there,
The Monarch's bones like ash lie cold.

* the king of Ch'in: the last king of the State of Ch'in and the first emperor of the Ch'in Empire, who claimed to be Emperor First.
* Six States: the six vassal states that Ch'in exterminated from 230 B.C. to 221 B.C., which were Han, Chao, Way, Ch'u, Yan, and Ch'i, before the ending of more than 500 years' civil war and the reunification of China based on a centralized power of the sovereign.
* tiger: a large carnivorous feline mammal of Asia, with vertical black wavy stripes on a tawny body and black bars or rings on the limbs and tail, praised as king of all animals.

* gold men: After the unification of China, as a precaution against possible rebellions, Emperor First gathered all weapons from the six states conquered and fused them into twelve bronze figures as tall as 15 meters and having feet six feet long and erected them in his palace.
* Case Dale: an ancient pass located to the east of the capital of Ch'in, and Lint'ao to the west.
* Mt. Summit: K'uaichi Mountains if transliterated, in present-day Chechiang Province, where Worm (Yü) convened a summit attended by vassal lords from all parts of China, hence the name.
* Ivory Mound: Langya T'ai if transliterated, a coastal mound built by Emperor First in modern-day Shantung Province.
* Mt. Black Steed: the mountain south of Lintung, an important offset of Mt. Ch'in Ridge, 1,302 meters above sea level, the location of the royal palace of Ch'in and tomb of Emperor First.
* whale: a large sea mammal larger than, but distinguished from, dolphins and porpoises, often a sign of great ambition and fortitude, and sometimes a symbol of opposition from an enemy.
* Mt. Fairyland: a fabled abode for immortals, what is P'englai in today's Shantung Province.
* Bliss Hsu: a Wordist (Taoist as is generally called) and alchemist in Ch'in, who tried to find elixir or panacea for the emperor and never returned from Japan on his second trip overseas.
* Ch'in: the Ch'in State or the State of Ch'in (905 B.C.- 206 B.C.), enfeoffed as a dependency of Chough by King Piety of Chough in 905 B.C. and enfeoffed as a vassal state by King Peace of Chough in 770 B.C. In the ten years from 230 B.C. to 221 B.C., Ch'in wiped out the other six powers and became the first unified regime of China, i.e. the Ch'in Empire.
* Three Springs: a poetic expression referring to where people are buried after death, and more often called Yellow Spring, as water down earth is believed to be yellow.

其 四

凤飞九千仞,
五章备彩珍。
衔书且虚归,
空入周与秦。
横绝历四海,
所居未得邻。
吾营紫河车,
千载落风尘。
药物秘海岳,
采铅青溪滨。
时登大楼山,
举首望仙真。
羽驾灭去影,
飚车绝回轮。
尚恐丹液迟,
志愿不及申。
徒霜镜中发,
羞彼鹤上人。
桃李何处开,
此花非我春。
唯应清都境,
长与韩众亲。

No. 4

The phoenix flies twenty miles high;
Five colors of its plumes sheen grand.
Billing a book, riding an air,

It alights on Chough-and-Ch'in Land.
Having travelled across four seas,
It finds the place not good at all.
Though it would make elixir rare,
To mundane dust it has to fall.
It'd concoct drugs in mountains calm
And beside a clear stream mine lead.
Then it climbs Mt. Great Mansion there
And looks at Fairtrue overhead.
It sees him go, riding a crane,
And can't await his coming back.
It sighs its drugs may come so late
That it fails in its wish, alack.
The mirror sees its hair grow gray;
The crane rider it's shy to see.
Tho peach trees bloom here and there;
The place is not where it can be.
To Fairyland it'd fly away
And for aye with immortals stay.

* phoenix: a legendary bird of great beauty, unique of its kind, which was supposed to live five or six hundred years before consuming itself by fire, rising again from its ashes to live through another cycle, a symbol of immortality. In Chinese mythology, the phoenix only perches on phoenix trees, i.e. firmiana, only eats firmiana fruit, and only drinks sweet spring water, and this mythic bird appears only in times of peace and sagacious rule.
* five colors: referring to five major colors: blue, red, white, black and yellow; a metonymy for various colors, like *The Word and the World* says: "Five colors dazzle the eyes, five sounds deafen the ears, five tastes baffle the palate, galloping to hunt drives one crazy, and rare goods reduce one to misconduct."
* Chough-and-Ch'in Land: the central part of China, which was the political center of the Kingdom of Chough together with its dependency of Ch'in.
* elixir: a hypothetical substance sought by medical alchemists to change base metals into

gold or prolong life indefinitely.
* Mt. Great Mansion: also known as Mt. Great Dragon, a mountain 20 kilometers south of Poolton (Ch'ihchow) under today's Anhui Province, looking like a great building or a huge dragon against the blue sky out of the town, hence the name.
* Fairtrue: synonym of Wordist immortal.
* crane: one of a family of large, long-necked, long legged, heronlike birds allied to the rails, a symbol of longevity and integrity in Chinese culture, only second to the phoenix in cultural importance.
* peach: any tree of the genus *Prunus Percica*, blooming brilliantly and bearing fruit, a fleshy, juicy, edible drupe, considered sacred in China, a symbol of romance, prosperity and longevity.
* Fairyland: referring to P'englai Isles beyond East Sea, a fairyland supported by giant turtles underneath and enclosed by a dark sea according to legend.

其 五

太白何苍苍,
星辰上森列。
去天三百里,
邈尔与世绝。
中有绿发翁,
披云卧松雪。
不笑亦不语,
冥栖在岩穴。
我来逢真人,
长跪问宝诀。
粲然启玉齿,
授以炼药说。
铭骨传其语,
竦身已电灭。
仰望不可及,
苍然五情热。
吾将营丹砂,
永与世人别。

No. 5

Mt. Venus with its trees scrapes clouds,
Which float about from star to star.
The sky's a hundred miles from earth,
And to humans it seems too far.
A green haired old man lives atop,
Donning clouds, lying on pine snow.
He contemplates in a rock cave,

Neither smiling nor speaking, no.
On my knees I ask for the knack
From the immortal I have met.
He smiles, exposing his white teeth
And tells me how drugs I can get.
I keep what he says deep in mind,
And thunder-like he does depart.
The task's something far beyond me,
I feel heat rising from my heart.
I'll purify cinnabar, well done,
Away from the world, from it gone.

* Mt. Venus: the highest peak of Ch'in Ridge, known for its height, coldness, dangerousness, strangeness and bountifulness, named after Venus, the Great White Star. Pai Li, of which Pai means Venus literally, was given the name Venus because his mother dreamed of Venus before labor, which suggests he was begotten by the spirit of the Great White Star.
* cinnabar: a mercuric mineral, the raw material for elixir in Wordist alchemy.

其 六

代马不思越,
越禽不恋燕。
情性有所习,
土风固其然。
昔别雁门关,
今戍龙庭前。
惊沙乱海日,
飞雪迷胡天。
虮虱生虎鹖,
心魂逐旌旃。
苦战功不赏,
忠诚难可宣。
谁怜李飞将,
白首没三边。

No. 6

The north horse misses not south Yüeh;
The south bird thinks not of north Yan.
All humors are shaped by the clime;
Change one's habits few people can.
Then they guarded the Wild Geese Pass,
And now they garrison Dragon Hall.
Sand's swirled hard to the desert sun,
And snow sweeps the Huns' sky to fall.
They are burning to go back home;
Now their bodies host louse and flea.
Their merits have won no reward,

And their fealty none cares to see.
Look there at General Li of Han,
Who died in shame, a gray-haired man.

* horse: a large herbivorous solid-hoofed quadruped (*Equus caballus*) with a coarse mane and tail, of various strains: Ferghana, Mongolian, Kazaks, Hequ, Karasahr and so on, and of various colors: black, white, yellow, brown, dappled and so on, commonly in the domesticated state, employed as a beast of draught and burden and especially for riding upon.
* Yüeh and Yan: two ancient states, respectively located in the south and north of China.
* the Wild Geese Pass: an important pass on the Great Wall, known as "the first pass of China". As it is a south-north hub, governors of all dynasties sent military forces there to guard against invasions from northern ethnic groups, usually called Huns.
* Dragon Hall: a holy altar where Hun chieftains held worship ceremonies.
* Hun: war-like nomadic peoples occupying vast regions from Mongolia to Central Asia in Chinese history, especially during the Han dynasty. They were a constant menace on China's western and northern borders.
* General Li: Broad Li (? – 119 B.C.) in full name, Kuang Li if transliterated, a renowned general who won many battles against the Huns in the Han dynasty. Two of his descendants left deep footprints in Chinese history, Hao Li (A.D. 351 – A.D. 417), King Martial Glare of West Cool (A.D. 400 – A.D. 421) and Yüan Li (A.D. 566 – A.D. 635), the founder and first emperor of T'ang.

其 七

五鹤西北来,
飞飞凌太清。
仙人绿云上,
自道安期名。
两两白玉童,
双吹紫鸾笙。
去影忽不见,
回风送天声。
我欲一问之,
飘然若流星。
愿餐金光草,
寿与天齐倾。

No. 7

The five cranes hover and whoop down,
Coming all the way from northwest.
The sage who's astride a green cloud
So says: My name is Rise-from-rest.
His four children so pure and white
Play mauve phoenix flutes in pair.
The sage suddenly disappears,
An echo blown clear through the air.
Like a meteor, off he has gone,
Tho I would catch up and ask why.
How I wish I gained elixir
To live well with Heaven for aye.

* crane: one of a family of large, long-necked, long legged, heronlike birds allied to the rails, a symbol of longevity and integrity in Chinese culture, only second to the phoenix in cultural importance.
* Rise-from-rest: an immortal living on Mt. Fairyland.
* flute: a tubular wind instrument of small diameter with holes along the side.
* elixir: a kind of cure-all, all alchemists in Chinese history have tried to make and all Wordists hope to find.
* Heaven: the space surrounding or seeming to overarch the earth, in which the sun, the moon, and stars appear, popularly the abode of God, his angels and the blessed, the dwelling place or state of existence of righteous souls after their life on earth, and in most cases suggesting supernatural power or sometimes signifying a monarch.

其 八

咸阳二三月，
宫柳黄金枝。
绿帻谁家子，
卖珠轻薄儿。
日暮醉酒归，
白马骄且驰。
意气人所仰，
冶游方及时。
子云不晓事，
晚献长杨辞。
赋达身已老，
草玄鬓若丝。
投阁良可叹，
但为此辈嗤。

No. 8

In Allshine, the second, third moon,
The court willows their gold twigs sway.
Who's the boy wearing a green hat,
Selling pearls, given to much play?
At nightfall, he comes back, so drunk,
His white horse gallops with a neigh.
His philandering much admired,
This gigolo would for long stay!
Yang, not a worldly man at all,
Gives his verse to the court so late.
His art is fine but he's too old,

Gray his sideburns and bald his pate.
Pity, he jumps down from the rail;
All sneer at him, hearing the tale.

* Allshine: Hsienyang if transliterated, the capital of the Ch'in Empire. It is so called because all its rivers and mountains could get sunshine from all around. It was built in 350 B.C. and Ch'in moved its capital here the next year from Oakshine (Liyang).
* the boy wearing a green hat: implying Yan Tung, a gigolo waiting on Princess Boarding Kiln (Kuant'ao) of Han. Yan used to sell pearls with his mother when he was a child, and therefore was able to enter the princess' park frequently. Having good looks, he was kept in the park to be raised by Princess Boarding Kiln.
* pearl: a lustrous, calcareous concretion deposited in layers around a central nucleus in the shells of various mollusks, and largely used as a gem, a symbol of love or friendship in Chinese culture.
* horse: a large herbivorous solid-hoofed quadruped (*Equus caballus*) with coarse mane and tail, of various strains and various colors, domesticated about four thousand years ago, reared as a pet, employed as a beast of draught and burden and especially for riding upon.
* Yang: Man Yang (Hsiung Yang) in full name, a great scholar, rhymed prose writer and official in the Han dynasty, whose great work *The Great One* has had a deep influence on works of later generations.

其 九

庄周梦胡蝶,
胡蝶为庄周。
一体更变易,
万事良悠悠。
乃知蓬莱水,
复作清浅流。
青门种瓜人,
旧日东陵侯。
富贵故如此,
营营何所求。

No. 9

Lush dreamed he was a butterfly;
A butterfly dreamed it was Lush.
One thing undergoes all changes;
All the world proceeds in a rush.
Water from Fairyland now flows
Over a shallow stream once more.
He, who by Blue Gate melon grows,
Was Marquis of East Hill of yore.
Wealth or honor is just like this;
Should one go after fame or bliss?

* Lush: Sir Lush, Chuangtzu if transliterated, an important philosopher in the Warring States period, one of the representatives of Wordism (Taoism). One of the most important Chinese classics is *Sir Lush*, a book of philosophical allegories written by Sir Lush.

* butterfly: any of various families of lepidopteran insects active in the day-time, having a sucking mouthpart, slender body, ropelike, knobbed antennae, and four broad, usually brightly colored, membraneous wings.
* Blue Gate: the east gate of Long Peace, the capital of T'ang.
* Fairyland: a fabled island on East Sea, a dwelling place of immortals and exalted spirits.
* Marquis of East Hill: a childe in the Ch'in dynasty. He was debased to grow melons by Blue Gate when Ch'in expired.

其 十

齐有倜傥生，
鲁连特高妙。
明月出海底，
一朝开光曜。
却秦振英声，
后世仰末照。
意轻千金赠，
顾向平原笑。
吾亦澹荡人，
拂衣可同调。

No. 10

In Ch'i a man, Lien Lu by name,
Is a talented sparkling one.
Like a pearl from beneath the sea,
He glistens to outshine the sun.
He's lobbied against Ch'in, so smart,
Winning all respect, so refined.
Prince Plain would give him much gold;
With a smile, he gently declined.
Unrestrained like this man am I;
To the vain world we say good-bye.

* Lien Lu: a famous strategist (305 B.C.- 245 B.C.) in the Warring States period, who once helped Prince Plain of Chao persuade the State of Way successfully to form an alliance against Ch'in.
* pearl: a lustrous, calcareous concretion deposited in layers around a central nucleus in

the shells of various mollusks, and largely used as a gem, medicine or given as a gift.
* sun: the heavenly body that is the center of attraction and the main source of light and heat in the solar system, a representation of Shine in contrast with Shade, the moon, in Chinese culture, a symbol of hope, life, strength, vigor, and youth.
* Ch'in: the Ch'in State or the State of Ch'in (905 B.C - 206 B.C.), enfeoffed as a dependency of Chough by King Piety of Chough in 905 B.C and enfeoffed as a vassal state by King Peace of Chough in 770 B.C. In the ten years from 230 B.C. to 221 B.C., Ch'in wiped out the other six powers and became the first unified regime of China, i.e. the Ch'in Empire.
* Prince Plain: Chao Sheng (? - 251 B.C.), a prince of the State of Chao and a renowned statesman and strategist in the Warring States period.

其十一

黄河走东溟，
白日落西海。
逝川与流光，
飘忽不相待。
春容舍我去，
秋发已衰改。
人生非寒松，
年貌岂长在。
吾当乘云螭，
吸景驻光彩。

No. 11

The Yellow flows to the east blue;
The sun sets beyond the west sea.
Rivers unrest, light on the go,
Time and tide wait for none and flee.
Prime and charm vanish all too soon;
One grows weak with his sideburns gray.
Life's not like a pine against snow;
How can our beauty for long stay?
On high a phoenix we should ride,
Absorbing glamour far and wide.

* the Yellow: the Yellow River, the second longest river in China, the cradle of Chinese civilization. As legend goes, the river derived from a yellow dragon that, couchant on Midland Plain, ate yellow soil, flooded crops, devoured people and stock, and was finally tamed by Great Worm, the First King of Hsia (cir. 21 B.C.- 16 B.C.). Its fertile

valleys were turned into fields of rice, barley and oscillating corn, amid gleaming streams and lakes.
* sun: the heavenly body that is the main source of light and heat in the solar system, a representation of Shine in contrast with Shade, the moon, in Chinese culture. It is a symbol of hope, life, strength, vigor, and youth.
* pine: any of a genus (*Pinus*) of evergreen trees of the pine family, a cone-bearing tree having bundles of two to five needle-shaped leaves growing in clusters, an important image in Chinese literature, a symbol of rectitude, longevity and so on.
* Phoenix: In Chinese myths, phoenixes, auspicious birds, unlike ordinary ones, only perch on parasol trees, and only eat bamboo shoots and pearly stone.

其十二

松柏本孤直，
难为桃李颜。
昭昭严子陵，
垂钓沧波间。
身将客星隐，
心与浮云闲。
长揖万乘君，
还归富春山。
清风洒六合，
邈然不可攀。
使我长叹息，
冥栖岩石间。

No. 12

Pines and cypresses stand erect;
Unlike peach and plum, they can't please.
Brightness Yan, who's a righteous man,
Will live in hills and fish at seas.
To seclusion he does retreat,
His heart like a cloud floating free.
Saying farewell to the Most High,
In the Richspring Hills he will be.
Like a breath of wind sweeping all,
He's hard to follow or o'erride.
Admiring him with a long sigh,
Among those rocks I would abide.

* pine: an evergreen tree of the genus *Pinus*, standing for staunchness and reliability in Chinese culture, especially when used in context with vines, an image of clinging wife.
* cypress: an evergreen tree of the family Cupressaceae, having durable timber, a symbol of rectitude, nobility and longevity in Chinese culture.
* peach: any of the plant (*Prunus Percica*), bearing a fleshy, juicy, edible drupe, cultivated in many varieties in temperate zones, considered sacred in China, a symbol of romance, prosperity and longevity.
* plum: a kind of plant or the edible purple drupaceous fruit of the plant which is any one of various trees of the genus *Prunus*, cultivated in temperate zones.
* Brightness Yan: Tsuling Yan (39 B.C.- A.D. 41) if transliterated, a renowned hermit in the Han dynasty. He showed his talent at an early age. After Hsiu Liu was enthroned to be the emperor of Han, Yan was invited several times to serve the court. Though the emperor was an acquaintance of his, Yan declined the offer and chose to live in seclusion in the Richspring Hills.
* the Most High: referring to Hsiu Liu (6 B.C.- A.D.57), the first emperor of Eastern Han (A.D. 25 - A.D. 220), which succeeded New Dynasty (A.D. 9 - A.D. 23) that usurped the throne of Western Han (202 B.C.- A.D. 8).
* the Richspring Hills: the hills where Brightness Yan reclaimed a farmland and went fishing in seclusion.

其十三

君平既弃世，
世亦弃君平。
观变穷太易，
探玄化群生。
寂寞缀道论，
空帘闭幽情。
驺虞不虚来，
鸑鷟有时鸣。
安知天汉上，
白日悬高名。
海客去已久，
谁人测沈冥。

No. 13

You Peace keeps away from the world,
And the world keeps You Peace away.
He observes the change of all things,
And serves all beings with the Way.
In solitude he learns the Word
And keeps his curtained room so still.
Fortune Cats come but at right time;
Phoenixes only to saints trill.
How does one know the Milky Way
And the sun that hangs in the sky?
The hiker's gone away for long,
Who can divine and tell me why?

* You Peace: Chünp'ing (86 B.C.- A.D. 10) if transliterated, a Wordist scholar and thinker at the end of the Western Han dynasty. He lived in seclusion by telling fortune in Silkton (Ch'engtu), and usually guided people to do good based on their potential, advocated the Wordist classic, *The Word and the World*, to benefit the people.
* the Word: referring to Tao if transliterated, the most significant and profoundest concept in Chinese philosophy. The Word is identifiable with the Word or Logos in the West, as there is an enormous amount of common ground in the two cosmologies and the doctrines concerning the most fundamental matters such as "the Word is the one" and "God is the One", and the personalization of Being, the progenitor of finite spirits, which are subordinate kinds of Being or merely appearances of the Divine, the One.
* Fortune Cat: a kind of benevolent beast in ancient Chinese myths. As legend goes, the beast is as large as the tiger, colored, with a tail longer than its body. In Chinese mythology, auspicious birds and beasts like phoenixes and fortune cats make their appearance only when benevolent governance is applied.
* phoenix: the king of all birds, an auspicious sign in Chinese civilization. In Egyptian mythology, it is a legendary bird of great beauty, unique of its kind, which was supposed to live five or six hundred years before consuming itself by fire, rising again from its ashes to live through another cycle, a symbol of immortality. In Chinese mythology, the phoenix is the most beautiful bird that only perches on phoenix trees, i.e. firmiana, only eats firmiana fruit, and only drinks sweet spring water, and this mythic bird appears only in times of peace and sagacious rule.
* the Milky Way: a luminous band circling the heavens composed of stars and nebulae; the Galaxy.

其十四

胡关饶风沙，
萧索竟终古。
木落秋草黄，
登高望戎虏。
荒城空大漠，
边邑无遗堵。
白骨横千霜，
嵯峨蔽榛莽。
借问谁凌虐，
天骄毒威武。
赫怒我圣皇，
劳师事鼙鼓。
阳和变杀气，
发卒骚中土。
三十六万人，
哀哀泪如雨。
且悲就行役，
安得营农圃。
不见征戍儿，
岂知关山苦。
争锋徒死节，
秉钺皆庸竖。
战士死蒿莱，
将军获圭组。
李牧今不在，
边人饲豺虎。

No. 14

The desert's been bleak since the past,
Which whirls a sky of wind and sand.
In autumn grass sears and leaves fall;
To gaze at Huns, uphill I stand.
The deserted town looks so bleak.
And nothing in the fief remains.
The rotten bones are chill with frost,
A field of brambles and no grains.
Who has destroyed the place like this?
Due to the Huns it's so become.
Now our sage lord flies into rage,
And will rise and beat the war drum.
Silence turns into bloody shouts;
Soldiers are sent from Middle Plain.
Three hundred and sixty thousand!
Their tragic tears running like rain.
To battlefields all having gone,
Who will the farmland till for grains?
Don't you see those guarding the front?
Don't you know they suffer all pains?
To charge ahead means run to die,
Though with halberds they try to stand.
The fighters fall flat into grass;
The generals win their ribbons grand.
Pity, Mu Li's not here this hour;
Tigers and wolves the folks devour.

* Hun: one of barbaric nomadic Asian peoples who frequently invaded China, a general

term referring to all northern or western invaders, who had no trade but battle and carnage, no fields or plough lands but only wastes where white bones lay scattered over yellow sands.
* Mu Li: Mu Li (? - 229 B.C.), a famous general of the State of Chao, one of the four most famous generals in the Warring States period.
* tiger: a large carnivorous feline mammal of Asia, with vertical black wavy stripes on a tawny body and black bars or rings on the limbs and tail, praised as king of all animals.
* wolf: a large carnivorous mammal related to the dog, regarded as ravenous, cruel, or rapacious, a metaphor for an invader or lecher in Chinese culture.

其十五

燕昭延郭隗，
遂筑黄金台。
剧辛方赵至，
邹衍复齐来。
奈何青云士，
弃我如尘埃。
珠玉买歌笑，
糟糠养贤才。
方知黄鹤举，
千里独徘徊。

No. 15

King Glare of Yan invites Wei Kuo
And for him builds a golden mound.
Hsin Chü arrives in Yan from Chao,
And from Ch'i, Yan Tsou comes around.
However, all those now in power
Reject me, treating me as dirt.
They spend much gold on dancing girls,
But keep talents with chaff, so curt.
Now I know why cranes fly away
And far off, in solitude stay.

---

* King Glare of Yan: King Glare of Yan (335 B.C.- 279 B.C.), the 39th monarch of Yan in the Warring States period, who built a golden mound to attract talents over the world, bringing the state to a flourishing age under his governance.
* Wei Kuo: Wei Kuo (351 B.C.- 297 B.C.), a minister of Yan, who suggested that King

Glare learn from the ancients to invite men of ability. Owing to his suggestion, Kuo was looked up to as the teacher of King Glare of Yan.

* Hsin Chu: Hsin Chu (? – 243 B.C.), a military strategist from Chao, who came to serve Yan and made some achievements.
* Yan: the State of Yan (1044 B.C.– 222 B.C.), a vassal state in the Spring and Autumn period, one of the Seven Powers in the Warring States period.
* Chao: the State of Chao (403 B.C.– 222 B.C.), a vassal state in the Spring and Autumn period, one of the Seven Powers in the Warring States period.
* Ch'i: the State of Ch'i (1000 B.C.– 221 B.C.), a vassal state of Chough, a powerful state in the Spring and Autumn period and the Warring State period.
* Yan Tsou: Yan Tsou (324 B.C.– 250 B.C.), a representative scholar of Wordism and the founder of Five Elements Theory. He, a native of Ch'in, was a promotor of Yan.
* crane: one of a family of large, long-necked, long legged, heronlike birds allied to the rails, a symbol of longevity and integrity in Chinese culture, only second to the phoenix in cultural importance.

其十六

宝剑双蛟龙,
雪花照芙蓉。
精光射天地,
雷腾不可冲。
一去别金匣,
飞沉失相从。
风胡灭已久,
所以潜其锋。
吴水深万丈,
楚山邈千重。
雌雄终不隔,
神物会当逢。

No. 16

Two swords like two dragons fly;
The snow gleams o'er lotuses pink.
Their shine invades Heaven and earth;
E'en thunder and lightning shrink.
One day from the cask they are lost,
So they are no longer a pair.
It's a long time since Zephyr died,
So hidden is their piercing glare.
Wu's water's fathomless, so deep,
Ch'u's hills upon hills roll away.
Female and male won't stay apart;
Divine things, they will meet one day.

* two swords: referring to the two renowned ancient swords, Kanchiang and Moyeh, a metaphor for one who has no opportunity to put his talent to use. The two swords were once collected by Huan Lei in the West Chin dynasty. He gave Kanchiang to his friend Hua Chang and kept Moyeh. But Kanchiang was lost after Chang was murdered. After Lei's death, when his son Hua Lei passed by Yanp'ing Ford, all of a sudden, Moyeh jumped off his waist to the water to join its partner Kanchiang, and the two swords turned into two dragons.
* lotus: one of the various plants of the waterlily family, noted for their large floating leaves and showy flowers, a symbol of purity and elegance in Chinese culture, unsoiled though out of soil, so clean with all leaves green.
* dragon: a fabulous serpent-like giant winged animal that can change its girth and length, a totem of the Chinese nation, a symbol of benevolence and sovereignty in Chinese culture, the totem of all Chinese across the world.
* Zephyr: a famous sword connoisseur from Ch'u in the Spring and Autumn period.

其十七

金华牧羊儿,
乃是紫烟客。
我愿从之游,
未去发已白。
不知繁华子,
扰扰何所迫。
昆山采琼蕊,
可以炼精魄。

No. 17

A shepherd in Gold Bloom there is;
An immortal sage he is called.
I would follow him to find truth,
But I am now old, gray and bald.
These worldly young men run about,
So hastened with a disturbed mind.
We can pick pistils at Mt. Queen,
Wherewith to train a soul refined.

* A shepherd in Gold Bloom: a shepherd called Ch'up'ing Huang was admired by a Wordist for his good deed, and therefore was brought to Mt. Gold Bloom to learn the Word. The shepherd became an immortal and named himself Red Pine afterwards.
* Mt. Queen: Mt. Kunlun if transliterated, is the most sacred mountain in China. It starts from the eastern Pamir Plateau, stretches across New Land (Hsinchiang) and Tibet, and extends to Blue Sea (Ch'inghai), with an average altitude of 5,500 – 6,000 meters. In Chinese myths, Mt. Queen is where Mother West dwells.

其十八

天津三月时，
千门桃与李。
朝为断肠花，
暮逐东流水。
前水复后水，
古今相续流。
新人非旧人，
年年桥上游。
鸡鸣海色动，
谒帝罗公侯。
月落西上阳，
余辉半城楼。
衣冠照云日，
朝下散皇州。
鞍马如飞龙，
黄金络马头。
行人皆辟易，
志气横嵩丘。
入门上高堂，
列鼎错珍羞。
香风引赵舞，
清管随齐讴。
七十紫鸳鸯，
双双戏庭幽。
行乐争昼夜，
自言度千秋。
功成身不退，
自古多愆尤。

黄犬空叹息,
绿珠成蚌雠。
何如鸱夷子,
散发棹扁舟。

No. 18

Close to Kingford Bridge the third moon,
Myriads of households see blooms blow.
In the morning the pistils blush;
At dusk they fall to the east flow.
The waves, chasing each other there,
Have been like this until today.
But so different people they are,
Who each year on the bridge play.
When at dawn cocks crow for the hour,
To morning court all grandees go.
When the moon falls beyond the court,
Half the town's filled with dawning glow.
When the levee's o'er and they leave,
Their robes and hats see the sun shine.
The horses like flying dragons run,
And their gold harnesses gleam fine.
All folks dodge their carts and steeds;
The grandees' mood exceeds Mt. Tower.
Then they enter their dining hall
And with dainties enjoy the hour.
The Ch'i lutes and flutes played so loud;
The Chao dancing girls their scent sway.
Seventy purple mandarin ducks
In the shade of the courtyard play.

They enjoy themselves day and night
And hope they can do this for e'er.
At their best if they don't retreat,
They will not end up well, o ne'er.
Ssu sighed a hunter he'd have been;
Shi, due to Green Pearl, went to hell.
Why not learn from Fan, hair dishevelled,
Boating on West Lake with his belle!

* Kingford Bridge: a bridge of great importance in Loshine, connecting two prosperous blocks of the ancient city.
* levee: a morning reception or an assembly at the court of a sovereign or at the house of a great personage. In ancient China, a levee at court was held every five days.
* Mt. Tower: located in the west of present-day Honan Province, one of the Five Mountains in Chinese culture. It is one of the five sanctuaries of Wordism, and the abode of God of Mt. Tower worshipped by Han Chinese, with an area of 450 square kilometers, consisting of Mt. Greatroom and Mt. Smallroom, having 72 peaks, 350 meters above sea level at the lowest and 1512 meters at the highest.
* lute: a stringed musical instrument, played by plucking the strings with fingers or a plectrum.
* flute: a tubular wind instrument of small diameter with holes along the side.
* mandarin ducks: duck-like love birds that always appear in pairs, a metaphor for couples in Chinese culture.
* Ssu: Ssu Li (284 B.C.- 208 B.C.), a renowned statesman, litterateur and calligrapher, whose political ideas have exerted a profound impact on China and laid the foundation for China's political system for more than two thousand years. After Emperor First of Ch'in died, Ssu was given a death sentence due to a false accusation. Before the execution, he sighed to his son that it would be impossible to hunt anymore. The allusion has often been quoted to indicate sinister risks in pursuit of a political life.
* Shi: referring to the litterateur Ch'ung Shi (A.D. 249 - A.D. 300), who died for refusing to give his consort Green Pearl away to a wicked official.
* Fan: referring to Li Fan (536 B.C.- 448 B.C.), a renowned statesman, strategist, economist and Wordist in the Spring and Autumn period. Fan changed his name to live in seclusion after he helped the State of Yüeh wipe out Wu.
* West Lake: west of Hangchow proper, one of the most famous attractions in China, with a rich historic legacy, like Su's Oyke, White Oyke, the Lone Hill, Petite's Tomb, Leifeng Pagoda and so on.

其十九

西上莲花山,
迢迢见明星。
素手把芙蓉,
虚步蹑太清。
霓裳曳广带,
飘拂升天行。
邀我登云台,
高揖卫叔卿。
恍恍与之去,
驾鸿凌紫冥。
俯视洛阳川,
茫茫走胡兵。
流血涂野草,
豺狼尽冠缨。

No. 19

From west I climb Mt. Lotus Flower,
And look up at the star on high.
Stroking the lotus with her hand,
Stepping on air, she walks the sky.
In rainbow robe with a long sash,
While rising, Heaven she does sweep.
She invites me to climb Cloud Mound,
Where to Shuching Wei I bow deep.
Riding a wild goose in the night,
I feel blown and thrown in the sky.
Looking down at the Loshine Plain,

> I see many Hun soldiers hie.
> The wild grass is with blood so drowned;
> The officials are wolves high-crowned.

* Mt. Lotus Flower: also known as Mt. Flora, Mt. West and Mt. Great Flower, one of the Five Mountains in China, representing the west.
* lotus: any of various waterlilies, especially the white or pink Asian lotus, used as a religious symbol in Hinduism and Buddhism. The lotus is a common image in Chinese literature, as two lines of a lyric by Hsiu Ouyang (1007-1072) read: "A thunder brings rain to the wood and pool, / The rain hushes the lotus, drips cool."
* Shuching Wei: an immortal. He once visited Emperor Martial of Han in a cart driven by a white deer. He disappeared, when feeling not welcome enough. When the emperor sent his son to find him, he was playing chess in a jade bed with fairies standing behind, and the prince could not get near.
* Hun: war-like nomadic peoples occupying vast regions from Mongolia to Central Asia in Chinese history, especially during the Han dynasty. They were a constant menace on China's western and northern borders.

其二十

昔我游齐都，
登华不注峰。
兹山何峻秀，
绿翠如芙蓉。
萧飒古仙人，
了知是赤松。
借予一白鹿，
自挟两青龙。
含笑凌倒景，
欣然愿相从。
泣与亲友别，
欲语再三咽。
勖君青松心，
努力保霜雪。
世路多险艰，
白日欺红颜。
分手各千里，
去去何时还。
在世复几时，
倏如飘风度。
空闻紫金经，
白首愁相误。
抚己忽自笑，
沉吟为谁故。
名利徒煎熬，
安得闲余步。
终留赤玉舄，
东上蓬莱路。

秦帝如我求，

苍苍但烟雾。

No. 20

I travelled Capital of Ch'i,

And then to Mt. Calyx did hike.

The mountains scraped the sky above,

Looking so green, green lotus-like.

There I met a saintly old man,

Whose name as I know was Red Pine.

He lent me a deer purely white,

And he rode two dragons divine.

Smiling, our shadows left behind,

We went up, soul with soul combined.

All choke with sadness and shed tears

When kin and friends say bye to me.

May they survive cold bites and frost,

With a young heart like a pine tree.

Life is hard, full of ups and downs;

The sun will always fade a rose.

Now as we part from each other,

When can we meet again? God knows.

Life is short howe'er long you wish,

Like a wind blowing and then gone.

You read *Sutra Gold*, but in vain,

With gray hair, all's been vainly done.

At this world I can't help but laugh;

Why on earth should I sing this song?

Let them wobble in ranks and fame;

I would be free, strolling along.

Red Pine went to Mt. Fairyland,
Leaving his ruby shoes aside.
Emperor of Ch'in would seek him,
But found haze spreading far and wide.

* Capital of Ch'i: Lintzu, an area of today's Tzupo, Shantung Province.
* Mt. Calyx: also named Mt. Flower or Mt. Sepal, northeast of present-day Chinan, Shantung Province. It is so named probably because of the lines in *The Book of Songs*: Cherry blossoms blow fine; / Even the sepals shine.
* Red Pine: an immortal who named himself Red Pine, formerly a shepherd called Ch'up'ing Huang who was admired by a Wordist for his good deeds and brought to Mt. Gold Bloom to learn the Word.
* deer: a ruminant (family *Cervidae*), having deciduous antlers, usually in the male only, as the moose, elk, and reindeer. Deer are closely related to Chinese life. Deer hide is a precious gift, especially presented to a female and a deer is usually a symbol of imperial power as it is often a target of pursuit.
* sun: the heavenly body that is the center of attraction and the main source of light and heat in the solar system, a representation of Shine in contrast with Shade, the moon, in Chinese culture, a symbol of hope, life, strength, vigor, and youth.
* rose: any of a genus of shrubs of the rese family, characteristically with prickly stems, alternate compound leaves, and five-parted, usually fragrant flowers of red, pink, white, yellow, etc, having many stamens. It is often used as a metaphor for beauty or love.
* *Sutra Gold*: a book on alchemy.
* dragon: a fabulous serpent-like giant winged animal, a totem of the Chinese nation, a symbol of benevolence and sovereignty in Chinese culture.
* Fairyland: a fabled island on East Sea, a dwelling place of immortals and exalted spirits.
* Ch'in: the Ch'in State or the State of Ch'in (905 B.C - 206 B.C.), enfeoffed as a dependency of Chough by King Piety of Chough in 905 B.C and enfeoffed as a vassal state by King Peace of Chough in 770 B.C. In the ten years from 230 B.C. to 221 B.C., Ch'in wiped out the other six powers and became the first unified regime of China, i.e. the Ch'in Empire.

其二十一

郢客吟白雪，
遗响飞青天。
徒劳歌此曲，
举世谁为传。
试为巴人唱，
和者乃数千。
吞声何足道，
叹息空凄然。

No. 21

A man from Yington sings *White Snow*,
Whose sound lingers up to the blue.
This song, howe'er, is sung in vain,
Who on earth will echo? So few.
When he tries to chant *Country Folks*,
Thousands of people there respond.
He falls silent. What can he say?
Sigh upon sigh, he does despond!

* Yington: Ying, the capital of the State of Ch'u, four kilometers north of today's Chaste Town (Chingchow), Hupei Province.
* *White Snow*: a song which is a representation of highbrow works, originally an elegant sophisticated tune of the State of Ch'u, played for the court, inaccessible to common people.
* *Country Folks*: a popular song from the State of Ch'u, enjoyed by common people, usually referring to vernacular art or anything that is vernacular.

其二十二

秦水别陇首,
幽咽多悲声。
胡马顾朔雪,
蹩躠长嘶鸣。
感物动我心,
缅然含归情。
昔视秋蛾飞,
今见春蚕生。
袅袅桑柘叶,
萋萋柳垂荣。
急节谢流水,
羁心摇悬旌。
挥涕且复去,
恻怆何时平。

No. 22

When the Ch'in takes leave of Mt. Bulge,
It feels so sad and choked a lot.
The Hun horse looks back at north snow;
With a long neigh, it would not trot.
This sight strikes me down to my heart,
Thus I intone a go-home lay.
Then I saw autumnal moths fly
And see spring silkworms creep today.
Sheen to sheen, mulberry leaves shine;
Green to green, willow branches sway.
My heart, like a flag, flows without stop,

And like a stream, cannot still stay.
Wiping off my tears, I would go;
When could I be freed of my woe?

* Mt. Bulge: a mountain located in the southeast of present-day Kansu Province, 2,928 meters above sea level and about 240 kilometers long from north to south, the borderline between Sha'anhsi Loess Plateau and West Bulge Loess Plateau, formerly inhabited by Western Arms, Ch'iang as is called today. It is usually used as a metaphor for the top of a mountain.
* Hun: one of barbaric nomadic Asian peoples who frequently invaded China, a general term referring to all northern or western invaders, who had no trade but battle and carnage, no fields or ploughlands but only wastes where white bones lay scattered over yellow sands.
* silkworm: the larva of a moth that produces a dense silken cocoon, especially the common silkworm from whose cocoon commercial silk is made. The silkworm was cultivated in 3000 B.C. when Lace Mum, who was Lord Yellow's concubine began to raise silkworms and make silk.
* mulberry: the edible, berry-like fruit of a tree (genus *Morus*) whose leaves are valued for silkworm culture, and the tree itself, first cultivated in the drainage area of the Yellow River in China about five thousand years ago, concurrent with the time when silkworms were raised.
* willow: any of a large genus of shrubs and trees related to the poplars, having generally smooth branches, and often long, slender, pliant, and sometimes pendent branchlets, which seem to be bidding farewell or sweeping amorously.

其二十三

秋露白如玉，
团团下庭绿。
我行忽见之，
寒早悲岁促。
人生鸟过目，
胡乃自结束。
景公一何愚，
牛山泪相续。
物苦不知足，
得陇又望蜀。
人心若波澜，
世路有屈曲。
三万六千日。
夜夜当秉烛。

No. 23

Autumn dew is like jade white,
Shining the blades of the court grass.
At this view, I cannot but sigh:
How time hastens the world to pass.
Life, bird-like, flies before our eyes;
All by itself, it disappears.
How foolish Lord Scene of Ch'i is!
Before Mt. Bull he sheds his tears.
Worldly greed none can satisfy;
Getting the butt, he longs for the end.
A human heart, like water, swells

>　　And like a road, is prone to bend.
>　　One Life's thirty-six thousand days;
>　　Each night let's enjoy candle rays.

* Lord Scene of Ch'i: a lord of Ch'i (? - 490 B.C.), a hegemon, in the Spring and Autumn period. He once wept at the sight of the landscape on Mt. Bull, sinking into deep melancholy of mortality. When all the retinue followed their lord and sobbed, only Sir Dusk remained sober and chuckled for the absurdity.
* Mt. Bull: also called Mt. Gold Bull, about 7.5 kilometers long and 2.5 kilometers wide in modern-day Feich'eng Shantung Province.
* candle: a cylinder of tallow, wax, or other solid fat, containing a wick, to give light when burning, first seen in literature in the Eastern Han dynasty. The most famous lines about candles are from a poem by a T'ang poet named Shangyin Li, "Silkworms stop offering silk when they die; / Candles become ash as their tears run dry."

其二十四

大车扬飞尘，
亭午暗阡陌。
中贵多黄金，
连云开甲宅。
路逢斗鸡者，
冠盖何辉赫。
鼻息干虹霓，
行人皆怵惕。
世无洗耳翁，
谁知尧与跖。

No. 24

The carts rumble, stirring up dust
That darkens the road at noon high.
The grandees squander so much gold;
Their houses rise to cloud the sky.
I meet cock fighters on the way;
How their clothes and canopies glare!
They breathe out air like clouds so loud
That travelers are given a scare!
None having good faith or belief,
Who can tell a saint from a thief?

---

* cock fighters: cock fighting has a long history in China, a main recreational activity all through history. The earliest cock fighting in China recorded in *Historical Records* was in 770 B.C.

* None having good faith or belief, / Who can tell a saint from a thief?: an allusion to

Freedom (Yu Hsu), a precedent of Wordists in the age of Mound and Hibiscus. When Mound wanted to offer his throne to Freedom, the latter regarded it as a shame and went to a river to wash his ears because he thought the offer had dirtied his ears. Freedom has since been regarded as a man of good faith and with discerning judgment of what is wrong or right.

其二十五

世道日交丧，
浇风散淳源。
不采芳桂枝，
反栖恶木根。
所以桃李树，
吐花竟不言。
大运有兴没，
群动争飞奔。
归来广成子，
去入无穷门。

No. 25

The world's gone astray from the Word;
Wickedness and vanity spread.
No one would gather laurel sprays,
They live near evil trees instead.
So plum and peach trees keep silence,
Just blooming on their own to blush.
The Way of Heaven is preset,
To which some day all souls will rush.
Sir Goodharvest will come once more;
With him I'll enter the Void Door.

* the Word: referring to Tao if transliterated, the most significant and profoundest concept in Chinese philosophy. According to Laocius's *The Word and the World*: "The Word is void, but its use is infinite. O deep! It seems to be the root of all things."
* laurel: an evergreen shrub with aromatic, lance-shaped leaves, yellowish flowers, and

succulent, cherry-like fruit, a symbol of glory usually in the form of a crown or wreath of laurel to indicate honor or high merit, especially when one had passed Grand Test in ancient China. In Chinese mythology, there is a laurel tree on the moon, and it would never fall even though Kang Wu has kept cutting it.
* plum: a kind of plant or the edible purple drupaceous fruit of the plant which is any one of various trees of the genus *Prunus*, cultivated in temperate zones.
* peach: any of the plant (*Prunus Percica*), bearing a fleshy, juicy, edible drupe, cultivated in many varieties in temperate zones, considered sacred in China, a symbol of romance, prosperity and longevity.
* the Way of Heaven: the natural or divine ultimate force in the cosmos, the Word or the Logos.
* Sir Goodharvest: a legendary immortal who is said to have lived 1,200 years when Lord Yellow visited him on Mt. Hollow, a sanctuary of Wordism.
* The Void Door: the gateway to the realm of the Word or the state of nothingness in Wordism.

其二十六

碧荷生幽泉，
朝日艳且鲜。
秋花冒绿水，
密叶罗青烟。
秀色空绝世，
馨香竟谁传。
坐看飞霜满，
凋此红芳年。
结根未得所，
愿托华池边。

No. 26

The lotus green grows in Dim Spring;
The dawning brightens her green hue.
Her blooms burst from autumn water;
Her dense leaves don thick smoky blue.
Her beauty ranks the best of all;
Who will her aroma far spread?
Frost will soon cover all the ground,
And blast the dazzle of her red.
Rooted up, nowhere to abide,
May she live by Flora Pool's side.

* lotus: one of the various plants of the waterlily family, noted for their large floating leaves and showy flowers, a symbol of purity and elegance in Chinese culture, unsoiled though out of soil, so clean with all leaves green.
* Dim Spring: name of a common pond.
* Flora Pool: Flora Palace in one of the four most famous royal parks in China, built in the T'ang dynasty.

其二十七

燕赵有秀色，

绮楼青云端。

眉目艳皎月，

一笑倾城欢。

常恐碧草晚，

坐泣秋风寒。

纤手怨玉琴，

清晨起长叹。

焉得偶君子。

共乘双飞鸾。

No. 27

The Border States boast a real belle;

Thin clouds hover o'er the glazed tiles.

Her brows intoxicate the moon;

Her ogle the whole town beguiles.

The verdant grass sways at late hours;

In autumn chill, she sits alone.

Her fair fingers run thru the lute

Till dawn and she gets up to moan.

Where could she go and a prince find

So to fly like two birds combined?

* the Border States: referring to two northern states, the State of Yan enfeoffed by King Martial and the State of Chao, built by the Chao's, descendants of a famous courtier of King Chow, the last king of Shang.
* the moon: the satellite of the earth, a representative of shade or feminity of things,

alluding to the belle in this poem. In a universe animated by the interaction of Shade and Shine energies, the moon is Shade visible, the very germ or source of Shade, and the sun is its Shine counterpart. It is the goddess of the moon and of months in Roman mythology, and in Chinese culture the imperial concubine of Lord Alarm (2480 B.C.–2345 B.C.), one of five mythical emperors in prehistorical China. The moon is celebrated with mooncakes by Chinese all over the world on Mid-autumn Day when the moon is at its full glory.

* lute: a Chinese lute, a stringed musical instrument, usually placed on a table, played by plucking the strings with finers or a plectrum.

其二十八

容颜若飞电,
时景如飘风。
草绿霜已白,
日西月复东。
华鬓不耐秋,
飒然成衰蓬。
古来贤圣人,
一一谁成功。
君子变猿鹤,
小人为沙虫。
不及广成子,
乘云驾轻鸿。

No. 28

Fair skin fades, gone off like a bolt;
Good scenes like a wind vanish soon.
The verdant grass turns white with frost;
The sunset sees the rising moon.
Thin hair can't stand an autumn chill;
Soon it's gray like a frosted reed.
Saints and sages do come and go;
But who of them can e'er succeed?
A gentleman becomes a crane,
And a flunky turns into sand.
Why not follow Sir Goodharvest
A flying wild goose to command?

- * the moon: the celestial body that revolves around the earth from west to east as a satellite, which appears at night and gives off shining silvery light, an image of purity and solitude in Chinese culture.
- * reed: the slender, frequently jointed stem of certain tall grasses growing in wet places or in grasses themselves. A frosted reed is an image of the white hair of one getting old or suffering a mishap.
- * crane: one of a family of large, long-necked, long legged, heronlike birds allied to the rails, a symbol of longevity and integrity in Chinese culture, only second to the phoenix in cultural importance.
- * Sir Goodharvest: a legendary immortal who is said to have lived 1,200 years when Lord Yellow visited him on Mt. Hollow. He told Lord Yellow like this:"I keep the One and stay in the balance of Shade and Shine, so I have lived for one thousand and two hundred years, with no sign of decrepitude."
- * wild goose: an undomesticated goose that is caring and responsible, taken as a symbol of benevolence, righteousness, good manner, wisdom, and faith in Chinese culture.

其二十九

三季分战国，
七雄成乱麻。
王风何怨怒，
世道终纷拏。
至人洞玄象，
高举凌紫霞。
仲尼欲浮海，
吾祖之流沙。
圣贤共沦没，
临歧胡咄嗟。

No. 29

The Three Ages saw all states fight;
Seven Powers caused much confusion.
The Virtue of Kingship did fail,
The world suffered all contention.
The saints saw thru the sign of things,
Raising high clouds purple and grand.
Confucius would raft 'cross the sea,
And Laocius went west to the sand.
Saints and sages like all men did fall;
I sigh: "Is there a way at all?"

* The Three Ages: Hsia (2070 B.C.- 1600 B.C.), Shang (1600 B.C.- 1046 B.C.) and Chough (1046 B.C.- 256 B.C.), the foundation of Chinese civilization. The end of the Three Ages ushered in a period of contentions and fights among vassal states.
* Seven Powers: referring to the seven most powerful states existing from 475 B.C. to

221 B.C., including Ch'i, Ch'u, Yan, Han, Chao, Way and Ch'in. The Warring States period ended in 221 B.C. when Ch'in wiped out the other six states and established the first unified empire in China's history.
* Confucius would raft 'cross the sea: According to *Analects*, Confucius said: "Now the Word is disobeyed. I would go across the ocean with a raft."
* Confucius: Confucius (551 B.C.- 479 B.C.), a renowned thinker, educator and statesman in the Spring and Autumn period. He was born into a declining aristocratic family in the State of Lu, founded an important school of Confucianism and has had an indelible influence on Chinese wisdom and culture, especially in terms of his doctrine of golden mean and adherence to the rite and music system.
* Laocius went west to the sand: According to historical records, Laocius went west and ended up nowhere in the desert. One source says that he went to India and founded Buddhism and he himself was Buddha.

其三十

玄风变太古,
道丧无时还。
扰扰季叶人,
鸡鸣趋四关。
但识金马门,
谁知蓬莱山。
白首死罗绮,
笑歌无时闲。
绿酒哂丹液,
青娥凋素颜。
大儒挥金椎,
琢之诗礼间。
苍苍三株树,
冥目焉能攀。

No. 30

The goodness of yore is no more;
The Word is lost, and lost for e'er.
Seeking wealth, fame and all things vain,
People run crazy here and there.
They fall prone but to power and ranks;
Who knows there's an Edenic clime?
They play with courtesans and belles,
Laughing, singing without free time.
At nectar those drinkers may jeer;
A charming lady will soon fade.
When the Confucians robbed a tomb,

The pearls with pebbles were mislaid.
Three pearl trees grow in the best clime,
Which, if with closed eyes, one can't climb.

* goodness: derived from the word "God", which is the Word incarnate, the prerequisite of being human. Only if one shows goodness to others and gets along well with others can he be a man. Goodness is a Chinese as well as human vein, the supermeme of all cultures.
* the Word: referring to Tao if transliterated, the most significant and profoundest concept in Chinese philosophy, identifiable with the Word or the Logos in the west. According to Laocius's *The Word and the World*: "The Word is void, but its use is infinite. O deep! It seems to be the root of all things." The Word is comparable to the Word or the Logos in western philosophy.
* courtesans: professional women singers or lutenists, like *geisha* in Japan. In Chinese blue brothel culture, Chinese scholars and officials often visited courtesans for literary or art recreational activities.
* When the Confucians robbed a tomb: According to a story recorded in *Sir Lush*, two Confucians made excuses for their robbery by quoting from Confucian classics. The story is quoted to satirize the hypocrisy of Confucians or Confucianism.
* pearl: a smooth, lustrous, usually white and bluish-gray, calcareous concretion deposited in layers around a central nucleus in the shells of various mollusks or oysters, and largely used as a gem, medicine or given as a gift, representing nobility, purity and dignity in Chinese culture.

其三十一

郑客西入关，
行行未能已。
白马华山君，
相逢平原里。
璧遗镐池君，
明年祖龙死。
秦人相谓曰，
吾属可去矣。
一往桃花源，
千春隔流水。

No. 31

Cheng entered Case Dale in the west
And all the way west he did speed.
Midway he met Mount Flora, who
Drove a carriage and a white steed.
Mount asked him to pass jade to Hoe,
With the word: Dragon dies next year.
The Ch'in folks spread the news to all
And said: Let's go, let's flee from here.
Then to Peach Blossom Source fled they
And from the world they were away.

* Cheng: referring to Jung Cheng, a messager of Emperor First. As legend goes, in 211 B.C. Cheng met a messenger from God of Mt. Flora, who gave Cheng a letter for the emperor, and Emperor First died the next year after receiving the letter.
* Case Dale: an ancient pass located to the east of the capital, and Lint'ao to the west.

* Mount Flora: an immortal in charge of Mt. Flora.
* Hoe: the immortal in charge of clouds and waters.
* Dragon: a code word referring to Emperor First of Ch'in.
* Ch'in: the Ch'in State or the State of Ch'in (905 B.C.- 206 B.C.), enfeoffed as a dependency of Chough by King Piety of Chough in 905 B.C and enfeoffed as a vassal state by King Peace of Chough in 770 B.C. In the ten years from 230 B.C. to 221 B.C., Ch'in wiped out the other six powers and became the first unified regime of China, i.e. the Ch'in Empire.
* Peach Blossom Source: a fictitious land in the representative masterpiece of Poolbright T'ao (Yüanming T'ao). In his writing, a group of Ch'in people fled to Peach Blossom Source to keep away from the turbulent days, and the people and their offsprings had lived away from the world for 500 years before a fisherman of Chin stumbled into the village. Peach Blossom Source, as a symbol of a peaceful, happy, free, and equal life, has become an ideal among Chinese scholars.

其三十二

蓐收肃金气，
西陆弦海月。
秋蝉号阶轩，
感物忧不歇。
良辰竟何许，
大运有沦忽。
天寒悲风生，
夜久众星没。
恻恻不忍言，
哀歌逮明发。

No. 32

The autumn wind blows on, so chill;
The crescent hangs o'er the sea west.
And o'er the steps cicadas shrill;
Work no more, we should have a rest.
How long can we have a good time?
One may rise there and may fall here.
It's a cold day with a sad sough;
The night lasts till stars disappear.
So aggrieved, nothing could I say;
Till dawn I sing a mournful lay.

* cicada: a homopterous insect that sings its song of summer and shrills in autumn, a symbol of death and resurrection in Chinese culture because of its metamorphosis and recycle. Therefore, in ancient China, a jade cicada figure was put in the mouth of a dead body with such an intention of eternal life.
* a sad sough: referring to an autumn wind.

其三十三

北溟有巨鱼，
身长数千里。
仰喷三山雪，
横吞百川水。
凭陵随海运。
烜赫因风起。
吾观摩天飞。
九万方未已。

No. 33

There is a giant fish in North Sea,
One thousand miles long, tail to fin.
It spurts snow to enshroud all hills,
And all rivers' flow it gulps in.
It turns up great waves in the sea,
And rises with wind from their top.
I see it whoop up to the sky,
And to the zenith without stop.

* a giant fish in North Sea: a symbol of absolute freedom according to *Sir Lush*, indicating that absolute freedom can only be obtained by forgetting the boundaries of object consciousness and self consciousness to reach the Void Door. The beginning chapter reads like this: There in North Sea is a fish called Minnow, whose body spans about a thousand miles. When transformed into a bird, it is called Roc, whose back spans about a thousand miles.
* zenith: the point directly overhead in the sky or on the celestial sphere, opposed to the nadir.

其三十四

羽檄如流星，
虎符合专城。
喧呼救边急，
群鸟皆夜鸣。
白日曜紫微，
三公运权衡。
天地皆得一，
澹然四海清。
借问此何为，
答言楚征兵。
渡泸及五月，
将赴云南征。
怯卒非战士，
炎方难远行。
长号别严亲，
日月惨光晶。
泣尽继以血，
心摧两无声。
困兽当猛虎，
穷鱼饵奔鲸。
千去不一回，
投躯岂全生。
如何舞干戚，
一使有苗平。

No. 34

The plumed order darts, meteor-like;

The tiger tally shakes the town.
The emergency call's so loud
That frightened birds cry before dawn.
The sun glaring high in the sky,
The three ministers judge and weigh.
Both Heaven and earth play their part;
The four seas remain clear all day.
Please let me know why such a haste.
Because recruitment's on in Ch'u.
They will go on march to Yünnan,
After in May they cross the Lu.
The cowardly recruits can't fight;
And it's hot, they can't go afar.
They take leave of their parents, sad;
The sun, the moon, how pale they are!
They cry in tears, they cry in blood;
Mutely they shout, mutely they wail.
They fight, like tigers tearing sheep;
They march, like fish fed to a whale.
None of a thousand can survive;
And no survivors wholesome stay.
Why not follow Hibiscus, who
To conquer Sprouts a spear did sway?

* the plumed order darts: urgent military orders in ancient China, usually attached with a plume to show urgency.
* tiger tally: a token issued to generals for troop movement. It is usually tiger-shaped, with one half kept by the monarch and the other by local generals, and generals can send troops only if the two halves are matched.
* sun: the heavenly body that is the center of attraction and the main source of light and heat in the solar system, a representation of Shine in contrast with Shade, the moon, in Chinese culture, a symbol of hope, life, strength, vigor and youth.

* the three ministers: supreme officials in charge of military, residence, water engineering and building.
* Both Heaven and earth play their part: in Laocius's *The Word and the World*:"The sky has gotten the One, hence blue and clear; the earth has gotten the One, hence staid and still."
* Ch'u: the State of Ch'u, usually referring to southern lands.
* the Lu: referring to the River Lu or River Goldensand, located in Yünnan Province. Ancients believed that there was miasma on the River Lu all the year round except for May.
* tiger: a large ferocious, predatory, carnivorous feline mammal, with stripes on a tawny body and black bars on the limbs and tail.
* sheep: a medium-sized domesticated ruminant of the genus *Ovis*, highly prized for its flesh, wool and skin, regarded as meek, mild and shy.
* whale: a giant cetaceous mammal of fish-like form, especially one of the larger pelagic species, as distinguished from dolphins and porpoises, a symbol of great ambition or threat.
* Hibiscus: Shun if transliterated, an ancient sovereign, a descendant of Lord Yellow (2717 B.C.- 2599 B.C.), a son-in-law of Mound (cir. 2377 B.C.- 2259 B.C.), regarded as one of Five Lords in prehistoric China.
* Sprouts: Three Sprouts, often called Miao or Hmong, an ethnic minority living in the southwest of China and some Asian countries, noted for their silver crowns and trinkets as well as dancing and herbal medicine.

其三十五

丑女来效颦，
还家惊四邻。
寿陵失本步，
笑杀邯郸人。
一曲斐然子，
雕虫丧天真。
棘刺造沐猴，
三年费精神。
功成无所用，
楚楚且华身。
大雅思文王，
颂声久崩沦。
安得郢中质。
一挥成斧斤。

No. 35

The ugly girl mimicked the belle,
Frightening her neighbors like that.
The stupid lad lost his right step,
And by his townsmen was laughed at.
Sir Brilliance sang a claptrap song,
So artificial, carved so much.
A monkey sculptured on a thorn
Wasted three years' efforts as such.
Dragon Killer had tried in vain,
Though smart, with talents thereamong.
King Civil in *Psalms Major* and

> *Odes* have lain waste there for so long.
> With the best partner for the play,
> The Ying man's axe we could sway.

* The ugly girl mimicked the belle: In *Sir Lush*, West Maid, one of the Four Belles in ancient China, often knitted her brows due to her heart disease. An ugly girl mimicked the belle and fancied she would be as beautiful as West Maid, but only to find that her neighbours were frightened away. The story is used to imply that one goes for wool and comes back shorn.
* The stupid lad lost his right step: It is said that a lad from Yan went to Chao's capital to learn how to walk elegantly, but failed and forgot the way he used to walk, so he could only crawl back.
* Sir Brilliance: a showy person using brilliant words to please.
* a monkey sculptured on a thorn: Lord of Yan was fond of miniature baubles, so a man from Way came and claimed to have the technique to carve a lively monkey on the end of a thorn. The lord was pleased and gave him a high reward, only to find he was cheated three years later, so he killed the cheat. The story implies deception can be fatal.
* Dragon Killer: There was a man selling all he had to learn how to kill dragons. After three years of training, however, it occurred to him that there was no dragon at all. Such talent is just an art of a high order but of little value.
* King Civil: King Civil (1152 B.C.- 1056 B.C.), a wise monarch of high reputation and the founder of Chough.
* *Psalms Major*: a part of *The Book of Songs*, the early collection of Chinese poems.
* *Odes*: a part of *The Book of Songs*, the early collection of Chinese poems.
* the Ying man's axe: A craftsman from Ying could cut off the powder on his partner's nose with his swift axe, but he could no longer perform it after his brave partner passed away.

其三十六

抱玉入楚国，
见疑古所闻。
良宝终见弃，
徒劳三献君。
直木忌先伐，
芳兰哀自焚。
盈满天所损，
沉冥道为群。
东海泛碧水，
西关乘紫云。
鲁连及柱史，
可以蹑清芬。

No. 36

With jade Ho came to the Ch'u State,
And was wronged once and again.
The treasure was rejected then,
Presented thrice at court in vain.
A straight tree is chopped down the first;
An orchid laments being burned.
Wax follows the footsteps of wane;
The Word welcomes all who are spurned.
Chunglien Lu went to the blue sea;
Laocius rode a cloud to the sand.
How I wish to follow these men
To tread their balm in Fairyland.

- Ho: Ho Pian in full name. Ho failed twice and lost his legs in an attempt to present his crude jade he found to monarchs of Ch'u before Lord Civil of Ch'u's enthronement. Ho held the jade stone crying bitterly for the previous misjudgment. Up to this point, the precious jade was finally appreciated by the new lord.
- the Ch'u State: a vassal state of Chough, one of the powers in the Warring States period, conquered and annexed by Ch'in in 223 B.C.
- orchid: any of a widely distributed family of terrestrial or epiphytic monocotyledonous plants having thickened bulbous roots and often very showy distinctive flowers, one of the four most important floral images in Chinese literature, which are wintersweet, orchid, bamboo, and chrysanthemum.
- the Word: referring to Tao if transliterated, the most significant and profoundest concept of cosomology and axiology in Chinese philosophy. The Word is fully elucidated in *The Word and the World*, the single book that Laocius wrote all his wisdom into. Its importance can be seen in this verse: "The Word is void, but its use is infinite. O deep! It seems to be the root of all things."
- Chunglien Lu: Chunglien Lu (305 B.C.- 245 B.C.), a sophist of Ch'i in the late Spring and Autumn period. He declined to be titled and awarded by Lord Plain of Chao, and left for East Sea.

其三十七

燕臣昔恸哭,
五月飞秋霜。
庶女号苍天,
震风击齐堂。
精诚有所感,
造化为悲伤。
而我竟何辜,
远身金殿旁。
浮云蔽紫闼,
白日难回光。
群沙秽明珠,
众草凌孤芳。
古来共叹息,
流泪空沾裳。

No. 37

Once, Tsou from the State of Yan wailed;
In the fifth moon, hoarfrost did fall.
The country girl's cry shook the skies;
The wind blew up to strike the hall.
Moved by their story and so moved,
Heaven and earth both for them wept
Why am I deposed and exiled,
Far away from the gold court kept?
The floating clouds veiled the palace
And the sun could hardly give light.
The weeds bullied the grass fragrant;

> The sand dirtied the queen pearl bright.
> I sigh with saints now and of yore,
> Shedding sad tears and shedding more.

* Tsou: Yan Tsou (324 B.C.- 250 B.C.) in full name, the founder of Five Element Theory, an official of the State of Yan. He wailed for his false imprisonment, which brought about frost even in summer.
* the State of Yan: Yan (1044 B.C.- 222 B.C.), a vassal state under Chough in the Spring and Autumn period, one of the Seven Powers in the Warring States period.
* The country girl's cry shook the skies: It's said that a widow of Ch'i was accused of a murder she had not committed, which aroused wind and thunder to struck the hall of court.
* pearl: a lustrous, calcareous concretion deposited in layers around a central nucleus in the shells of various mollusks, and largely used as a gem, regarded as a treasure or a symbol of love and friendship.

其三十八

孤兰生幽园，
众草共芜没。
虽照阳春晖，
复悲高秋月。
飞霜早淅沥，
绿艳恐休歇。
若无清风吹，
香气为谁发。

No. 38

The lonely orchid in the yard
Fades together with the grass dry.
Although I bathe in warm spring light,
I mourn the autumn moon on high.
The flying frost hastens a rain;
The brightness will end, I'm afraid.
If without the wind blowing on,
For whom does balm the air pervade?

* orchid: an elegant thick-leaved plant having white, rosy or purple flowers, one of the four most important images in Chinese literature, which are wintersweet, orchid, bamboo, and chrysanthemum.
* the moon: the planet of the earth, which appears at night and gives off shining silvery light, an image of loneliness and altitude as it is the only one of its kind at night.

其三十九

登高望四海，
天地何漫漫。
霜被群物秋，
风飘大荒寒。
荣华东流水，
万事皆波澜。
白日掩徂辉，
浮云无定端。
梧桐巢燕雀，
枳棘栖鸳鸾。
且复归去来，
剑歌行路难。

No. 39

How Heaven and earth turn and turn!
I climb up the height and behold.
Everything is shining with frost，
The wind blows the wasteland so cold.
Like water, ranks and fame flow east；
Like billows, everything surges on.
The westering sun will soon set；
The aimless clouds float up and down.
Sparrows nestle on parasol trees；
Phoenixes perch on thorny grass.
Let me go home, go back home now；
O sword song, it's a hard way, alas.

- * sparrow: a small, plain-colored passerine bird related to the finches, grosbeaks and buntings, a very common bird in China, a symbol of insignificance.
- * parasol tree: Chinese parasol tree (*Firmiana simplex*), tree of the hibiscus family native to Asia, growing as tall as 12 metres, having deciduous leaves and small greenish white flowers that are borne in clusters.
- * phoenix: In Chinese myths, phoenixes, auspicious birds, unlike ordinary ones, only perch on parasol trees, and only eat bamboo shoots and pearly stone.
- * sword song: alluding to Pai Li's swordsmanship. When a bursting young man, Pai Li exhibited a swashbuckling penchant, took to knight-errantry, and learned swordsmanship from Min P'ei, the universally acknowledged swordsman in the T'ang dynasty, and as Pai Li boasted, he even cut down a few combatants with his cutlass. Interestingly, Pai Li and Min P'ei were two of "the Three Paragons" of the age by imperial edict: Pai Li in songs and odes, Min P'ei in sword dance, and Hsu Chang in cursive calligraphy.

其四十

凤饥不啄粟，
所食唯琅玕。
焉能与群鸡，
刺蹙争一餐。
朝鸣昆丘树，
夕饮砥柱湍。
归飞海路远，
独宿天霜寒。
幸遇王子晋。
结交青云端。
怀恩未得报。
感别空长叹。

No. 40

On millet phoenixes don't feed;
Only bamboo shoots do they need.
How can a phoenix vie with hens
And, frowning, for a meal compete?
At dawn on a hill tree it cheeps;
At dusk by a pool stone it cries.
Its sea way back home rolls afar,
And it perches on the chilled skies.
Haply it meets the Prince of Front,
And together to clouds they fly.
Not having repaid his great grace,
To the vast sky it heaves a sigh.

* millet: a member of the foxtail grass family, or its seeds, cultivated as a cereal, used as a stable food in ancient times, having been cultivated in China for more than 7,300 years, one of the earliest crops in the world.
* phoenix: the king of all birds, an auspicious sign. Unique of its kind, it was supposed to live five or six hundred years before consuming itself by fire, rising again from its ashes to live through another cycle, a symbol of immortality. In Chinese mythology, a phoenix only perches on parasol trees and only eats bamboo shoots.
* bamboo shoots: tender bamboo sprouts, which may be dried for storage, are used as a delicacy in China.
* Prince of Front: Crown Prince of Front(567 B.C.- 549 B.C.), the first son of King Spirit of Chough. He was an intelligent and courageous young man. Though a prince, he had few desires and was keen on the Word. As legend goes, after his early death he rose to the sky, astride a white crane, hence becoming an immortal.

其四十一

朝弄紫泥海，
夕披丹霞裳。
挥手折若木，
拂此西日光。
云卧游八极，
玉颜已千霜。
飘飘入无倪，
稽首祈上皇。
呼我游太素，
玉杯赐琼浆。
一餐历万岁，
何用还故乡。
永随长风去，
天外恣飘扬。

No. 41

At dawn you wade a muddy pond;
At dusk irised red clouds you don.
You wave to pluck an emerald twig,
And dance beneath the tilting sun.
Astride a cloud you surf the sky;
Your face has been frosted enow.
Up, up, to the welkin you float;
And to Lord of Heaven you bow.
You ask me to travel the space
And upon me nectar bestow.
A meal's time is an eon on earth;

Homeland? Nowhere else I should go.
With the wind I will for e'er fly,
Afloat, afloat beyond the sky.

* "you" in this poem refers to Newmoon East (Shuo Tungfang) (154 B.C.- 93 B.C.), a jocular and witted official serving Emperor Martial of Han.
* Lord of Heaven: the supreme sovereign of the universe, identifiable with God in the west, also called Lord of Jade, Father in Heaven, Upper Lord of the Cosmos, Highest Celestial Saintly Merciful August Lord of the Profound Dome of the Sky and so on.
* nectar: in Chinese and Greek mythologies, the drink of the gods or fairies, and in botany, the saccharine substance secreted by some plants and forming the base of natural honey.

其四十二

摇裔双白鸥,
鸣飞沧江流。
宜与海人狎,
岂伊云鹤俦。
寄形宿沙月,
沿芳戏春洲。
吾亦洗心者,
忘机从尔游。

No. 42

A pair of seagulls white spread wings
And over the Blue River cry.
They may with a fisherman play;
Why need they with clouded cranes fly?
Falling asleep on moonlit sand
And having fun at a spring shoal,
I, washed and purified all o'er,
Will travel with you soul to soul.

* seagull: a kind of sea bird, any gull or large tern, a symbol of clean integrity. The seagulls in the Wordist book *Sir Line* (Liehtzu) are particularly sensitive to impurity of motive and will make friends only with the completely guileless and disinterested.
* the Blue River: an unspecific river in this poem.
* crane: one of a family of large, long-necked, long-legged, heronlike birds allied to the rails, a symbol of longevity and integrity in Chinese culture, only second to the phoenix in cultural importance.

其四十三

周穆八荒意,
汉皇万乘尊。
淫乐心不极,
雄豪安足论。
西海宴王母,
北宫邀上元。
瑶水闻遗歌,
玉杯竟空言。
灵迹成蔓草,
徒悲千载魂。

No. 43

King Solemn traveled the wild land;
Lord Martial reigned the greatest clime.
As they sought pleasure with no bounds,
Could they be best lords of all time?
King Solemn dined with Mother West;
Lord Martial feasted Lady Up.
King Solemn and West left their songs;
Lord Martial drank an empty cup.
Their footprints turned out to be grass,
Which does the age-old soul harass.

* King Solemn: King Solemn of Chough (cir. 1054 B.C.- 949 B.C.), the fifth sovereign of Chough, in reign for 55 years, the longest in Chough's history.
* Lord Martial: Emperor Martial (156 B.C.- 87 B.C.), the seventh emperor of Han, a prominent statesman, strategist and poet, and a pursuer of immortality as well.

* Mother West: a sovereign goddess living on Mt. Queen in Chinese myths. She was originally described as human-bodied, tiger-toothed, leopard-tailed and hoopoe-haired, regarded as a goddess in charge of women protection, marriage and procreation, and longevity.
* Lady Up: a fairy existing in myths, who visited Lord Martial in North Palace.
* Lord Martial drank an empty cup: Lord Martial ordered that a bronze man be made to hold a jade cup to collect dew, aiming to be immortal by drinking it with jade filings.

其四十四

绿萝纷葳蕤，
缭绕松柏枝。
草木有所托，
岁寒尚不移。
奈何夭桃色，
坐叹葑菲诗。
玉颜艳红彩，
云发非素丝。
君子恩已毕，
贱妾将何为。

No. 44

The creepers and trailers do climb
Around the pine twigs manifold.
Even grass and plants have their place,
Not going away when it's cold.
What a pity, the charming girl
Sighs, gathering turnips, alack.
Her rosy cheeks still radiate;
Her sable hair remains as black.
Now that her man's love is off gone,
What can she do? What can be done?

* creepers and trailers: usually used as metaphors for wives, because they crawl on something, like a wife leaning on her husband.
* pine: an evergreen tree of the genus *Pinus*, standing for staunchness and reliability in Chinese culture, especially when used in context with vines, an image of clinging wife.
* turnip: the fleshy globular edible root of either of two brassicaceous biennial herbs, *Brassica rapa* and the rutabaga.

其四十五

八荒驰惊飙,
万物尽凋落。
浮云蔽颓阳,
洪波振大壑。
龙凤脱罔罟,
飘摇将安托。
去去乘白驹,
空山咏场藿。

No. 45

A storm assaults the border land;
All blossoms fade or withered be!
The floating clouds eclipse the sun;
The roaring waves upturn the sea.
The loving pair escape the trap;
Where can they abide, free of harm?
Off, off, of ponies white astride,
They come to chant on a hill farm.

* A storm assaults the border land: indicating Lushan An's Rebellion. In the eleventh moon of A.D. 755, Lushan An turned traitor and captured cities and forts in a few months, forcing the emperor to flee to Ssuch'uan.
* the loving pair: indicating Emperor Deepsire and his imperial consort, Jade Ring.
* Off, off, of ponies white astride: deriving from *The Pony White* in *The Book of Songs*, which was written for detaining a noble guest. The guest in the poem was talented enough to be promoted in rank, but he preferred to live in seclusion.

其四十六

一百四十年，
国容何赫然。
隐隐五凤楼，
峨峨横三川。
王侯象星月，
宾客如云烟。
斗鸡金宫里，
蹴鞠瑶台边。
举动摇白日，
指挥回青天。
当涂何翕忽，
失路长弃捐。
独有扬执戟，
闭关草太玄。

No. 46

Now, it's a hundred forty years,
How stately our T'ang, our great land!
Dim, dim, the high five-phoenixed towers
O'erlook the three rivers, so grand.
Lords like stars supporting the moon;
Guests like clouds coming up and down.
Cock fighting in the palace gold;
Ball kicking in Forbidden Town.
Their movements quiver the white sun;
Their shouting pierces the blue sky.
How arrogant all those in power!

How depressed the souls left to sigh!
There was a man, Man Yang by name;
Reading *The Great One* was his aim.

- T'ang: the T'ang Empire (A.D. 618 - A.D. 907), a great empire after Sui, one of the most powerful dynasties in Chinese history. The T'ang dynasty was the golden age of Chinese Poetry—In the number of poems and variety of poetic forms, the beauty of imagery and broadness of themes, T'ang Poetry surpasses all that had preceded it.
- The five-phoenixes towers: referring to the Entrance Towers to Forbidden Town in East Capital Loshine (Loyang).
- the three rivers: the Ching, the Wei, and the Lo, three important rivers west of Case Dale.
- the moon: the celestial body that revolves around the earth from west to east as a satellite, which appears at night and gives off shining silvery light, an image of altitude and solitude in Chinese culture.
- cock fighting: an activity enjoying a great popularity in palaces.
- ball kicking: football playing that originated in the Warring States period or even as early as in the Age of Lord Yellow (2717 B.C.- 2599 B.C.).
- Man Yang: Man Yang (53 B.C.- A.D. 18), Hsiung Yang if transliterated, born in Silkton, present-day Ch'engt'u, Ssuch'uan, a great scholar, rhymed prose writer, official in the Han dynasty, whose *The Great One* has had a deep influence on works of later generations. According to *History of the Han Dynasty*, when other officials flattered those in power, only Man Yang kept to himself to write his philosophical work, *The Great One*.
- *The Great One*: a philosophical work in the style of euph by Male Yang, a euphuist dissertation themed on the profundity of the Word and thereupon modeling the schema of cosmological genesis and the evolution of things.

其四十七

桃花开东园，
含笑夸白日。
偶蒙东风荣，
生此艳阳质。
岂无佳人色，
但恐花不实。
宛转龙火飞，
零落早相失。
讵知南山松。
独立自萧瑟。

No. 47

Peach blossoms burst there in East Park;
They praise the white sun with a smile.
Thanks to the east wind, they now burst,
With such brilliant charm to beguile.
Aren't the beauties blooming like that?
They may not bear fruit, I'm afraid.
Dragon Fire Star will appear soon;
All those blossoms will droop to fade.
Do you know the pine does not bow?
Uphill, it stands against a sough.

* peach blossoms: flowers of a peach tree, which beautiful ladies are compared with.
* Dragon Fire Star: one in the East Constellation. It appears at dusk in the fifth moon and reaches its highest height, and as it descends in the seventh moon, when summer gives place to autumn.
* pine: a cone-bearing tree having needle-shaped evergreen leaves growing in clusters, a symbol of longevity and rectitude in Chinese culture.

其四十八

秦皇按宝剑,
赫怒震威神。
逐日巡海右,
驱石驾沧津。
征卒空九寓,
作桥伤万人。
但求蓬岛药,
岂思农扈春。
力尽功不赡,
千载为悲辛。

No. 48

Emperor First holding his sword,
His anger frightened God the Lord.
To view the sun he toured seaside;
With stone God made for him a ford.
Soldiers from nine realms were employed,
Of whom ten thousand died on site.
He sought elixir from the isle,
Not caring the folks' joy or plight.
All his efforts were spent in vain;
This sad tale would for e'er remain.

* Emperor First: Emperor First (259 B.C.- 210 B.C.), the founding emperor of Ch'in, who wiped out all the other states and established the first unified empire in China. He was universally acknowledged as a great politician, strategist, reformer, and an iron hand tyrant, who laid the political layout of China after the Ch'in dynasty till now.

* God the Lord: the One, Supreme Being, ever-existing and eternal; the infinite creator, sustainer and ruler of the cosmos with the attributes of being omniscient, omnipotent and omnipresent, or else called Father in Heaven or with a natural propensity, the Word, the One, Heaven and so on.
* With stone God made for him a ford: As legend goes, in order to tour where the sun rises, Emperor First of Ch'in built a stone bridge with the help of Sea God.
* elixir: panacea that Wordists tried to seek. Wordism began with its doctrine of inaction and later advanced to fanciful superstitions of celestial realms and supernatural beings and of death-conquering herbs and pellets.

其四十九

美人出南国，
灼灼芙蓉姿。
皓齿终不发，
芳心空自持。
由来紫宫女，
共妒青蛾眉。
归去潇湘沚，
沉吟何足悲。

No. 49

The beauty is from southern land,
Radiant like a lotus in bloom.
Her white teeth have no chance to show;
Her glamour is locked in her room.
In palaces now as of yore,
The most beautiful bears the curse.
Why not go to a shoal in Hsiang
And happily recite our verse?

* lotus: one of the various plants of the waterlily family, noted for their large floating leaves and showy flowers, a symbol of purity and elegance in Chinese culture, unsoiled though out of soil, so clean with all leaves green.
* Hsiang: referring to the River Hsiang, a branch of the Yangtze River, located in present-day Hunan Province.

其五十

宋国梧台东，
野人得燕石。
夸作天下珍，
却哂赵王璧。
赵璧无缁磷，
燕石非贞真。
流俗多错误，
岂知玉与珉。

No. 50

East of Parasol Mound in Sung
A folk found a stone, a stone mere.
He bragged it was the best of all
And at King of Chao's jade did sneer.
The king's jade had no spot or stain;
The folk's stone can't stand any wear.
The vulgar tend to make mistakes;
Can they tell jade from stone? O ne'er.

* Parasol Mound: unidentified. There was one bearing the name in Ch'i in the Warring States period, which is 28 meters high and 220 meters in circumference, the largest mound of rammed earth in Ch'i's palace. The poet might have made a mistake when saying it was in Sung.
* King of Chao's jade: the most well-known jade in China's history discovered by Ho Pian. It originally belonged to the State of Ch'u, and was given as a gift to King of Chao. After being sent to Ch'in as a war trophy, unfortunately, it was lost, nowhere to be found as time passes.

其五十一

殷后乱天纪，
楚怀亦已昏。
夷羊满中野，
菉葹盈高门。
比干谏而死，
屈平窜湘源。
虎口何婉娈，
女嬃空婵媛。
彭咸久沦没，
此意与谁论。

No. 51

The Lord of Yin thwarted God's Way;
The King of Ch'u had a fussed head.
A sage does wander in the wild;
Weeds in high mansions sprawl and spread.
Pikan died for his good advice;
Yüan Ch'ü jumped to the Hsiang, downstream.
Though a narrow escape is dear;
Girl Sis, though fair, did in vain beam.
It is long since Hsien P'eng got drowned;
Who will give advice above ground?

* the Lord of Yin: indicating King Chow (1105 B.C.- 1046 B.C.), the last king of Shang, who had executed severe laws and waged wars in the east, which triggered conflicts among reigning groups and weakened the foundation of Shang's reign. In folks' version, King Chow was usually described as a violent tyrant indulging in luxury

and desires.
* God's Way: the Way of Heaven, the ultimate principle in the universe.
* the King of Ch'u: the King of Ch'u (355 B.C.- 296 B.C.), a king reigning over Ch'u in the Warring States period. He saw the prosperity of Ch'u during his early reign, but failed due to his demotion of Yüan Ch'ü, misled by Ee Chang, the lobbyist of Ch'in.
* Pikan: Pikan (1110 B.C.- 1047 B.C.), the prime minister of Shang, who had served the court as an imperial tutor since he was 20. He was loyal and caring for the people, usually remonstrated King Chow with blunt words. Pikan's admonition finally irritated King Chow and he was martyred, his heart taken out.
* Yüan Ch'ü: Yüan Ch'ü (340 B.C.- 278 B.C.), a great patriotic poet and official of Ch'u, the archetype of the incorruptible and faithful minister, repeatedly wronged by the king. His suicide at last by drowning in the Milo River is still commemorated at Dragon Boat Festival every year throughout China.
* Girl Sis: Yüan Ch'ü's sister, who persuaded Yüan Ch'ü not to remonstrate anymore.
* Hsien P'eng: a noble official of Shang who drowned himself for his failed remonstrance.

其五十二

青春流惊湍，
朱明骤回薄。
不忍看秋蓬，
飘扬竟何托。
光风灭兰蕙，
白露洒葵藿。
美人不我期，
草木日零落。

No. 52

The spring goes off like a fast flow;
The summer will arrive here soon.
The thistledown I dare not watch;
Where will it land, on and on blown?
The orchid's brightened by the sun;
The mallow glistens with dew white.
The beauty does not come to me;
Plants and grass wither, what a blight!

* thistledown: the pappus of a thistle, a kind of vigorous prickly plant with cylindrical or globular heads of tubular purple flowers, an important image in Chinese literature, a metaphor for vagrants or strayers.
* orchid: any of a widely distributed family of terrestrial or epiphytic monocotyledonous plants having thickened bulbous roots and often very showy distinctive flowers, one of the four most important floral images in Chinese literature, which are wintersweet, orchid, bamboo, and chrysanthemum.
* sun: the heavenly body that is the center of attraction and the main source of light and heat in the solar system, a representation of Shine in contrast with Shade, the moon,

in Chinese culture, a symbol of hope, life, strength, vigor and youth.
* mallow: *Malva verticillata* or any plant of the genus *Malva* with roundish leaves, the first of the five popular vegetables in ancient China.

其五十三

战国何纷纷,
兵戈乱浮云。
赵倚两虎斗,
晋为六卿分。
奸臣欲窃位,
树党自相群。
果然田成子,
一旦杀齐君。

No. 53

The Warring States fought without end;
Halberds, swords and spears collided.
The Chao State leaned on tigers two;
Chin was by six lords divided.
Vile courtiers would usurp the crown;
All gangs arose to swank and sway.
There was a man Farmcrops by name,
Who murdered Lord of Ch'i one day.

* The Warring States: mainly referring to the seven most powerful states that fought against each other for hegemony, Ch'i, Ch'u, Yan, Han, Chao, Way, and Ch'in.
* The Chao State: the State of Chao (403 B.C.- 222 B.C.), a vassal state in the Spring and Autumn period, one of the Seven Powers in the Warring States period.
* tigers two: referring to P'o Lien, the eminent commander, and Hsiangju Lin, the outstanding statesman and diplomat. They were both a deterrent to the strong Ch'in.
* Chin was by six lords divided: In the last stage of the Spring and Autumn period, the State of Chin waned and was controlled by six lords. After tangled warfare among the six lords, three remained (Chao, Way, Han) and partitioned Chin, which was a

representative watershed of the Spring and Autumn period and the Waring States period.
* Farmcrops: a prime minister of Ch'i. In 481 B.C., Farmcrops launched a coup by killing the Lord of Ch'i and enthroned his younger brother. After that, Farmcrops monopolized the reign of Ch'i.

其五十四

倚剑登高台，
悠悠送春目。
苍榛蔽层丘，
琼草隐深谷。
凤鸟鸣西海，
欲集无珍木。
鸒斯得所居，
蒿下盈万族。
晋风日已颓，
穷途方恸哭。

No. 54

With my sword on, a mound I climb
And see a spring field rolling wide.
Green hazels shade the layered knoll;
Magic herbs in the deep dale hide.
A phoenix, cheeping by West Sea,
Would light but finds no good wood.
Cawing crows perch in her abode;
The wormwood grows, a multitude.
The world has become worse and worst;
No way out, into tears all burst.

* hazel: a bushy shrub or small tree of the birch family (genus *Corylus*) yielding a hard-shelled edible nut enclosed in a leafy involucre.
* phoenix: an auspicious bird, the best of all, which only perches on parasol trees and only eat bamboo shoots and pearly stone.

* West Sea: a lake also called Blue Sea (Ch'inghai) or Kokonor, the great salt lake more than 3,300 meters above sea-level in today's Ch'inghai Province.
* crow: an omnivorous, raucous, oscine bird of the genus *Corvus*, with glossy black plumage. It is regarded as an ominous bird, a metaphor for death because it is a scavenger, feeding on carrion.
* wormwood: any of a genus (*Artemisia*) of herbs or small shrubs related to the sagebrush, especially a common species, aromatic, tonic, bitter, and used in making absinthe.

其五十五

齐瑟弹东吟，
秦弦弄西音。
慷慨动颜魄，
使人成荒淫。
彼美佞邪子，
婉娈来相寻。
一笑双白璧，
再歌千黄金。
珍色不贵道，
讵惜飞光沈。
安识紫霞客，
瑶台鸣素琴。

No. 55

Ch'i's lute is good for airs from east;
Ch'in's strings fit the music of west.
The tunes move all faces and hearts;
The audience is with lust obsessed.
The youngsters so handsome but mean
To curry favor come along.
A pair of jade for a sweet smile,
A box of gold for one more song.
If one loves wealth, he spurns the Word,
Letting all treasures fly away.
Don't you know the sagacious man,
Who by Jade Pool the lute did play?

* lute: a stringed musical instrument, played by plucking the strings with fingers or a plectrum.
* the Word: referring to Tao if transliterated, the most significant and profoundest concept in Chinese philosophy. It is the Creator of all. According to Laocius's *The Word and the World*: "The Word is void, but its use is infinite. O deep! It seems to be the root of all things." The Word is identifiable with the Word or Logos in the West, as there is an enormous amount of common ground in the two cosmologies and the doctrines concerning the most fundamental matters such as "the Word is the One" and "God is the One", and the personalization of Being, the progenitor of finite spirits, which are subordinate kinds of Being or merely appearances of the Divine, the One.
* Jade Pool: a fairy pool on Mt. Queen, by which Mother West holds banquets.

其五十六

越客采明珠，
提携出南隅。
清辉照海月，
美价倾皇都。
献君君按剑，
怀宝空长吁。
鱼目复相哂，
寸心增烦纡。

No. 56

A man from Yüeh found a bright pearl;
To sell it he came from South Land.
Its gleam outshone the moon at sea;
Its price the whole town could not stand.
His tribute met with the crown's sword;
He let out a cry to the sky.
One proffered a fish eye and sneered;
How could he suffer the hard try?

* Yüeh: referring to South Yüeh, a mountainous and costal area, rich in pearls, in what is approximately today's Kuangtung Province.
* pearl: a lustrous, calcareous concretion deposited in layers around a central nucleus in the shells of various mollusks, and largely used as a gem, a symbol of love and friendship in Chinese culture.
* the moon: the satellite of the earth, a representation of feminity in contrast with the sun, a presentation of masculinity. In a universe animated by the interaction of Shade (female) and Shine (male) energies, the moon is literally Shade visible.
* fish eye: a metaphor for something cheap or fake, especially when collocated with

"pearl", for example, "pass fish eyes for pearls" means "mix the genuine with the fake". It is said that a man bought a big pearl and his neighbor was jealous. On one occasion, the neighbor found a big fish eye and trumpeted he had a pearl. Hence, fish eyes have been used to indicate fake items.

其五十七

羽族禀万化，
小大各有依。
周周亦何幸，
六翮掩不挥。
愿衔众禽翼，
一向黄河飞。
飞者莫我顾，
叹息将安归。

No. 57

Birds there are, each after their kind,
Differently born, differently bred.
How sad Chirpchirp, a bird so called!
Its gigantic wings it can't spread.
To drink, it borrows others' wings,
And does to the Yellow River fly.
Those who fly do not regard me;
Where shall I live? So sad, I sigh.

* the Yellow River: the second longest river in China, flowing through Loess Plateau, hence yellow water all the way. 5,464 kilometers long, with a drainage area of 752,443 square kilometers, it has been regarded as the cradle of Chinese civilization. As legend goes, the river derived from a yellow dragon that, couchant on Midland Plain, ate yellow soil, flooded crops, devoured people and stock, and was finally tamed by Great Worm, the First King of Hsia (cir. 21 B.C.- 16 B.C.). Its fertile valleys were turned into fields of rice, barley and oscillating corn, amid gleaming streams and lakes.
* Chirpchirp: a legendary bird in Chinese mythology, which is clumsy with big wings, a heavy head and a crooked tail. It often feels hungry and needs others' help to take flight.

其五十八

我到巫山渚，
寻古登阳台。
天空彩云灭，
地远清风来。
神女去已久。
襄王安在哉。
荒淫竟沦替。
樵牧徒悲哀。

No. 58

I come to the foot of Mt. Witch;
To view relics I climb Sun Mound.
All hued clouds vanish from the sky;
A wind blows chillness from around.
It's long since Goddess disappeared
And where is King Hsiang now, o where?
The dissolute play is still on,
E'en fishers and herdsmen despair.

* Mt. Witch: a mythical and religious mountain, which was thought to be a range of mountains in Sha'anhsi.
* Sun Mound: the place where Goddess of Mt. Witch stays.
* Goddess: Goddess of Mt. Witch, a good-looking fairy who shapes herself as clouds at dawn and turns to rain at dusk. In the myths, King Huai of Ch'u once met her and had an intercourse overnight in his dream. The story was recorded by Jade Sung, a student of Yüan Ch'ü.
* King Hsiang: King of Ch'u (263 B.C.), who underwent the waning of Ch'u during his reign and died of illness.

其五十九

恻恻泣路歧，
哀哀悲素丝。
路歧有南北，
素丝易变移。
万事固如此，
人生无定期。
田窦相倾夺，
宾客互盈亏。
世途多翻覆，
交道方崄巇。
斗酒强然诺，
寸心终自疑。
张陈竟火灭，
萧朱亦星离。
众鸟集荣柯，
穷鱼守枯池。
嗟嗟失权客，
勤问何所规。

No. 59

Chu Yang seeing crossroads would howl;
Sir Ink meeting dyeing would cry.
Crossroads lead to all directions;
Dyeing is prone to change for aye.
Everything is preset like this;
Nothing steady can so remain.
T'ien and Tou rivaled and fought on;

Their hangers-on swapped so to gain.
The world has many turns and twists;
Friendship meets lots of ups and downs.
A promise made when you are drunk
Gives rise to your own doubts and frowns.
Chang and Ch'en, true friends, become foes;
Hsiao and Chu, close pals, fiercely vie.
All birds wish to perch in dense woods;
Fish stranded keep to a pond dry.
Those who have lost power greetings send;
But what's the use? Too late to mend.

* Chu Yang: Chu Yang (395 B.C.- 335 B.C.), a great philosopher in the Warring States period, who advocated the thoughts of Laocius and Sir Lush. Opposite to Sir Ink, Chu Yang put stress on keeping to one's nature and egoism—"A hair of mine I won't sacrifice". When Chu Yang came to a crossroads, unable to decide which road to take, he thought of the crossroads in life and wept for any carelessness that might lead to a wrong path.
* Sir Ink: Sir Ink (cir. 476 B.C.- 390 B.C.), a philosopher, educator, scientist, and martial strategist in the late Spring and Autumn period and the early Warring States period, and the founder of Inkism which was regarded as one of the two most prestigious schools along with Confucianism. He came up with the Inkist ideas such as universal love, denouncing unjust war, and respecting scholars, which has exerted a great influence in Chinese history. Sir Ink saw silk dyeing and sobbed because in his eyes, any dye could make silk into some other color, which implies that the appearance may conceal its nature, so one should be cautious when employing people.
* T'ien and Tou: referring to Fen T'ien and Ying Tou, two important officials in the Han dynasty. When Tou was in power, hangers-on scrambled to visit Tou, but when T'ien succeeded, they all turned to T'ien.
* Chang and Ch'en: referring to Er Chang and Yu Ch'en, who both participated in the uprising against Ch'in. They were sworn friends when in hardship, but foes when in success. Chang killed Ch'en in the war.
* Hsiao and Chu: referring to Yu Hsiao and Po Chu in the Han dynasty. With the help of Hsiao's recommendation, Chu made achievements in his official career. Unfortunately, they had a wedge in their relationship afterwards and became foes at last.

乐府三十首
Conservatoire, 30 Poems

远　别　离

远别离，
古有皇英之二女，
乃在洞庭之南，
潇湘之浦。
海水直下万里深，
谁人不言此离苦？
日惨惨兮云冥冥，
猩猩啼烟兮鬼啸雨。
我纵言之将何补？
皇穹窃恐不照余之忠诚，
雷凭凭兮欲吼怒。
尧舜当之亦禅禹。
君失臣兮龙为鱼，
权归臣兮鼠变虎。
或云：尧幽囚，舜野死。
九疑联绵皆相似，
重瞳孤坟竟何是？
帝子泣兮绿云间，
随风波兮去无还。
恸哭兮远望，
见苍梧之深山。
苍梧山崩湘水绝，
竹上之泪乃可灭。

Apart from Their Man

Apart from their man,
Two belles called Grand and Bloom, of yore,
Strayed south of Lake Cavehall
And along the Hsiang, ashore.
The sea a thousand miles deep,
Who does not feel their disunion sore?
The sun so pale, oh, the clouds drifting,
Orangutans wail and demons guffaw.
Who can understand what I deplore?
My loyalty Heaven above can't show,
O thunder claps, throwing a rain to pour.
Mound and Hibiscus demised throne to Worm.
Losing his men, Dragon like fish has no claw;
Having got power, mice show a tiger's paw.
I hear Mound was jailed and Hibiscus died in a moor.
Mt. Nine Doubts rolling, the peaks look the same;
Where is Hibiscus's tomb, why and wherefore?
They cried in a grove of bamboo,
And jumped into the waves, ne'er more.
While wailing, they gazed afar,
Seeing Mt. Nine Doubts high soar.
Their tears on mottled bamboo blend with gore
Till the mount falls and the Hsiang flows no more.

* Grand and Bloom: Fairgrand and Shebloom in full name, the daughters of Mound (chief of tribal alliance in early historical times) in the myths. They were married to Hibiscus, who later became their father's successor and helped him out of unfavorable conditions. They drowned themselves in the River Hsiang at the news of their husband's death. Later generations called them Madams Hsiang because their spirits lingered on the south of Lake Cavehall and the banks of the River Hsiang.

* Lake Cavehall: a lake in present-day Hunan Province, with an area of 3,879.2 square kilometers and 803.2 kilometers in circumference.
* orangutan: a large anthropoid ape (genus *Pongo* or *Simia*), having brown-reddish hair, brown skin, small ears, doglike teeth, narrow lips, and long arms reaching to the ankles.
* Mound: Mound (2377 B.C.- 2259 B.C.), Yao if transliterated. Divine and noble, Mound has been regarded as one of Five Lords in ancient China.
* Hibiscus: Hibiscus (cir. 2277 B.C.- 2178 B.C.), Shun if transliterated, the Double-pupiled One, an ancient sovereign, a descendant of Lord Yellow (2717 B.C.-2599 B.C.), regarded as one of Five Lords in prehistoric China.
* Worm: the founding lord of Hsia, who took over the leadership from Hibiscus. It was said that Mound was put in jail, having lost his morality, and Hibiscus died in a moor when he was in a tour. The poet borrowed the ancient legend to imply that the reign of T'ang was in danger of being destroyed.
* Heaven: the space surrounding or seeming to overarch the earth, in which the sun, the moon, and stars appear, popularly the abode of God, his angels and the blessed, and in most cases suggesting supernatural power or sometimes signifying a monarch.
* Mt. Nine Doubts: located in Hunan Province. As said, it's where Hibiscus was buried.
* mottled bamboo: a kind of bamboo with natural mottles on it. As said, after Hibiscus's death, Grand and Bloom wailed in a bamboo grove, and their tear drops on bamboos made them mottled. Out of grief, the two consorts jumped into the River Hsiang.

公 无 渡 河

黄河西来决昆仑，
咆哮万里触龙门。
波滔天，尧咨嗟。
大禹理百川，
儿啼不窥家。
杀湍湮洪水，
九州始蚕麻。
其害乃去，茫然风沙。
被发之叟狂而痴，
清晨临流欲奚为。
旁人不惜妻止之，
公无渡河苦渡之。
有长虎可搏，河难凭，
公果溺死流海湄。
鲸白齿若雪山，
公乎公乎挂罥于其间。
箜篌所悲竟不还。

A Mad Man Drowned

The Yellow River from Mt. Queen did pour,
Rushing down to Dragon Gate with a roar.
The sky-flushing waves Mound did loud deplore.
Worm, to control the flooded plains,
Kids wailing, didn't indoors go.
When he had reined the great deluge,

All folks on earth began to grow.
The flood under control, sandstorms remained so.
A mad man, disheveled hair drooping low,
In the morn jumped to a rushing flow.
No one would ever stop him but his wife;
He could not tide over, but he would go.
Tigers he could fight; rivers he could not.
The man got drowned, by eddies whirled to flow.
The whale's teeth like mountains covered with snow,
O silly man, silly man, you were hung between, a tragic show.
The lute cello rang sad: o no, o no.

* the Yellow River: the second longest river in China, regarded as the cradle of Chinese civilization. It is 5,464 kilometers long, with a drainage area of 752,443 square kilometers. As legend goes, the river derived from a yellow dragon that, couchant on Midland Plain, ate yellow soil, flooded crops, devoured people and stock, and was finally tamed by Great Worm, the First King of Hsia (cir. 21 B.C.– 16 B.C.).
* Mt. Queen: Mt. Kunlun if transliterated, the most sacred mountain in China. It starts from the Eastern Pamir Plateau, stretches across New Land (Hsinchiang) and Tibet, and extends to Ch'inghai, with an average altitude of 5,500 – 6,000 meters. In Chinese myths, Mt. Queen is where Mother West dwells.
* Dragon Gate: Mt. Dragon Gate, located in modern-day Sha'anhsi Province, where the Yellow River runs through.
* Mound: Mound (2377 B.C.– 2259 B.C.), Yao if transliterated. Divine and noble, Mound has been regarded as one of Five Lords in ancient China.
* Worm, to control the flooded plains: Worm went out for water control for eight years, so dedicated that he passed by his home three times without entering.

蜀　道　难

噫吁嚱,危乎高哉!
蜀道之难,难于上青天!
蚕丛及鱼凫,
开国何茫然!
尔来四万八千岁,
不与秦塞通人烟。
西当太白有鸟道,
可以横绝峨眉巅。
地崩山摧壮士死,
然后天梯石栈相钩连。
上有六龙回日之高标,
下有冲波逆折之回川。
黄鹤之飞尚不得过,
猿猱欲度愁攀援。
青泥何盘盘,
百步九折萦岩峦。
扪参历井仰胁息,
以手抚膺坐长叹。
问君西游何时还?
畏途巉岩不可攀。
但见悲鸟号古木,
雄飞雌从绕林间。
又闻子规啼夜月,愁空山。
蜀道之难,难于上青天,
使人听此凋朱颜!
连峰去天不盈尺,
枯松倒挂倚绝壁。

飞湍瀑流争喧豗，
砯崖转石万壑雷。
其险也如此，
嗟尔远道之人胡为乎来哉！
剑阁峥嵘而崔嵬，
一夫当关，万夫莫开。
所守或匪亲，化为狼与豺。
朝避猛虎，
夕避长蛇；
磨牙吮血，
杀人如麻。
锦城虽云乐，
不如早还家。
蜀道之难，难于上青天，
侧身西望长咨嗟！

The Shu Way Is Hard

Oh, wow, my! What a height, so high!
The Shu way is so hard, harder than climbing the sky!
When did Silkworm and Fishduck
Begin their realm? It's hard to say.
Since then it's been forty eight thousand years;
Between here and Ch'in Land there is no way.
Mt. Venus in the west birds can fly o'er,
On to the top of Mt. Brow flap they may.
The earth sank, mountains crushed, the brave men died,
Hence the sky ladder and stack path relay.
Up, the peak barring Apollo's cart by six dragons drawn;
Down, the waves swirling and surging up to the Milky Way.

Yellow cranes flying there at the height cringe;
Chimpanzees would climb but to start they sway.
The Clay Ridge circles up,
Bending and twisting around the rocks gray.
From star to star you hold your breath to feel,
And palming your chest, you sit down to sigh.
Now going west, when will you come back then?
It's dangerous to climb the crags so high.
Behold, the birds wail over olden trees,
Male leading female, round the wood they fly.
Hark, on the barren hill, the cuckoos to the moon cry.
The Shu way is so hard, harder than climbing the sky;
At this you are too scared to run your eye.
The range is less than a foot from the blue;
Rotten pines hang upside down in cliffs high.
Water dashes rocks and turns like thunder;
Waterfalls and whirlpools noisily vie.
It's so dangerous!
Why have you come here all the way from afar, why?
Sword Pavilion towering juts steeply up;
If one man holds the pass, all invaders will die.
Those stationed are kindred and kin,
Otherwise, they'd rebel like wolves sly.
At dusk snakes you evade;
At dawn tigers you shun;
A snake may bite for fun;
A tiger may bloody run.
Tho Silkton is such a good place,
You'd better go back home anon.
The Shu way is so hard, harder than climbing the sky!
Turning west to gaze, hopelessly you sigh.

* Shu: one of the earliest kingdoms in China, founded by Silkworm according to legend.
* Silkworm: the founder of the Kingdom of Shu, who taught his people how to raise silkworms, hence regarded as God of Silkworm-breeding.
* Fishduck: one of the earliest kings of Shu, regarded as Gods of Fishing.
* Mt. Venus: the highest peak of Ch'in Ridge and also the highest peak in China east of Blue Sea-Tibetan Plateau, a Wordist sanctuary, known for its height, coldness, dangerousness, strangeness and bountifulness.
* Mt. Brow: one of the four Buddhist mountains, located in Ssuch'uan Province, named for its elegant brow-shaped silhouette viewed from a distance.
* The earth sank, mountains crushed, the brave men died: According to legend, King of Shu sent five strong men to pick up the five belles given by King Hui of Ch'in. On their way back, they saw a serpent sneak into a cave. A brave man seized its tail, and the other four pulled it out with all their strength. In an instant, the earth sank and the mountain crushed and buried the men and the belles. Thus, the mountain cracked into five peaks, which made a way to Shu.
* Apollo's cart: As legend goes, Apollo or God of Sun (a Goddess named Good Air, actually) rode a cart pulled by six dragons across the sky every day.
* dragon: Though variously understood as a large reptile, a marine monster, a jackal and Satan incarnate, it is also a kind protector in folklore and myth in Western culture, a mascot on the national flag of Wales. And in the East, it has been represented as a fabulous serpent-like giant winged animal that can change its length and girth, a totem of the Chinese nation and a symbol of benevolence and sovereignty in Chinese culture.
* the Milky Way: the Silver River in Chinese mythology, a luminous band circling the heavens composed of stars and nebulae; the Galaxy.
* the Clay Ridge: located on the border of present-day Kansu and Sha'anhsi provinces. There are rainy cliffs precipitous enough to block the passage by clay.
* the cuckoos to the moon cry: It is said that during the Shang dynasty, Cuckoo (Yü Tu), a caring king of Shu, abdicated the throne due to a flood and lived in reclusion. After his death, he became a cuckoo, wailing day and night, shedding tears and blood.
* tiger: a large carnivorous feline mammal, with stripes on a tawny body and black bars on the limbs and tail.
* snake: an ophidian reptile, having a greatly elongated, scaly body, no limbs, and a specialized swallowing apparatus, a symbol of indifference, malevolence, cattiness, and craftiness in Chinese culture.
* Sword Pavilion: a strategic pass with a plank road built along cliffs in modern-day Ssuch'uan Province.
* Silkton: the other name of Ch'engtu for it was a town of silk.

梁　甫　吟

长啸梁甫吟，
何时见阳春？
君不见，
朝歌屠叟辞棘津，
八十西来钓渭滨。
宁羞白发照清水，
逢时吐气思经纶。
广张三千六百钓，
风期暗与文王亲。
大贤虎变愚不测，
当年颇似寻常人。
君不见，
高阳酒徒起草中，
长揖山东隆准公。
入门不拜逞雄辩，
两女辍洗来趋风。
东下齐城七十二，
指挥楚汉如旋蓬。
狂客落魄尚如此，
何况壮士当群雄！
我欲攀龙见明主，
雷公砰訇震天鼓。
帝旁投壶多玉女，
三时大笑开电光，
倏烁晦冥起风雨。
阊阖九门不可通，
以额扣关阍者怒。

白日不照我精诚，
杞国无事忧天倾。
猰貐磨牙竞人肉，
驺虞不折生草茎。
手接飞猱搏雕虎，
侧足焦原未言苦。
智者可卷愚者豪，
世人见我轻鸿毛。
力排南山三壮士，
齐相杀之费二桃。
吴楚弄兵无剧孟，
亚夫咍尔为徒劳。
梁甫吟，声正悲。
张公两龙剑，
神物合有时。
风云感会起屠钓，
大人㠛屼当安之。

Ode to Father Liang

O I sing *Ode to Father Liang*;
When can I sunny spring behold?
Don't you espy
The slaughterer from Mornsong leave Thornford
And comes west to fish at eighty years old?
His gray hair seen in water hurts his heart;
But when it's right time, he talks smart and bold.
He's fished three thousand six hundred days;
The same view with King Civil he does hold.
When he will jump to prey a fool can't tell,

Though he looks like an ordinary mould.
Don't you espy
The drunkard comes out of grass in High Sun,
And the high-bridged nose he stands up to greet?
He never bows but his eloquence shines;
He shouts Lord out of washing with girls sweet.
He gains seventy two towns with his tongue,
And commands Ch'u and Han troops, a great feat.
A lowly man like him can do like this,
Let alone a hero with worth complete.
His Majesty great I'd like to advise;
Because war drums like thunder shake the skies.
The crown's playing pot-filling with ladies,
While laughing and talking, all smiling eyes.
But outside a storm with dark clouds does rise.
The nine Heavenly Gates are closed to all;
The guards reject me and do me despise.
Heaven, why is my loyalty not shown?
Much ado about nothing, they warn me.
They are men eaters showing off their fangs;
I'm like a mild deer not hurting the lea.
Like macaques fighting vultures and tigers,
We're at stake, as dangerous as can be.
A wise man retreats while a fool looks proud;
The world may see me clever, free of strain.
In dealing with three robust men in Ch'i,
The prime minister just used peaches twain.
Seeing Wu and Ch'u's lords not using Chü,
General Chou laughed they would fight in vain.
Ode to Father Liang, o what a sad song,
When can I the two swords combine

To fulfil the mission divine?
　　　When can I help His Majesty with war?
　　　All talents will play their part, vexed no more.

* Father Liang: a hill at the foot of Mt. Arch, a place that a large number of corpses were buried together.
* *Ode to Father Liang*: alias *O Father Liang*, a folk tune used as an elegy.
* slaughterer: referring to Great Grand (1156 B.C.- cir. 1017 B.C.), surnamed Chiang, styled Flying Bear, an influential strategist and statesman. A slaughterer at his early age, he remained diligent in hardship, expecting to display his talent for the country one day, but did not make any achievements until 70. He went west at the age of 72, fishing as he waited for King Civil, and finally won his appreciation.
* Mornsong: the capital of Shang (1600 B.C.- 1046 B.C.) in its last years and the capital of the State of Watch (1115 B.C.- 209 B.C.), in today's Ch'i County, Honan Province.
* Thornford: name of an old ferry, in present-day Honan Province.
* King Civil: the founder of Chough.
* Chough: the State of Chough (1046 B.C.- 256 B.C.), the third kingdom in Chinese history, comprising Western Chough and Eastern Chough.
* the drunkard: referring to Shihch'i Li, an unrestrained scholar who served as a counsellor of Pang Liu, who became the founding emperor of Han.
* High Sun: the capital of Dark Crown's kingdom, in present-day Hopei Province, also Dark Crown's alias when he reigned in High Sun. Dark Crown (2342 B.C.- 2245 B.C.), Chuanhsu if transliterated, was one of Five Emperors in prehistoric China.
* pot-filling game: In myth, Father East often played pot-filling game with fairy ladies. He cast 1,200 darts a time. If all darts missed the pot, Heaven would laugh at him by lightning.
* deer: a ruminant (family *Cervidae*), having deciduous antlers, usually in the male only, as the moose, elk, and reindeer.
* macaque: a monkey with a stout body, short tail, cheek pouches, and pronounced muzzle.
* vulture: a large bird of prey, related to the eagles, hawks, and falcons, having the head and neck naked or partly naked, feeding mostly on carrion.
* tiger: a large carnivorous feline mammal, with stripes on a tawny body and black bars on the limbs and tail.
* three robust men: There were three robust men serving King Scene of Ch'i. They were strong enough to fight tigers. Ying Yan, the prime minister, suggested getting rid of

them by giving two peaches to those two who were meritorious. The three fought for the reward brutally, as a result, and all committed suicide out of shame.
* Chü: referring to Chümeng, a gallant in the Fore-Ch'in period, who often saved people from danger.
* Yafu Chou: Yafu Chou (199 B.C.- 143 B.C.), a famous general in the Han dynasty. When seven dukes rebelled, the emperor sent general Yafu Chou to suppress them.
* the two swords: referring to the two renowned ancient swords, Kanchiang and Moyeh. They were once collected by Huan Lei in the West Chin dynasty. He gave Kanchiang to his friend Hua Chang and kept Moyeh. But Kanchiang was lost after Chang was murdered. After Lei's death, when his son Hua Lei passed by Yanp'ing Ford, all of a sudden, Moyeh jumped off his waist to the water to join its partner Kanchiang, and the two swords turned into two dragons.

乌 夜 啼

黄云城边乌欲栖，
归飞哑哑枝上啼。
机中织锦秦川女，
碧纱如烟隔窗语。
停梭怅然忆远人，
独宿孤房泪如雨。

Crows Cawing at Dusk

Crows will perch by the town in sand galore;
They fly back to the boughs and loudly caw.
Upon her loom the beauty weaves brocade,
While murmuring toward the curtain shade.
She stops her shuttle and does him recall;
Her room so vacant, like rain her tears fall.

* crow: an omnivorous, raucous, oscine bird of the genus *Corvus*, with glossy black plumage. It is regarded as an ominous bird, a metaphor for death because it is a scavenger, feeding on carrion. It is a common image in Chinese literature, which can be found in *The Book of Songs* compiled 2500 years ago: "Crows are all black, it's said, / So as foxes are red."
* the town in sand galore: a border town encompassed with flying sand in the desert.
* the beauty: referring to Hui Su, wife of T'ao Tou, who was exiled. Su wove her affection for her husband into a plalindrome brocade of 840 words.

乌 栖 曲

姑苏台上乌栖时，
吴王宫里醉西施。
吴歌楚舞欢未毕，
青山欲衔半边日。
银箭金壶漏水多，
起看秋月坠江波。
东方渐高奈乐何！

Crows Perching

When crows come to perch upon Kusu Mound;
West Maid in Wu's Harem drinks, as if drowned.
Wu songs and Ch'u dance, the play's going on;
The green hills west will swallow half the sun.
The gold hourglass sees leaking more and more;
The moon falls to the waves that wash the shore.
The day's breaking while their spirits still soar.

* crow: an omnivorous, non-migratory, raucous, oscine bird of the genus *Corvus*, with glossy black plumage and a typical harsh call. It is regarded as an ominous bird, a messenger from hell because it can smell those dying and feeds on carrion as a scavenger.
* Kusu Mound: a palace King Fuch'ai built for West Maid.
* West Maid: once a laundry lady in the State of Yüeh, which was then a tributary to the State of Wu. Because of her beauty, West Maid was selected to be trained in Yüeh's palace, and sent to King of Wu as a spy. Immediately, she won the king's affection and favor with her bewitching charm and performance art of dancing. As a result, the State

of Wu waned and perished.
* hourglass: a vessel made of glass or some similar material, used for measuring time by the running of water or sand from the upper into the lower compartment.
* the moon: the satellite of the earth, a representation of feminity in contrast with the sun, a presentation of masculinity. In a universe animated by the interaction of Shade (female) and Shine (male) energies, the moon is literally Shade visible.

战 城 南

去年战,桑干源,
今年战,葱河道。
洗兵条支海上波,
放马天山雪中草。
万里长征战,
三军尽衰老。
匈奴以杀戮为耕作,
古来唯见白骨黄沙田。
秦家筑城避胡处,
汉家还有烽火燃。
烽火燃不息,
征战无已时。
野战格斗死,
败马号鸣向天悲。
乌鸢啄人肠,
衔飞上挂枯树枝。
士卒涂草莽,
将军空尔为。
乃知兵者是凶器,
圣人不得已而用之。

A Battle South of the Town

Mulberry Dry Source saw a battle last year;
This year a war was waged on the Leek Flow.
Weapons were washed with waves in Tajik Sea;

Horses were fed on grass in Mt. Sky snow.

Fighting thirty thousand miles off,

All soldiers are tired and old grow.

The Huns kill like tilling the field;

Since the past, they've seen just white bones and yellow sand.

There loom the walls built in Ch'in against Huns;

Here beacon towers founded by Han still stand.

The beacon fires are kept, still on,

The wars and battles not yet done.

Some steeds die in the battles wild;

Some horses defeated to the sky sadly neigh.

Crows peck intestines of the dead;

Then they fly and hang them on boughs to sway.

Soldiers sprinkle grass with their blood;

Generals can but grow hair gray.

As known to all, weapons are ominous;

Saints do not put them to use while they may.

* Mulberry Dry Source: the Mulberry Dry River, 30 kilometers south of today's Great Union (Tat'ung), Shanhsi Province, so named because it usually dries when mulberries ripe. It is the upper reach of the E'er Quiet River, a branch of the Sea River, the fifth largest water systems in China.
* the Leek Flow: name of a watercourse, which has two sources—One is Mt. Leek, which is today's Pamirs, the other Khotan in today's New Land (Hsingchiang).
* Tajik Sea: or Ntiaochia Sea, which is today's Persian Gulf.
* horse: a large herbivorous solid-hoofed quadruped (*Equus caballus*) with coarse mane and tail, of various strains: Ferghana, Mongolian, Kazaks, Hequ, Karasahr and so on and of various colors: black, white, yellow, brown, dappled and so on, domesticated about four thousand years ago, employed in agriculture, transportation and warfare.
* Mt. Sky: also named Mt. Heaven, one of the seven mountain chains in the world, 2,500 kilometers long, 250 to 350 kilometers wide on average. Mt. Sky in this poem probably refers to the Khangai Mountains in today's Mongolia, namely Mongolian People's Republic.

* Ch'in: the Ch'in State or the State of Ch'in (905 B.C - 206 B.C.), enfeoffed as a dependency of Chough by King Piety of Chough in 905 B.C and enfeoffed as a vassal state by King Peace of Chough in 770 B.C.. In the ten years from 230 B.C. to 221 B.C., Ch'in wiped out the other six powers and became the first unified regime of China, i.e., the Ch'in Empire.
* Hun: nomadic barbarians west and north of China, who had no trade but battle and carnage, no fields or ploughlands but only wastes where white bones lay scattered over yellow sands.
* beacon tower: a prominent building set on a wall or hill or a similar position, as a guide or warning to garrison generals or others.
* steed: a horse; especially a spirited war horse. The use of horses in war can be traced back to the Shang dynasty (1600 B.C.- 1046 B.C.), when a department of horse management was established. A verse from *The Book of Songs* tells of Lord Civil of Watch's industriousness: "In state affairs he leads; / He has three thousand steeds."

将 进 酒

君不见,
黄河之水天上来,
奔流到海不复回!
君不见,
高堂明镜悲白发,
朝如青丝暮成雪!
人生得意须尽欢,
莫使金樽空对月。
天生我才必有用,
千金散尽还复来。
烹羊宰牛且为乐,
会须一饮三百杯。
岑夫子,
丹丘生,
将进酒,
杯莫停。
与君歌一曲,
请君为我倾耳听。
钟鼓馔玉不足贵,
但愿长醉不觉醒。
古来圣贤皆寂寞,
惟有饮者留其名。
陈王昔时宴平乐,
斗酒十千恣欢谑。
主人何为言少钱,
径须沽取对君酌。
五花马,

千金裘，

呼儿将出换美酒，

与尔同销万古愁。

Do Drink Wine

Don't you espy

The Yellow River surge down from the sky,

Up to the sea it does tumble and flow?

Don't you espy

To my white hair in the mirror I sigh,

As at dawn is black and at dusk turns snow?

Do enjoy life while in prime you run high;

Not to the moon just your empty cup ply.

So born by Heaven we must be of use;

Spend all the money and more will come up.

Cook lamb, kill cattle just for joy profuse;

Do gulp down three hundred fills from your cup.

Ts'en, my teacher,

Redknoll, friend mine,

Don't put down cups,

Do drink the wine.

I'll sing you a song of cheer,

Please listen, prick up your ear.

Bells, drums and dainties are precious no more;

Drink ourselves drunk, ne'er sober, lying down.

Obscure are the sages and saints of yore,

Only drinkers can enjoy high renown.

At olden times Prince Ch'en held a great feast;

He drank barrels and barrels with no stall.

How can a host claim to have money least?
I shall buy more and drink up to you all.
Dapples be sold,
And furs like gold.
Call our son to pawn them, buy wine, buy more,
With you I will drink off our age-long sore.

* wine: Drinking plays an important part in the lives of most Chinese, especially Chinese poets, acting as a form of enlightenment comparable to Zen practice. Wine is a must at a feast, as is said, without wine, there will be no feast.
* the Yellow River: the second longest river in China, flowing through Loess Plataeu, hence yellow water all the way. 5,464 kilometers long, with a drainage area of 752,443 square kilometers, it has been regarded as the cradle of Chinese civilization. As legend goes, the river derived from a yellow dragon that, couchant on Midland Plain, ate yellow soil, flooded crops, devoured people and stock, and was finally tamed by Great Worm, the First King of Hsia (cir. 21 B.C.- 16 B.C.).
* Heaven: the space surrounding or seeming to overarch the earth, in which the sun, the moon, and stars appear, popularly the abode of God, his angels and the blessed, and in most cases suggesting supernatural power or sometimes signifying a monarch.
* Ts'en and Redknoll: Pai Li's Wordist friends.
* Prince Ch'en: referring to Chih Ts'ao (A.D. 192 – A.D. 232), the third son of the overlord Ts'ao Ts'ao. So talented and dissolute, he failed to ascend the throne but succeeded as a poet, remembered as a representative of Making Peace Literature in Chinese history.
* dapple: an animal whose skin or fur is spotted, a horse in this poem.

行行且游猎篇

边城儿,
生年不读一字书,
但知游猎夸轻趫。
胡马秋肥宜白草,
骑来蹑影何矜骄。
金鞭拂雪挥鸣鞘,
半酣呼鹰出远郊。
弓弯满月不虚发,
双鸧迸落连飞髇。
海边观者皆辟易,
猛气英风振沙碛。
儒生不及游侠人,
白首下帷复何益!

The Young Hunters

The lads in Border Town
Do not read for life, all illiterate;
They but know play and hunting, bragging: great.
Fall wind blowing grass white, Hun steeds they ride;
They gallop, trailing shadows, how elate!
Their gold whips slash their sheath, whirling up snow;
Half drunk, with hawks to the suburbs they go.
Bows fully bent, targets are rightly shot;
With one arrow hurled, two owlets are got.
All viewers this dangerous play evade,

The lads' spirits sand and moraine pervade.
How can scholars with these hunters compare?
What's the use of them but growing gray hair?

* Hun steeds: horses from areas northwest of China, of which the sky horse or Pegasus is the most famous.
* hawk: a diurnal bird of prey, notable for keen sight and strong flight, usually used as a metaphor for one who takes military means in contrast with a dove, one who tries to find peaceful solutions.

飞龙引二首

Riding a Dragon, Two Poems

其 一

黄帝铸鼎于荆山，
炼丹砂。
丹砂成黄金，
骑龙飞上太清家。
云愁海思令人嗟，
宫中彩女颜如花。
飘然挥手凌紫霞，
从风纵体登鸾车。
登鸾车，
侍轩辕，
遨游青天中，
其乐不可言。

No. 1

Lord Yellow cast tripods in the Chaste Hills
To refine cinnabar.
Cinnabar having become gold,
He rode a dragon for the sky afar.
We feel lost and in vain sigh to the brume;
The maids in the harem like blossoms bloom.
How I wish to sway a cloud and depart
And with wind climb onto the phoenix cart.
Onto the phoenix cart,

To serve Cartshaft with heart,

The blue we tour, on high we soar.

What a bliss, we can't expect more!

* Lord Yellow: Lord Yellow (2717 B.C.– 2599 B.C.) is one of the five heavenly figures in myth and the earliest ancestor of Chinese people. It is said that Lord Yellow made a tripod in the Chaste Hills. As the tripod was finished, a dragon came down to visit him. He and more than 70 accompanied officials and consorts all rode on the dragon and flew up to the sky.
* tripod: a cooking utensil or cauldron with three feet or legs, usually cast with bronze, popular in ancient China, a symbol of a powerful family.
* cinnabar: a crystallized red mercuric sulfide, HgS, the chief ore of mercury, the raw mineral material for elixir in Wordist alchemy.
* the Chaste Hills: there are five mountain ranges bearing the name. This place is unidentified in this poem.
* dragon: a fabulous serpent-like giant winged animal, a totem of the Chinese nation, a symbol of benevolence and sovereignty in Chinese culture.
* Cartshaft: an alias of Lord Yellow, the first of five prehistoric lords of China.

其 二

鼎湖流水清且闲,
轩辕去时有弓剑,
古人传道留其间。
后宫婵娟多花颜,
乘鸾飞烟亦不还,
骑龙攀天造天关。
造天关,闻天语,
屯云河车载玉女。
载玉女,过紫皇,
紫皇乃赐白兔所捣之药方。
后天而老凋三光,
下视瑶池见王母,
蛾眉萧飒如秋霜。

No. 2

Lake Tripod is limpid, brimming with mirth.
Then Lord Yellow left, his sword left on earth;
E'er since, all tales have been told of its worth.
In the harem there, to bloom the belles vie;
The saints riding phoenixes thru clouds fly;
I'd drive my dragon to the Gate of Sky.
To the Gate of Sky to hear what gods say,
And ride with Jade Maid to the Milky Way.
To the Milky Way, we ascend to Lord Jade;
Lord Jade will offer me the knack for elixir brewed by White Hare.
With Goddess I'd live till stars lose their glare,
Then I'd see Queen Mother in Jade Court there.

Her brows look gray, and like frost is her hair.

* Lake Tripod: in present-day Lingpao, Honan Province.
* Lord Yellow: alias Cartshaft, the first of the five heavenly gods in myth and the earliest ancestor of Chinese people. As is said, Lord Yellow made a tripod in the Chaste Hills. As the tripod was done, a dragon came down to visit him. He and his 70 or more officials and consorts all rode on the dragon and flew to the sky. In the myth, when Lord Yellow and his retinue rode the dragon away, they left some junior officials on earth, who could but pull the dragon's beard in vain. All they got was only a strand of beard and the sword dropped from Lord Yellow.
* phoenix: an auspicious bird, unique of its kind, which only perches on parasol trees and eats bamboo shoots.
* dragon: Though variously understood as a large reptile, a marine monster, a jackal and so on in Western culture, it has been esteemed as a fabulous serpent-like giant winged animal, a totem of the Chinese nation and a symbol of benevolence and sovereignty in Chinese culture.
* Jade Maid: a fairy who often showed up with her partner Gold Lad.
* the Milky Way: a luminous band circling the heavens composed of stars and nebulae; the Galaxy.
* Lord Jade: the celestial being of the highest rank in Wordism.
* White Hare: In Chinese myths, there is a hare on the moon ramming elixir.
* Queen Mother: Mother West, a mythological being in Chinese culture.
* Jade Court: i.e. Jade Pool, where Queen Mother hosts banquets.

天 马 歌

天马来出月支窟,
背为虎文龙翼骨。
嘶青云,振绿发,
兰筋权奇走灭没。
腾昆仑,历西极,
四足无一蹶。
鸡鸣刷燕晡秣越,
神行电迈蹑慌惚。
天马呼,飞龙趋,
目明长庚臆双凫。
尾如流星首渴乌,
口喷红光汗沟朱。
曾陪时龙蹑天衢,
羁金络月照皇都。
逸气棱棱凌九区,
白璧如山谁敢沽。
回头笑紫燕,
但觉尔辈愚。
天马奔,恋君轩,
駷跃惊矫浮云翻。
万里足踯躅,
遥瞻阊阖门。
不逢寒风子,
谁采逸景孙。
白云在青天,
丘陵远。
崔嵬盐车上峻坂,

倒行逆施畏日晚。
伯乐翦拂中道遗,
少尽其力老弃之。
愿逢田子方,
恻然为我悲。
虽有玉山禾,
不能疗苦饥。
严霜五月凋桂枝,
伏枥衔冤摧两眉。
请君赎献穆天子,
犹堪弄影舞瑶池。

The Sky Horse

The sky horse comes from Kusana, alack,
With pterygoid bones and stripes on the back.
It neighs to the sky, swaying its green mane;
With tendons rare, it runs off, not seen again
It flies o'er Mt. Queen, up to the west tip,
Four hoofs in the air, ne'er a slip.
At dawn it preens in Yan and grazes Yüeh when dark;
Like lightning it runs with whirs, you can hark.
The sky horse whirls past, like a dragon stark;
Shoulders protruding, its eyes spark.
Like a flash its tail and like a crow its head,
Like blood its sweat and from its mouth light red.
With royal steeds it once trod Thoroughfare;
With its golden harness, to the court it does glare.
Its glamour dazzles all creatures on earth;
Its value like jade piled up, who knows its worth?

It turns to smock at a swift steed,
Feeling that it's foolish indeed.
The sky horse gallops, for royal carts yearns,
And leaping, jumping, floating clouds it turns.
But it falters to hesitate,
Gazing far into Heaven's Gate.
If Sir Chilly Wind is not here,
Who can value a pony dear?
White clouds float across the blue sky;
The hills rolling off do tower high.
The salt cart's going up the slope;
It slips backward. Now late, how can it cope?
Only Glee will to its sorry state sigh;
Doing its best when young, when old laid by.
May it bump into Sir Farm Square,
With enough sympathy, he's fair.
Tho on Mt. Queen there's fodder fine;
Too far away, no chance to dine.
Frost in the fifth moon laurel twigs weigh down;
No fodder in the mange but its sad frown.
Who can redeem it as a tribute, pray;
It can dance and swirl well for a horse play.

* the sky horse: According to historical records, the sky horse from Kusana is a precious kind. As it sprints, its shoulders swell and it sweats as if bleeding.
* Mt. Queen: Mt. Kunlun if transliterated, regarded as the most sacred mountain in China. It starts from the Eastern Pamir Plateau, stretches across New Land (Hsinchiang) and Tibet, and extends to Ch'inghai, with an average altitude of 5,500 - 6,000 meters. In Chinese myths, Mt. Queen is where Mother West dwells.
* Yan and Yüeh: ancient states in the Spring and Autumn period, which are now used to indicate northern and southern parts of China.
* dragon: a fabulous serpent-like giant winged animal, a symbol of benevolence and

sovereignty in Chinese culture.
* Sir Chilly Wind: a horse connoisseur in ancient times.
* Glee: a horse connoisseur living in the Spring and Autumn period, now referring to a person who discovers, recommends, raises and uses talents.
* Sir Farm Square: a Wordist, renowned for his knowledge and nobility.
* Frost in the fifth moon: a phrase borrowed from Yan Tsou's story, in which one who suffers from false imprisonment touches Heaven.
* laurel: an evergreen shrub with aromatic, lance-shaped leaves, yellowish flowers, and succulent, cherry-like fruit, a symbol of glory usually in the form of a crown or wreath of laurel to indicate honor or high merit, especially when one had passed Grand Test in ancient China. In Chinese mythology, there is a laurel tree on the moon, and it would never fall even though Kang Wu has kept cutting it.

行路难三首
It's a Hard Go, Three Poems

其 一

金樽清酒斗十千,
玉盘珍馐直万钱。
停杯投箸不能食,
拔剑四顾心茫然。
欲渡黄河冰塞川,
将登太行雪满山。
闲来垂钓坐溪上,
忽复乘舟梦日边。
行路难,行路难,
多歧路,今安在?
长风破浪会有时,
直挂云帆济沧海。

No. 1

Bounteous they are, the gold cups and pure wine,
The jade plates, dainties, and all those things fine!
Sad, I lay down chopsticks and thank my host;
My sword unsheathed, looking on, I feel lost.
I would cross the Yellow, but it's ice-clogged;
I would climb Mt. Great Go, but it's snow-fogged.
When free, I'd fish downstream, singing a croon,
And in dream cruise around the sun and moon.
It's a hard go! It's a hard go!

Where am I now? The path misleads me so.
Someday, I will put up a towering sail,
And to the ocean, waves and winds I'll hail.

* the Yellow: the Yellow River, the second longest river in China, flowing through Loess Plataeu, hence yellow water all the way. 5,464 kilometers long, with a drainage area of 752,443 square kilometers, it has been regarded as the cradle of Chinese civilization. As legend goes, the river derived from a yellow dragon that, couchant on Midland Plain, ate yellow soil, flooded crops, devoured people and stock, and was finally tamed by Great Worm, the First King of Hsia (cir. 21 B.C.- 16 B.C.).
* Mt. Great Go: Mt. T'aihang if transliterated, meandering on the border of Shanhsi, Honan and Sha'anhsi, an important mountain range in East China and a geographic watershed.

其　二

大道如青天，
我独不得出。
羞逐长安社中儿，
赤鸡白雉赌梨栗。
弹剑作歌奏苦声，
曳裾王门不称情。
淮阴市井笑韩信，
汉朝公卿忌贾生。
君不见
昔时燕家重郭隗，
拥篲折节无嫌猜。
剧辛乐毅感恩分，
输肝剖胆效英才。
昭王白骨萦蔓草，
谁人更扫黄金台？
行路难，归去来！

No. 2

The way of life is broad like the sky;
But I've no way to go, no way.
It's a shame to join the fops in the town;
Red cocks, white pheasants, cockfighting all day.
Poor, Feng sang his sad lay and played his sword;
To bow to power does not with me accord.
The hooligans jeered: Hsin Han was so tame;
The grandees in Han envied Ee Chia's fame.
Don't you espy

Then, King of Yan held Kui Kuo in esteem,
No suspicion, no jealousy, no scheme?
Chü Hsin and Ee Yüeh did whate'er they could;
Sacrifice their life to the lord they would.
Now King of Yan's tomb is rampant with grass;
Who will show respect for talents, alas?
A hard way, alack! Now I will go back!

* cock: the male, usually full grown, of the domesticated fowl, having a high red crown, hence an image of a leader or champion.
* pheasant: a long-tailed gallinaceous bird noted for the gorgeous plumage of the male, often regarded as wild chicken in Chinese culture.
* cockfights: cockfighting has a long history in China, a main recreational and gaming activity throughout history. The earliest cock fighting in China recorded in *Historical Records* was in 770 B.C.
* Hsuan Feng: a strategist in the Spring and Autumn period, Lord Mengch'ang's hanger-on, who used to play his sword and sing a sad lay to express his complaint.
* Hsin Han: Hsin Han (cir. 231 B.C.- 196 B.C.), a founding commander of the Han regime. He had been poor and shown a good endurance of humiliation. Once a young man made fun of him and forced him to crawl through his legs, and Han did so without changing his expression.
* Ee Chia: Ee Chia (200 B.C.- 168 B.C.), a political commentator, litterateur, who gained his fame when he was young. When he served as an official, he was envied by those higher-ranking ministers.
* Kui Kuo: Kui Kuo (351 B.C.- 297 B.C.), a minister of Yan, who suggested that King Glare of Yan learn from the ancients to invite men of ability. King Yan adopted his suggestion and showed great respect to the talents joining Yan, which attracted talents like Ee Yüeh, Yan Tsou and Hsin Chü. Owing to this suggestion, the State of Yan flourished, and King Yan held Kuo in esteem as a royal teacher.
* Hsin Chü: Hsin Chü (? - 243 B.C.) a military strategist from Chao, who later served Yan.
* Ee Yüeh: a prominent military commander. In the year 284 B.C., he commanded the five-nation allied forces to attack the State of Ch'i and set an example of the weak overcoming the strong in war history.

其 三

有耳莫洗颍川水，
有口莫食首阳蕨。
含光混世贵无名，
何用孤高比云月？
吾观自古贤达人，
功成不退皆殒身。
子胥既弃吴江上，
屈原终投湘水滨。
陆机雄才岂自保？
李斯税驾苦不早。
华亭鹤唳讵可闻？
上蔡苍鹰何足道？
君不见
吴中张翰称达生，
秋风忽忆江东行。
且乐生前一杯酒，
何须身后千载名？

No. 3

Don't wash your ears with water from the Ying;
Don't eat fungi on Mt. Firstshine o'er there.
In this world you'd restrain and bide your time;
Why withdraw and with the pure moon compare?
The able and sagacious men in the past
All died, who, at their best, did not give ground.
Tzuhsu's body was thrown down to the Wu;
Yüan Ch'ü jumped plop to the Hsiang and got drowned.

Chi Lu, so able, couldn't save himself;

Ssu Li ended up in the tragic state.

Could Chi Lu hear cranes on the carved roof crow?

Could Ssu Li go hunting out of East Gate?

Don't you espy

Han Chang from Wu, so broad-minded a man,

Went back to eat perch at an autumn sough?

Be happy and drink your cup while in prime;

Don't care your fame ten centuries from now.

* wash your ears: When Mound asked Freedom, noble and talented, to ascend the throne, he thought it was a humiliation and declined, and when Mound gave him an appointment, he felt sullied even the moment he heard it and washed his ears by the River Ying.
* the Ying River: also known as the East Stream or the Sandy Ying River, originating from the east peak of Mt. Tower, 620 kilometers long, which is the biggest branch of the Huai River.
* eat fungi on Mt. Firstshine: referring to the story of Bowone and Straightthree. As they failed to admonish King Martial of Chough, they left Chough and refused to take crops reaped under the reign of Chough. They lived on fungi on Mt. Firstshine and finally starved to death.
* Firstshine: Mt. Firstshine, located in today's Weiyüan County. It is the highest of all mountains there, so it is the first to receive sunshine, hence the name, and it is famous because two princes from the State of Lonebamboo called Bowone (Po-ee if transliterated) and Straightthree (Shuch'i if transliterated) died of starvation here for their rectitude.
* the moon: the planet of the earth, which appears at night and gives off shining silvery light, a source of brightness and an image of purity and solitude in Chinese culture.
* Tzuhsu: referring to Tzuhsu Wu (559 B.C.- 484 B.C.), a senior official of Wu. At his old age, his suggestion was denied and he was alienated by the king. The king of Wu was irritated by the latter's complaints, so he gave him a sword to commit suicide. After his death, the king put his body in a leather bag and threw it into a river.
* Yüan Ch'ü: Yüan Ch'ü (340 B.C.- 278 B.C.), a great patriotic poet and aristocrat of Ch'u, who threw himself into a river, so aggrieved at his broken state.
* Chi Lu: Chi Lu (A.D. 261 - A.D. 303), a well-known litterateur and calligrapher in

Chin, killed for false accusation by a eunuch. Before his execution, he cried: "Could I hear cranes crowing again on the carved roof?"

* Ssu Li: Ssu Li (284 B.C. - 208 B.C.), a renowned statesman, litterateur and calligrapher, whose political ideas have had a profound impact on China and laid the foundation for China's political system for more than two thousand years. After Emperor First of Ch'in died, Ssu was given a death sentence due to a false accusation. Before his execution, he sighed to his son that it would be impossible to hunt anymore.
* Han Chang: a high-ranking official in charge of personnel management in Loshine in the Western Chin dynasty. An autumn sough brought to him the taste of delicious perch in his hometown, so he resigned and went back home, leaving worldly affairs behind.
* perch: a small, spiny-finned, predaceous fresh water fish (genus *Perca*), a table delicacy in China.

长 相 思

长相思，在长安。
络纬秋啼金井阑，
微霜凄凄簟色寒。
孤灯不明思欲绝，
卷帷望月空长叹。
美人如花隔云端！
上有青冥之长天，
下有渌水之波澜。
天长路远魂飞苦，
梦魂不到关山难。
长相思，摧心肝！

Long Longing

My longing stretches to the capital.
Neath the rails cheep crickets ephemeral;
My mat feels cold as frost begins to fall.
The lone lamp dims and my sad tears run dry;
Rolling up the curtain, to the moon I sigh.
The belle looms like a rosebud in the sky.
High above extends the infinite blue;
Down below a tumult of waves do flow.
Time hangs on my hand and the way's far-flung;
The mountain passes cannot hear my song.
My longing, rending my heart, stretches long.

* cricket: a leaping orthopterous insect, with long antennae and three segments in each tarsus, the male of which makes a chirping sound by friction of forewings, a common image of a quiet night in Chinese literature.
* the moon: the satellite of the earth, an important image in Chinese literature or culture as it can evoke many associations such as solitude and nostalgia on the one hand, and purity, brightness and happy reunions on the other. Philosophically, it is the very germ or source of *Shade*, and the sun is its *Shine* counterpart. It is the goddess of the moon and of months in Roman mythology, and in Chinese culture the imperial concubine of Lord Alarm (2480 B.C.- 2345 B.C.), one of five mythical emperors in prehistorical China. The moon is celebrated with mooncakes on Mid-autumn Day when the moon is at its full glory.

上 留 田 行

行至上留田,
孤坟何峥嵘。
积此万古恨,
春草不复生。
悲风四边来,
肠断白杨声。
借问谁家地,
埋没蒿里茔。
古老向余言,
言是上留田,
蓬科马鬣今已平。
昔之弟死兄不葬,
他人于此举铭旌。
一鸟死,百鸟鸣。
一兽走,百兽惊。
桓山之禽别离苦,
欲去回翔不能征。
田氏仓卒骨肉分,
青天白日摧紫荆。
交柯之木本同形,
东枝憔悴西枝荣。
无心之物尚如此,
参商胡乃寻天兵。
孤竹延陵,
让国扬名。
高风缅邈,
颓波激清。

尺布之谣，

塞耳不能听。

Upper Reclaimed Farm

I've come to Upper Reclaimed Farm；

How lonely the tomb rank with grass!

And this tomb, with an age-old spite,

Has no more spring blossoms, alas.

A sad wind blows from all around；

Sadly, the poplars seem to cry.

May I ask whose graveyard it is,

Which in rampant warmwood does lie?

An old folk comes on to tell me：

It's Mister Farm's tomb, as is said.

Where bitter fleabanes sprawl and spread.

When he died, his body his brothers threw；

The folks raised for him a flag blue.

When a bird does die, all other birds cry；

When a beast does fall, all other beasts squall.

The fowls to go apart have a sad heart；

While backward they start, so keenly they smart.

When the Farms divided would go away,

Chinese red buds looked as if to decay.

The trees entwined have been the same made；

The east twigs flourish and the west ones fade.

The things without a heart are kind like this；

Why do people struggle, barred by Abyss.

The brothers demised throne；

Their kingdoms are well known.

High virtues far away,
Decadence on the way.
To all sarcasms or sneers,
People turn off their ears.

* Upper Reclaimed Farm: a conservatoire tune, originally name of a place.
* poplar: any of a genus (*Populus*) of dioecious trees and bushes of the willow family, widely distributed in northern and central China.
* fowl: the common domestic cock, hen or chicken, poultry in general. The domestication of the fowl in China was begun more than 5,000 years ago according to archaeological finds.
* Mr. Farm: referring to the owner of Upper Reclaimed Fram.
* bitter fleabane: one of various plants of composite family, supposed to repel fleas.
* The brothers demised throne: It implies two stories in ancient China. The first story reads like this. Bowone and Straightthree were royal brothers of the Kingdom of Lonebamboo. The King of Lonebamboo designated his son Straightthree as Crown Prince. After the king's death, Straightthree abdicated in favor of his elder brother Bowone and the latter refused, for it was against their father's will. Both brothers left the kingdom. The second story is like this. King of Wu wished to give the throne to his youngest son Chicha, so the elder sons Chufan, Yuchi and Yumei gave up the right of succession voluntarily. Chicha politely declined it, and the brothers decided to pass the throne to the youngest by committing suicide. Chicha still refused and let his nephew succeed to the throne.

春　日　行

深宫高楼入紫清，
金作蛟龙盘绣楹。
佳人当窗弄白日，
弦将手语弹鸣筝。
春风吹落君王耳，
此曲乃是升天行。
因出天池泛蓬瀛，
楼船蹙沓波浪惊。
三千双娥献歌笑，
挝钟考鼓宫殿倾，
万姓聚舞歌太平。
我无为，人自宁。
三十六帝欲相迎，
仙人飘翩下云軿。
帝不去，留镐京。
安能为轩辕，
独往入窅冥。
小臣拜献南山寿，
陛下万古垂鸿名。

A Spring

The high tower in the palace scrapes the sky;
With carved gold dragons on, the columns stand.
A belle by the window basks in the sun;
Over the plucked strings runs her tender hand.

A spring wind blows the tune to the Lord's ears,
Which is *Ascending the Sky*, an old song.
As it's from Heaven Pool and fairy isles,
The tower ships shaking the waves plow along.
Three thousand beauties sing songs and they smile;
The bells and drums the halls and courts beguile.
All folks gather to sing of the gay while.
Now in void I stay; all have a good day.
Thirty-six gods to alight come their way;
And fairies alight from their cart to stay.
Our Lord is not gone; he stays in the town.
How can He go like Cartshaft did,
To the sky, back and forth, up and down?
Long live Your Majesty now I would pray;
May your good name last for e'er, for e'er stay.

* sun: the heavenly body that is the center of attraction and the main source of light and heat in the solar system, a representation of Shine in contrast with Shade, the moon, in Chinese culture, a symbol of hope, life, strength, vigor and youth.
* *Ascending the Sky*: a poem composed by Chih Ts'ao, a prince and a poet in the Three Kingdoms period.
* thirty-six gods: There are thirty-six gods representing thirty-six skies in Wordist mythology, created based on the cosmology that the Word begets everything. The thirty-six skies include nine layers of sky and each layer covers four directions that again represent four seasons.
* Cartshaft: alias Lord Yellow (2717 B.C.- 2599 B.C.), one of the five heavenly figures in myth and the earliest ancestor of Chinese people. It is said that Cartshaft made a tripod in the Chaste Hills. As the tripod was finished, a dragon came down to visit him. He and more than 70 accompanied officials and consorts all rode on the dragon and flew up to the sky.

前有一樽酒行二首
A Golden Cup Ahead, Two Poems

其 一

春风东来忽相过，
金樽渌酒生微波。
落花纷纷稍觉多，
美人欲醉朱颜酡。
青轩桃李能几何，
流光欺人忽蹉跎。
君起舞，日西夕。
当年意气不肯倾，
白发如丝叹何益。

No. 1

An east wind blows 'cross my face and blows up,
Rippling the green wine in my golden cup.
The blossoms flutter down in such a rush;
The beauties seeming to be drunk all blush.
How long can peaches and plums keep their prime;
The elapse bullying us, don't waste our time.
I would dance with you; the west sun is askew.
When young, our fancies we couldn't surpass;
We pity our gray hair in vain, alas!

---

* wine: one of the most important beverages in Chinese culture, of which brown wine was brewed more than three thousand years ago and white wine (spirit) became popular in the Sung dynasty. Wine has an important position in Chinese life, such as literary creation, cultural activities, health care, cookery and so on.

* plums and peaches: a metonymy for plants in general; a metaphor for disciples or students, and sometimes symbolizing a flashy life.

其 二

琴奏龙门之绿桐,
玉壶美酒清若空。
催弦拂柱与君饮,
看朱成碧颜始红。
胡姬貌如花,
当垆笑春风。
笑春风,舞罗衣,
君今不醉将安归?

No. 2

I play the lute made of paulownia fine;
The jade kettle is brimming with pure wine.
Plucking the lute strings, with you I would drink;
Seeing our faces blushing, turning pink.
The Hun girls like sweet blossoms smile;
By the platform they all beguile.
They all beguile, their skirts they swirl;
If you are not drunk, don't you go home, pearl.

* lute: a Chinese lute, a stringed musical instrument, usually placed on a table, played by plucking the strings with fingers or a plectrum.
* paulownia: any of a genus of Chinese trees of the figwort family, with heart-shaped leaves and panicles of handsome, fragrant and purple flowers.
* the Hun girls: northern or western nomadic young women selling wine in their wineshops in the capital or other parts of China in the T'ang dynasty, featured with a high nose, charming eyes and blonde hair, and brimming with enthusiasm and ardor.
* pearl: a smooth, lustrous, usually white and bluish-gray, calcareous concretion

deposited in layers around a central nucleus in the shells of various mollusks or oysters, and largely used as a gem, medicine or given as a gift, a metaphor for the dearest one and a representation of nobility, purity and dignity in Chinese culture.

夜 坐 吟

冬夜夜寒觉夜长，
沉吟久坐坐北堂。
冰合井泉月入闺，
金缸青凝照悲啼。
金缸灭，啼转多。
掩妾泪，听君歌。
歌有声，妾有情。
情声合，两无违。
一语不入意，
从君万曲梁尘飞。

A Night Croon

The winter night cold, she feels the night long;
In North Hall she sits still and croons a song.
The well frozen, the moon enters the room;
The golden lamp sheds cold light on her gloom.
Out goes the lamp chill; sadder grows her trill.
She sweeps off her tears; a man's song she hears.
His song sounds so glad; her love goes like mad.
Two hearts are combined, hence they have one mind.
If a word can't stir up her love,
Ten thousand tunes will ring in vain above.

* the moon: the satellite of the earth, an important image in Chinese literature or culture as it can evoke many associations such as solitude and nostalgia on the one hand, and purity, brightness and happy reunions on the other. Philosophically, it is the very germ or source of *Shade*, and the sun is its *Shine* counterpart. The moon absorbed the Fallen Immortal utterly, appearing in over a third of his poems.

野 田 黄 雀 行

游莫逐炎洲翠，
栖莫近吴宫燕。
吴宫火起焚巢窠，
炎洲逐翠遭网罗。
萧条两翅蓬蒿下，
纵有鹰鹯奈若何。

Siskins in the Field

In emeralds of Flame Isle, do not stay;
From nests in Wu's palace, keep away.
A palace fire will all the nests enwrap;
The emerald will mislead you to a trap.
Siskins can only under bushes flap;
Even eagles or hawks don't have their hap.

* Flame Isle: modern-day Hainan Island, so called because it is very hot there in summer and very warm in winter, generally known as a penal colony in ancient China.
* A palace fire: referring to the fire that burned Wu's Palace. According to historical records, in the 11th year of Emperor First's reign (the first emperor of Ch'in), a courtier in Wu's Palace tried to light up nesting swallows and accidentally started a fire that burnt down the nests and the palace.
* siskin: a finch, related to the golden finch, olive-green and yellow barred with black.
* eagles or hawks: diurnal birds of prey, notable for keen sight and strong flight, which are usually used as a metaphor for those who take military means in contrast with doves, those who try to find peaceful solutions.

箜 篌 谣

攀天莫登龙，
走山莫骑虎。
贵贱结交心不移，
唯有严陵及光武。
周公称大圣，
管蔡宁相容。
汉谣一斗粟，
不与淮南春。
兄弟尚路人，
吾心安所从。
他人方寸间，
山海几千重。
轻言托朋友，
对面九疑峰。
开花必早落，
桃李不如松。
管鲍久已死，
何人继其踪？

Ballad of the Harp

Climbing the sky, don't dragons ride;
Scaling a hill, leave tigers aside.
Are there friends in different ranks staying true?
We have none but Sir Yanridge and Kuangwu.
Prince of Chough was a saint so grand;

Kuan and Ts'ai's guile he couldn't stand.
Sewn can be cloth, piled can be grain,
But Lord and prince as feuds remain.
Brothers are like strangers as such;
Where could I be reassured much?
People are kept off heart to heart,
Like hills thousands of miles apart.
When in friends one tries to put trust,
Be faced with Mt. Nine Doubts he must.
Early blooming flowers early fall;
Peaches and plums can't match pines tall.
Long long ago, Kuan and Pao died;
Who can go with them side by side?

- dragon: Though variously understood as a large reptile, a marine monster, a jackal and so on in Western culture, it has been esteemed as a fabulous serpent-like giant winged animal, a totem of the Chinese nation and a symbol of benevolence and sovereignty in Chinese culture.
- tiger: a large ferocious carnivorous feline mammal, with stripes on a tawny body and black rings on the limbs and tail, praised as king of all animals.
- Sir Yanridge and Kuangwu: Sir Yanridge was a renowned hermit in the Eastern Han dynasty. Kuangwu, meaning Lightmight, is Hsiu Liu's posthumous title. Hsiu Liu won the throne with the help of Sir Yanridge. After Hsiu Liu was enthroned, he invited Yanridge several times to serve the court, but Yanridge declined the offer and lived in seclusion. Their friendship was so solid that the emperor even allowed Yanridge to share his bed with him. Their story symbolizes true friendship.
- Prince of Chough: the 4th son of King Civil, brother of King Martial. After King Martial died, the king was too young to reign, so Prince of Chough became a regent. During his regency, he put forward fundamental laws and regulations in various aspects, and improved the patriarchal clan system, the feudal system, and the well-farm system.
- Kuan and Ts'ai: King Civil's 3rd and 5th son. Dissatisfied with the regency, suspecting that it was detrimental to the young king, they coerced Wukeng, the son of King Chow of Yin, into rebellion. Prince of Chough, taking the order from the king, suppressed

the rebellion, killed Kuan and sent Ts'ai into exile. In the 7th year of regency, Prince of Chough gave the power back to the king.
* Sewn can be cloth, piled can be grain: In the 6th year of Emperor Civil of Han, his brother Chang Liu rebelled, hence the brothers became feuds. So, it's said that cloth or grain can be unified but hostile brothers remain divided.
* Mt. Nine Doubts: the mountain where Hibiscus was buried. It was so named because it confused people by similar peaks and landscape.
* Kuan and Pao: referring to Chung Kuan and Shuya Pao, a model of true friends. Kuan and Pao did business together and Kuan took more profits, but Pao did not think he was greedy, for he knew that Kuan was poorer; Kuan failed in his pursuit of an official career for several times, but Pao did not think he was unworthy, for he knew that everyone had his time; Kuan escaped from battlefields three times, but Pao did not think he was a coward because he knew Kuan had his mother to serve.

雉朝飞

麦陇青青三月时，
白雉朝飞挟两雌。
锦衣绮翼何离褷，
犊牧采薪感之悲。
春天和，
白日暖。
啄食饮泉勇气满，
争雄斗死绣颈断。
雉子斑奏急管弦，
倾心美酒尽玉碗。
枯杨枯杨尔生稊，
我独七十而孤栖。
弹弦写恨意不尽，
瞑目归黄泥。

A Pheasant Flies

In the third moon, the wheat fields look so green;
A white pheasant with two females do preen.
Their plumes like silken clothing brightly sheen;
The shepherd gathering firewood feels keen.
The spring is so fair;
There flows a warm air.
Having had food and drink, in spirits high,
The males fight till their necks break and they die.
Pheasants Bright played so fast does hearts combine;

The jade bowls are brimming with mellow wine.
Bare poplars, bare poplars, you have sprouts new;
Seventy years old, how lonely I grow!
The strings so plucked cannot express my woe;
With eyes closed, to Hades I'll go.

* wheat: a grain yielding an edible flour, the annual product of a cereal grass (genus *Triticum*), introduced to China from West Asia more than 4,000 years ago, used as a staple food in China and most of the world. In its importance to consumers, it is second only to rice.
* pheasant: a long-tailed gallinaceous bird noted for the gorgeous plumage of the male.
* *Pheasants Bright*: a song of a pheasant's love for her chicks and the pains of their parting.
* poplar: any of a genus (*Populus*) of dioecious trees and bushes of the willow family, widely distributed in the northern hemisphere.
* Hades: the abode of the dead, and a euphemism for hell. It is called Yellow Spring in Chinese culture, because deep down earth water is yellow, and Yellow Spring belongs in the Nine Hells and Nine Springs.

上　云　乐

金天之西，
白日所没。
康老胡雏，
生彼月窟。
巉岩容仪，
戍削风骨。
碧玉炅炅双目瞳，
黄金拳拳两鬓红。
华盖垂下睫，
嵩岳临上唇。
不睹诡谲貌，
岂知造化神。
大道是文康之严父，
元气乃文康之老亲。
抚顶弄盘古，
推车转天轮。
云见日月初生时，
铸冶火精与水银。
阳乌未出谷，
顾兔半藏身。
女娲戏黄土，
团作愚下人。
散在六合间，
濛濛若沙尘。
生死了不尽，
谁明此胡是仙真。
西海栽若木，

东溟植扶桑。
别来几多时,
枝叶万里长。
中国有七圣,
半路颓洪荒。
陛下应运起,
龙飞入咸阳。
赤眉立盆子,
白水兴汉光。
叱咤四海动,
洪涛为簸扬。
举足蹋紫微,
天关自开张。
老胡感至德,
东来进仙倡。
五色师子,
九苞凤凰。
是老胡鸡犬,
鸣舞飞帝乡。
淋漓飒沓,
进退成行。
能胡歌,
献汉酒。
跪双膝,
并两肘。
散花指天举素手。
拜龙颜,
献圣寿。
北斗戾,
南山摧。
天子九九八十一万岁,

长倾万岁杯。

Wen K'ang, a Hun

Beyond the sky, the west
Is where the sun does rest.
A Hun, Wen K'ang as hight,
Born at the moon's first light.
His face like a high crag,
He's robust with a shag.
His blue eyes sparkle and brilliantly glare;
His red sideburns go well with his blond hair.
His eyelashes his eyes equip;
His nose towers on his upper lip.
Without seeing such a weird face,
How do you know the divine grace?
The Word is K'ang's father strict and divine;
The One is K'ang's mother smiling to shine.
Stroked was Pangourd from head to heel;
Turned was the sky and turned the wheel.
Clouds spreading, the sun and moon were begot;
Fire essences and mercury were wrought.
When the sun was still in the dale,
The moon was half wrapped with a veil.
When Nuwa kneaded yellow clay,
Foolish humans were made to play.
Dispersed all over the vast land,
These humans were like grains of sand.
From birth to death, the life goes on,
Who knows this Hun is an immortal one?

By West Sea grows a knowledge tree;
On East Shore soughs a mulberry.
How many years now have gone past;
Twigs and leaves their shadows down cast.
Middle Kingdom has seven saints;
A flood causes many restraints.
His Majesty comes on to rise,
Like a dragon to Allshine flies.
Red Brows help Basin to throne;
White Water maintains Han alone.
With shouts and scolds, the sea does quake;
With tides and waves, the earth does shake.
Do climb up the Emperor Star;
Heaven's Gate is for you ajar.
The Hun is moved by your great worth;
To give you a spray, he comes forth.
The five-colored lions do there sway;
The nine-bud phoenix does there play.
They are cocks and dogs of the Huns;
In Emperor's town they're good ones.
They keep order and they are fine.
They go or they come in a line.
Hun songs they can sing;
Han wine they here bring.
Aground they kneel there;
Their elbows they pair.
Now a fairy throws blooms with her hand fair.
To Him they kowtow;
For His Bliss they bow.
The Dipper may break;
The mountains may quake.

> The Son of Heaven will live long, eighty thousand years old;
> A long life cup he will oft hold.

* Hun: one of barbaric nomadic Asian peoples who frequently invaded China, a general term referring to all northern or western invaders.
* the Word: referring to Tao if transliterated, the most significant and profoundest concept in Chinese philosophy. According to Laocius's *The Word and the World*: "The Word is void, but its use is infinite. O deep! It seems to be the root of all things."
* Pangourd: a legendary figure who separated Heaven from earth. He was the earliest man in China's mythology. As legend goes, Pangourd woke up in the chaos before the world was formed. He swayed his axe and cut, and what was light and clear rose up to be the sky, and what was heavy and turbid sank to be earth. He stood, head to the sky and feet on the earth, for thirty-six thousand years lest Heaven and the earth merge again. As Heaven and earth were finally formed, he lay down to take a rest. At this moment, his breath turned to be winds and clouds, his left eye turned into the sun, his right eye turned into the moon, and his limbs and trunk into mountains, blood into rivers, and hair into stars.
* Nüwa: the goddess of creation in ancient Chinese mythology. As said, she made seventy things every day, used yellow clay to make humans in imitation of her own image, and created a marital system for humans. When Heaven and earth cracked, she melt colorful stones to mend them, saving humans from the disaster.
* West Sea: a lake also called Blue Sea (Ch'inghai), in today's Ch'inghai Province.
* Seven Saints: referring to the seven emperors of the early T'ang dynasty.
* dragon: a fabulous serpent-like giant winged animal, a totem of the Chinese nation, a symbol of benevolence and sovereignty in Chinese culture.
* Allshine: the capital of Ch'in, 30 kilometers from Long Peace, that is, the capital of T'ang and today's Hsi-an.
* Red Brows: referring to Red Brows Army, notorious peasant rebels in ancient China. They rose in rebellion against the Han Empire in A.D. 18, and proclaimed Basin, a descendant of the Han, as their emperor. Red Brows were defeated by Hsiu Liu (Emperor Lightmight) in the year of A.D. 27.
* Basin: Basin Liu, a descendant of the Lis, the royal family, who was made a puppet emperor by Red Brows with the reign title Establishment (A.D. 25 – A.D. 27), and when dethroned, was well treated by Emperor Lightmight, the founder of Eastern Han (A.D. 25 – A.D. 220).
* White Water: Hsiu Liu's fiefdom. At the end of Western Han, a great sign showed and

Hsiu Liu sent his army from there and founded the regime of Eastern Han eventually.
* five-colored lions: a magnificent looking lion. The lion is a large, yellowish-brown or tawny carnivorous mammal (Panthera leo) of the cat family, native to Africa, Southwest Asia and South America, introduced to China, given as a gift to a Chinese emperor, in the Western Han dynasty.
* nine-bud phoenix: In Chinese mythology, a phoenix has six icons and nine buds. The six icons are head for Heaven, eyes for the sun, back for the moon, wings for wind, feet for the earth and tail for a weft; the nine buds are mouth for life, heart for moderation, ears for hearing, tongue for flexion, plumage for hues, crown for colors, claws for hooks, voice for high sound, and abdomen for a decorated room.
* lion: a large, yellowish-brown or tawny feline carnivorous mammal, a symbol of courage or a metaphor for a man of leonine character or mien.
* the Dipper: a constellation composed of seven bright stars, which looks like a spoon in the sky.
* Son of Heaven: a metaphor for a king or emperor to suggest divine kingship.

夷则格上白鸠拂舞辞

铿鸣钟，
考朗鼓。
歌白鸠，
引拂舞。
白鸠之白谁与邻，
霜衣雪襟诚可珍。
含哺七子能平均。
食不噎，
性安驯。
首农政，
鸣阳春。
天子刻玉杖，
镂形赐耆人。
白鹭之白非纯真，
外洁其色心匪仁。
阙五德，
无司晨，
胡为啄我葭下之紫鳞。
鹰鹯雕鹗，
贪而好杀；
凤凰虽大圣，
不愿以为臣。

Turtledove White and a Stroke Dance Light

Strike the bell aloud;

Beat the drum, so proud;

Sing *Turtledove White*;

Dance a stroke, dance light.

Who is the the turtledove's neighbour, who?

How valuable is her clothing like snow!

Seven children she does brood and breed;

They eat the same seed;

They eat as they need.

Farming's the first thing;

The folks welcome spring.

Jade sticks His Majesty has made;

With carved turtles, they're elders' aid.

White herons' feathers are white, but not true;

The color is clean but the heart is skew.

Cocks' virtues they've none,

Not heralding dawn.

They peck purple-scaled fish in the reed pond I own.

Hawks, vultures, eagles, ospreys,

Greedily they kill.

Tho phoenixes are worthy birds,

To be their peer is not their will.

* *Turtledove White*: an ancient song of white turtledoves. The white turtle appeared in Hotspring's age, that is, in the beginning of the Shang dynasty, regarded as something peculiar because turtledoves might have various colors but white at that time.
* turtledove: a kind of dove (genus *Streptopelia*), noted for its affection for mate and young.
* heron: a long-necked and long-legged wading bird, feeding on fish, a symbol of freedom, purity, longevity and happiness in Chinese culture.
* cock: the male, usually full grown, of the domesticated fowl, having a high red crown, hence an image of a leader or champion.
* hawks, vultures, eagles, ospreys: large birds of prey, usually regarded as fierce and

greedy, feeding on hares and fish, and sometimes on carrion.
* phoenix: a legendary bird, king of all birds, a symbol of good luck and nobility, a totem of the Chinese nation.

日 出 入 行

日出东方隈，
似从地底来。
历天又复入西海，
六龙所舍安在哉？
其始与终古不息，
人非元气，
安得与之久徘徊？
草不谢荣于春风，
木不怨落于秋天。
谁挥鞭策驱四运？
万物兴歇皆自然。
羲和！羲和！
汝奚汩没于荒淫之波？
鲁阳何德，
驻景挥戈？
逆道违天，矫诬实多。
吾将囊括大块，
浩然与溟涬同科！

The Sun Rises

The sun rises from the East Bend,
Like from below, it does ascend.
Day after day, it tours the sky and sets west;
Is it where the Six Dragons used to rest?
It is like this as it has been, here and there;

Men are not Vital Air;

How can they stay with it for e'er?

Grass does not thank the stroke of the spring fay;

Trees do not blame the chill of autumn day.

Who'll whip to urge the turning of seasons?

Rise or rest, all beings have their reasons.

She-her, She-her,

Why did you try to drive the sun to the ocean?

Shine Lu, what's that you play?

Wave your spear to stop its motion?

Such acts against Heaven, so stupid, so absurd!

O Heaven, earth and humans, the third,

We should join the One, with Vital Air blurred.

* the Six Dragons: referring to the sun. In Chinese mythology, a goddess named She-her rides a cart pulled by six dragons across the sky every day to bring light to the world, hence the Six Dragons as the metonymy for the sun.
* Vital Air: a term used by ancient philosophers, especially Wordists, referring to the air that existed before the formation of Heaven and earth. It is regarded as the most original and essential element.
* She-her: the mother of the sun or the dyad of Goddess of Sun and Goddess of Calendar in Chinese mythology. As is said, She-her, as Goddess of Sun, drives the sun across the sky.
* Shine Lu: It is said that Shine Lu had a fierce battle with the State of Han in the Warring States period. When dusk was falling, Lu waved his spear to force the sun to move 45 kilometers back.
* Heaven: the space surrounding or seeming to overarch the earth, in which the sun, the moon, and stars appear, popularly the abode of God, his angels and the blessed, and in most cases suggesting supernatural power or sometimes signifying a monarch.
* the One: a philosophical concept of Wordism, the beginning of all things, as is defined in *Sir Lush*, "In the beginning was the None, having nothing, having no name. Then there arose the One, and nothing was formed yet." And in Laocius's *The Word and the World*: "The sky has gotten the One, hence blue and clear; the earth has gotten the One, hence staid and still." Similarly, in the West, God is the One, Self-subsisting Reality. The One in the West and the One in the East are actually one, identifiable though in different languages.

胡　无　人

严风吹霜海草凋，
筋干精坚胡马骄。
汉家战士三十万，
将军兼领霍嫖姚。
流星白羽腰间插，
剑花秋莲光出匣。
天兵照雪下玉关，
虏箭如沙射金甲。
云龙风虎尽交回，
太白入月敌可摧。
敌可摧，旄头灭，
履胡之肠涉胡血。
悬胡青天上，
埋胡紫塞傍。
胡无人，汉道昌。
陛下之寿三千霜。
但歌大风云飞扬，
安得猛士兮守四方。

Hun, There Will Be None

Cold wind blows; desert plants and grass decay.
Lo, those bows and arrows, Hun horses neigh.
To fight, the three hundred thousand troops crave,
Under Commander Swift Huo, who's so brave.
On waist, meteor arrows tied with plumes white;

In hand, glaring sword stuck with lilies bright.
The royal troops fight Huns at Jade Pass in snow;
Our armors are by foes' arrows pierced through.
Dragons and tigers will enemies kill!
Venus enters the moon; foes will die soon.
The enemies will meet their chief's defeat.
Their intestines we tread through blood so red.
Hang their heads on high, near the sky;
Throw their bodies there on fronts bare.
Hun, There Will Be None; China is a great one!
Long live Your Majesty, so suave and grave!
Still we should sing: The clouds with the wind wave;
To guard our frontiers where can I find the brave?

* Hun: one of barbaric nomadic Asian peoples who frequently invaded China, a general term referring to all northern or western invaders.
* Swift Huo: referring to P'iaoyao Huo (140 B.C.- 117 B.C.), a renowned general, prominent strategist and patriotic hero in the Han dynasty. He made his first show at 17, leading 800 fierce cavalrymen to penetrate the enemy lines and defeat the Huns. Swift fought against the Huns in three major wars and each time returned with victory. He died of a disease at 24, leaving his achievements as the highest glory for Chinese military commanders.
* Jade Pass, built in the Han dynasty, an important military fort and passage on the Silk Road. It was named for jade business between Han and the western regions.
* dragons and tigers: a metaphor for brave soldiers.
* Venus: the second planet from the sun, the most brilliant object in the heavens except the sun and the moon. In Chinese astrology, there will be a disaster when Venus shows up across the sky in the daytime.
* the moon: the celestial body that revolves around the earth from west to east as a satellite, which appears at night and gives off shining silvery light, an image of purity and solitude in Chinese culture.
* The clouds with the wind wave: The lines sung come from High Wind, a song composed by Pang Liu, the founding emperor of Han.

北 风 行

烛龙栖寒门，
光曜犹旦开。
日月照之何不及此？
惟有北风号怒天上来。
燕山雪花大如席，
片片吹落轩辕台。
幽州思妇十二月，
停歌罢笑双蛾摧。
倚门望行人，
念君长城苦寒良可哀。
别时提剑救边去，
遗此虎文金鞞靫。
中有一双白羽箭，
蜘蛛结网生尘埃。
箭空在，
人今战死不复回。
不忍见此物，
焚之已成灰。
黄河捧土尚可塞，
北风雨雪恨难裁。

North Wind

Candle Dragon lives in Cold Gate;
Its light withdraws but at night late.
The sun or the moon will not shed light here or nearby;

Only north wind howls with anger down from the sky.
Snowflakes o'er Mt. Yan, as large as a mat,
Are blown onto Lord Yellow Mound like that.
The twelfth moon sees a wife in Remote Town
Sing not, smile not, but knotted in a frown.
There she does passers-by behold,
Thinking of her man guarding the Great Wall so cold.
You went to the border with your sword mere,
Your tiger skin quiver left with me here.
Two arrows tied with white plumes held inside,
On it spiders weaving their web abide.
Arrows laid in vain,
You killed in action will ne'er life regain.
This token, useless, I will crash;
I'll burn it, burn it into ash.
The Yellow River can be stuffed though deep;
The sleet whirled by north wind I can hardly reap.

* Candle Dragon: In Chinese myths, Candle Dragon is a human-faced, dragon-bodied, limbless creature. It lives in the North Pole, which is never sunlit. When it opens its eyes, day breaks; when it closes its eyes, night falls.
* Mt. Yan: one of the most famous mountains in Northern China, rolling from Changchiak'ou to Mountain-sea Pass, 420 kilometers long, 200 kilometers wide at most.
* Lord Yellow Mound: a big mound on Mt. Fisher 7.5 kilometers northeast of Level Dale (P'ingku), now a district under Peking, as is believed to be Lord Yellow's mausoleum.
* Remote Town: a town roughly located in present day Tahsing County, near Peking.
* the Great Wall: usually called Ten Thousand Li Great Wall, a giant project undertaken in different periods of Chinese history to defend China from northern nomadic invasions.
* spider: a wingless arachnid having an unsegmented abdomen and capable of spinning silk in the construction of webs for the capture of prey such as flies and insects, usually regarded as a mascot in China, a symbol of good luck or good news to come,

sometimes also bespeaking desolation, especially in a deserted room.
* the Yellow River: the second longest river in China, flowing across Loess Plateau, hence yellow. It is 5,464 kilometers long, with a drainage area of 752,443 square kilometers, having nurtured the Chinese nation, regarded as the cradle of Chinese civilization. After being tamed by Worm, the first king of Hsia, its fertile valleys were turned into fields of rice, barley and oscillating corn, amid gleaming streams and lakes.

侠 客 行

赵客缦胡缨，
吴钩霜雪明。
银鞍照白马，
飒沓如流星。
十步杀一人，
千里不留行。
事了拂衣去，
深藏身与名。
闲过信陵饮，
脱剑膝前横。
将炙啖朱亥，
持觞劝侯嬴。
三杯吐然诺，
五岳倒为轻。
眼花耳热后，
意气素霓生。
救赵挥金槌，
邯郸先震惊。
千秋二壮士，
烜赫大梁城。
纵死侠骨香，
不惭世上英。
谁能书阁下，
白首太玄经。

The Knights

The knight wore a tassel in hair,
His sword gave off a frosty glare.
A saddle silver, a horse white,
Galloping thru the street like light.
Within ten steps, he may kill one,
A thousand miles, foes he has none.
Task done, he goes off all alone,
His merit to the world unknown.
Once Faithridge drank with knights in breeze,
Swords drawn out and placed on their knees.
With his roast he cheered Hai Chu up
And to Ying Hou toasted a cup.
Each drank three cups, promising: Right,
Compared with this, mountains are light.
They felt heated from ear to ear;
Up the sky burst their will and cheer.
To save Chao he waved a gold ball,
Shaking Hantan the capital.
For millenniums the two knights' tale
Has spread in Great Beam to prevail.
Tho dead, they've left their balmy trace,
Heroes in the world, heroes ace.
Being a scholar who would care,
Reading in the room with gray hair?

* Faithridge: Prince Faithridge (Hsin Ling) (? - 243 B.C.), Prince of Way, the youngest son of King Glare of Way, a famous militarist and politician in the Warring

States period. He was courteous to talents, attracting 3,000 hangers-on. Hai Chu, a butcher, and Ying Hou, a porter, were treated with great courtesy and became his hangers-on.

* Chao: the State of Chao (403 B.C.- 222 B.C.), a vassal state in the Spring and Autumn period, one of the Seven Powers in the Warring States period.
* Hantan: the capital of Chao, a major city in today's Hopei Province. When threatened by the troops of Ch'in, Chao asked Faithridge for help. Hou suggested stealing the military tally, and Chu killed the commander with his gold hammer, so that Way's army was under Faithridge's command. In this way, Faithridge successfully saved Hantan.
* Great Beam: the capital of Way, present-day K'aifeng, Honan Province.

乐府三十七首
Conservatoire, 37 Poems

关 山 月

明月出天山，
苍茫云海间。
长风几万里，
吹度玉门关。
汉下白登道，
胡窥青海湾。
由来征战地，
不见有人还。
戍客望边色，
思归多苦颜。
高楼当此夜，
叹息未应闲。

The Moon over Mt. Pass

The moon appears out of Mt. Sky,
Between the sea and clouds on high.
For one thousand miles sweeps a sough,
A-blowing through Jade Gate Pass now.
The Hans march on the White Mound way;
The Huns gaze on the Blue Sea Bay.
Since ancient times they have here fought,
And no one has returned, oh, naught.
Hardship drives all the soldiers mad;
Nostalgia drowns their faces sad.
Tonight inside that tower so high,

There will be no cease of their sigh.

* the moon: the planet of the earth, which appears at night and gives off shining silvery light, an image of purity and solitude in Chinese culture.
* Mt. Pass: usually referring to Mt. Lane on the border of today's Sha'anhsi and Kansu provinces, an important strategic vantage point and a gateway to the Silk Road.
* Mt. Sky: Mt. Heaven, one of the seven mountain chains in the world, 2,500 kilometers long, 250 to 350 kilometers wide on average.
* Jade Gate Pass: located in the northwest of Tunhuang, an important artery to West Regions of China, built in the Han dynasty, located in the north of today's Tunhuang, Kansu Province. As is recorded, to guard against Hun invasions, Emperor Martial of Han formed alliance with nations in the western regions to initiate the route between east and west, and instituted four sires and built two passes with beacons west of the Yellow River. Fortresses were made from Lingchü to Wine Spring in 111 B.C. and more fortresses made from Wine Spring to Jade Gate.
* the White Mound way: Pang Liu, the founding emperor of Han, led his army to fight against the Huns and was trapped on the White Mound for seven days.
* Hun: one of barbaric nomadic Asian peoples who frequently invaded China, a general term referring to all northern or western invaders.
* the Blue Sea Bay: Blue Sea Lake or Kokonor, the great salt lake more than 10,000 feet above sea-level in today's Ch'inghai Province, so called because the lake looks blue.

独漉篇

独漉水中泥,
水浊不见月。
不见月尚可,
水深行人没。
越鸟从南来,
胡鹰亦北渡。
我欲弯弓向天射,
惜其中道失归路。
落叶别树,
飘零随风。
客无所托,
悲与此同。
罗帏舒卷,
似有人开。
明月直入,
无心可猜。
雄剑挂壁,
时时龙鸣。
不断犀象,
绣涩苔生。
国耻未雪,
何由成名。
神鹰梦泽,
不顾鸱鸢。
为君一击,
鹏抟九天。

Someone Wades

Someone wades, stirring mud around;
In the muddy pool no moon's found.
It is all right if no moon's found;
But as it's deep, one may be drowned.
The Yüeh birds from the south here hie;
The Hun hawks to their home north fly.
I would draw my bow and shoot to the sky;
They may go astray on their way I sigh.
Leaves fall down from the trees
And are blown by the breeze.
I have nowhere to lie,
Just like them I do sigh.
It seems my bed net's stirred,
Someone comes, as if heard.
It's moonlight coming on;
There's no doubt, it's the one.
The male sword on the wall
Once gives a dragon call.
That sharpened rhino blade
Is o'er there with moss laid.
I haven't cleansed our shame;
How can I carve my name?
It's said an eagle divine
Won't on owls and kites dine.
Its aim is to fly high
To catch hawks in the sky.

- Yüeh: the State of Yüeh (2032 B.C.– 222 B.C.), a vassal state under Hsia, Shang and Chough in Southeast China in the Spring and Autumn period. As a regime it was first founded by Nothing Left (Wuyü), King Young Health (Shaok'ang) of Hsia' son born of a concubine.
- Hun: war-like nomadic peoples inhabiting vast regions from Mongolia to Central Asia in Chinese history, especially during the Han dynasty. They were a constant menace on China's western and northern borders.
- Our shame: referring to Lushan An's Rebellion (A.D. 755 – A.D. 763). In the spring of 755, under the pretext of ridding the court of the prime minster, Lushan An raised the standard of rebellion. He quickly captured the city of Loshine, occupied the entire territory north of the Yellow River, and was soon marching eastward on Long Peace. He had proclaimed himself the Emperor of Great Yan. This rebellion led to a loss of a large number of people and a sharp decline of T'ang's national power, a turning point of the T'ang Empire.
- eagle: a diurnal bird of prey of the family Accipitridae of worldwide distribution, notable for keen sight and strong flight, usually praised as a hero in Chinese culture.
- owl: a predatory nocturnal bird, having large eyes and head, short, sharply hooked bill, long powerful claws, and a circular facial disk of radiating feathers, regarded as ominous in Chinese culture.
- kite: a certain bird of prey of the hawk family, having long, pointed wings and a forked tail, usually regarded as shrewed and greedy.

登高丘而望远

登高丘，
望远海。
六鳌骨已霜，
三山流安在？
扶桑半摧折，
白日沈光彩。
银台金阙如梦中，
秦皇汉武空相待。
精卫费木石，
鼋鼍无所凭。
君不见
骊山茂陵尽灰灭，
牧羊之子来攀登。
盗贼劫宝玉，
精灵竟何能？
穷兵黩武今如此，
鼎湖飞龙安可乘？

Climbing High to Gaze Afar

I climb a high mound
And gaze to the sea.
The six turtles are but bones now;
Where have the three hills flown to be?
The magic mulberry is broken;
No glamour of it does remain.

The silver mound and gold gate, but a dream,
August and Martial have waited in vain.
Jayway's wasted much stone and wood;
Turtles find them to no avail.
Don't you espy
The tombs on Mt. Black Steed have fallen to dust
That only kids or shepherds come to scale?
Having been robbed of all treasures,
What on earth can their spirits do?
Having gone all out for war till today,
Could they ride dragons to Lake Tripod blue?

* the six turtles: As is said, there was a huge gully in the east of Rising Sea (Pohai), and there were five fairy mountains floating on waves. God was afraid that they might drift away and the immortals and fairies lose their dwellings, so he ordered fifteen giant turtles to bear the mountains on their back in turn. In this way, the mountains were fixed. And there was a State of Giants on the sea, and a giant man from the state took several steps to the mountains and caught six turtles. The six turtles were burnt for divination, and as a result, two mountains drifted to the extreme north and sank into water.
* the three hills: In historical records, ancient kings were eager to find the three mountains for elixir. It is said that the creatures on the mountains were all white and buildings were all gold. Looked at from a remote distance, they looked as if floating on clouds; once near, they were actually under water; if one got closed to them, a wind would blow him away.
* the magic mulberry: a mythical plant, growing by the abyss where the sun rises.
* August: referring to Emperor First of Ch'in who annexed other six powerful states of the Seven Powers.
* Martial: referring to Lord Martial of Han, who prospered the country in all aspects.
* Jayway: According to legend, a daughter of Magic Farmer's was drowned in East Sea and turned into a bird named Jayway. It looked like a crow or jay, but with an annular head, a white beak, and red feet. It was born to carry stone and wood in an attempt to fill up the sea.
* the tombs on Mt. Black Steed: the mountain where August, i. e. Emperor First was

buried. It was said that the tomb was extremely luxurious, but before it was completed, an uprising army burnt the palaces and destroyed the tomb. And a rumor spread that the tomb was burnt when a shepherd accidentally ignited it as he was trying to find his lost sheep around the tomb.

* dragon: a fabulous serpent-like giant winged animal, a symbol of benevolence and sovereignty in Chinese culture.
* Lake Tripod: Lord Yellow became immortal at Lake Tripod and rode a dragon flying to the sky.

阳 春 歌

长安白日照春空，
绿杨结烟垂袅风。
披香殿前花始红，
流芳发色绣户中。
绣户中，相经过。
飞燕皇后轻身舞，
紫宫夫人绝世歌。
圣君三万六千日，
岁岁年年奈乐何。

Song of a Sunny Spring

Long Peace meets spring from the sunlit skies;
The mist o'er willows with the breeze does rise.
In front of Balm Hall flowers begin to flush;
To the painted door their fragrance does rush.
Their fragrance does rush, and there it floats, hush!
Flying Swallow gets up and light she dances;
Lady Purple Hall's song the world entrances.
The Most High's life, thirty-six thousand days,
Year after year, what amusements, what plays!

* Long Peace: Ch'ang'an if transliterated, the capital of the T'ang Empire, with 1,000,000 inhabitants, the largest walled city ever built by man.
* Balm Hall: name of one of the harems in Emperor Martial Reign of the Western Han dynasty.

* Flying Swallow: referring to Feiyan Chao (45 B.C.- 1 B.C.). Starting as a dancer in the residence of Princess Yang'o, she attracted Emperor Complete of Han's attention, hence she was made an imperial concubine and later the empress. As her sister Hote Chao came and attracted the emperor, Swallow gradually lost the emperor's attention.
* Lady Purple Hall: one of Emperor Martial's most favored imperial concubines.

杨 叛 儿

君歌杨叛儿，
妾劝新丰酒。
何许最关人，
乌啼白门柳。
乌啼隐杨花，
君醉留妾家。
博山炉中沉香火，
双烟一气凌紫霞。

Traitor Young

You sing the tune *Traitor Young*,
I invite you to Newrich wine.
Which is the most stirring one?
Crows on the tree by White Gate whine.
In poplar blossoms the whine's drowned;
You, now drunk, with me this night spend.
The incense is dying out on Mt. Fight;
Two curls of smoke to purple clouds ascend.

* *Traitor Young*: a children's rhyme originally, developed into a conservatoire tune later.
* Newrich: a county, located in the northeast of Lintung, celebrated for fine wine. Pang Liu, Emperor Highsire, the founder of Han, born in Rich in East China, rose from grassroots, wiped out Hsiang's army and established Han, with Long Peace as its capital. As his father missed the beauty and wine of his hometown, Pang Liu made a copy of his hometown and moved the best brewers and even dogs and chickens from

Rich, and ever since Newrich wine has been well-known, attracting generations of litterateurs to sing praise of it.
* White Gate: In ancient China, eight directions are called eight gates, and the southwest gate was called White Gate.
* poplar: any of a genus (*Populus*) of dioecious trees and bushes of the willow family, widely distributed in the northern hemisphere.
* incense: an aromatic substance that exhales perfume during combustion, burnt before a Buddhist, Wordist or any religious or ancestral figure as an act of worship.
* Mt. Fight: a kind of censer named Mt. Fight, with overlapping mountains carved on its lid. Once incense is ignited, this censer looks just like Mt. Fight on the sea. Another source says the censer looks like Mt. Flora, where King Glare of Ch'in wrestled with a god from Heaven, hence Mt. Fight, the alias of Mt. Flora. There have been quite a few poems themed on Mt. Fight Censer since the Southern Dynasties period (A.D. 420 - A.D. 589).

双　燕　离

双燕复双燕，
双飞令人羡。
玉楼珠阁不独栖，
金窗绣户长相见。
柏梁失火去，
因入吴王宫。
吴宫又焚荡，
雏尽巢亦空。
憔悴一身在，
孀雌忆故雄。
双飞难再得，
伤我寸心中。

The Swallows' Disaster

The two swallows fly higher and higher;
How this pair of mates I admire!
In the attic they build their nest;
Indoors each strokes the other's crest.
Then the cypress beams are on fire;
For Wu's palace there they aspire.
In due time, Wu's Palace is burned;
The nest with their chicks is upturned.
The loss of husband does her ail;
This widowed female wants her male.
They can't fly in pairs any more;

My heart's inflicted with a sore.

* swallow: a passerine bird, with short broad, depressed bill, long pointed wings, and forked tail, noted for fleeting flight and migratory habits. In Chinese culture, swallows are welcome to live with a family with their nest on a beam of a sitting room.
* cypress: an evergreen tree of the family Cupressaceae, having durable timber, a symbol of rectitude, nobility and longevity in Chinese culture.
* Wu: the State of Wu (12 Century B.C.- 473 B.C.), a vassal state in the lower reaches of the Long River, i.e., the Yangtze River, annexed by the State of Yüeh.
* the cypress beams: Cypress Beams Hall in Lord Martial's palace caught a fire around A.D. 104.
* Wu's Palace: Kouchien (520 B.C.- 465 B.C.), King of Yüeh, successfully wiped out the State of Wu for revenge, and burnt Wu's Palace around 473 B.C.

山 人 劝 酒

苍苍云松，
落落绮皓。
春风尔来为阿谁？
蝴蝶忽然满芳草。
秀眉霜雪颜桃花，
骨青髓绿长美好。
称是秦时避世人，
劝酒相欢不知老。
各守麋鹿志，
耻随龙虎争。
欻起佐太子，
汉王乃复惊。
顾谓戚夫人，
彼翁羽翼成。
归来商山下，
泛若云无情。
举觞酬巢由，
洗耳何独清。
浩歌望嵩岳，
意气还相倾。

The Hermits Toasting

Green，green，these cloud pine trees；
Glad，glad，those with gray hair.
Then for whom there resonates a spring breeze?

Butterflies flutter o'er grass here and there.
Tho tinged with hoarfrost they look still in prime,
With robust bones, firm sinews, all too fine.
They say they're hermits to evade Ch'in's time,
Not feeling old, each to each toasting wine.
Swamp deer's will they would abide by,
Shamed that tigers and dragons vie.
That fact they would help the crown prince
Takes His Majesty by surprise.
The Lord turns to Lady Ch'i hence:
These old men have told their whys.
They come back to the Shang Hills then,
Like clouds with no feeling between.
They pray to Ch'ao, and Hsu, the man,
Who once washed his ears to be clean.
Singing loud, to Mt. Tower I gaze,
Admiring their great airs and ways.

* Ch'in: the first unified regime of China, i.e. the Ch'in Empire.
* His Majesty: referring to Pang Liu, the founding emperor of Han. The emperor wanted to give his throne to Lady Ch'i's son instead of the crown prince. To win the throne, the queen, mother of the crown prince, treated the four old men of the Shang Hills with courtesy and invited them to assist the crown prince. Since the four men were talents that Pang Liu longed for, he could only tell Lady Ch'i that it was too late to dethrone the crown prince.
* Lady Ch'i: a favoured concubine of Pang Liu, the founding emperor of Han. After the emperor's death, the queen became queen mother. The evil empress threw Lady Ch'i into captivity, having her hair cut and her neck bundled with an iron ring, and ordered her to husk rice. At last, Lady Ch'i was dismembered, eyes gouged out, ears stuffed with copper, tongue cut off, throat silenced with medicine, so she was made what is called "human swine", and was thrown into a lavatory to die in pain.
* the Shang Hills: behind the town of today's Shanglo, about 1,100 meters above sea level, where the four hermits known as Four Gray Heads lived in reclusion, now noted

as the First Hermitage in China.
* Ch'ao and Hsu: referring to Father Ch'ao and Yu Hsu (Freedom), hermits during Mound's reign. It is said that Yu Hsu was unhappy at Mound's offer of his throne to him, so he washed his ears with clean water.
* washed his ears: The allusion to washing ears is a classical one, referring to Freedom, a hermit living by the Ying River, who washed his ears when offered the throne so as to get the sound of the proposal out of them.
* Mt. Tower: located in the west of present-day Honan Province, one of the Five Mountains in Chinese culture.

于阗采花

于阗采花人，
自言花相似。
明妃一朝西入胡，
胡中美女多羞死。
乃知汉地多名姝，
胡中无花可方比。
丹青能令丑者妍，
无盐翻在深宫里。
自古妒蛾眉，
胡沙埋皓齿。

The Bloom Picker in Khotan

The bloom picker in Khotan says:
Blossoms with blossoms are the same.
When Lady Glare was married to a Hun,
So many Hun beauties would die with shame.
They know the Hans have so many girls fair;
No Hun beauties there can with them compare.
Paintings can make ugly ones brightly sheen;
Nosalt, who's so plain, takes the role of Queen.
Belles are envied now as of yore,
Some buried in West, seen no more.

---

* Khotan: also known as Kotan or Hotan, a town on the southern branch of the Silk Road in New Land (Hsinchiang) in China. Khotan was once a center of a Buddhist

empire. The old capital, Yoktan, is about 10 kilometers west of the current city.
* Lady Glare: Lady Glare (cir. 52 B.C.- cir. A.D. 8), Chaochün Wang if transliterated, a lady in the seraglio of the emperor of the Han dynasty, one of the Four Belles in China. A maid of honour in the beginning, she was selected in 33 B.C. to marry the Hun chieftain who had proposed a royal marriage to consolidate mutual peace between two parties. She was one of the earliest victims of the political marriages, which the ruling house of China was compelled to make from time to time with the chieftains of the barbarian tribes in order to avoid their savage incursions into China, the Middle Kingdom.
* Hun: one of barbaric nomadic Asian peoples who frequently invaded China, a general term referring to all northern or western invaders.
* Nosalt: a famous ugly woman in history. She was married to King Hsuan of Ch'i (cir. 350 B.C.- 301 B.C.) in virtue of her wisdom and good advice.
* West: alias Western Regions, the areas inhabited by Huns and other nomadic people governed by China, for example, the Han Empire and the T'ang Empire, generally stretching from Jade Gate Pass and Sun Pass to Pamir Plateau and Balkhash Lake, and sometimes even to Caspian Sea and Black Sea.

鞠 歌 行

玉不自言如桃李，
鱼目笑之卞和耻。
楚国青蝇何太多，
连城白璧遭谗毁。
荆山长号泣血人，
忠臣死为刖足鬼。
听曲知甯戚，
夷吾因小妻。
秦穆五羊皮，
买死百里奚。
洗拂青云上，
当时贱如泥。
朝歌鼓刀叟，
虎变磻溪中。
一举钓六合，
遂荒营丘东。
平生渭水曲，
谁识此老翁。
奈何今之人，
双目送飞鸿。

A Football Song

Jade, silent, will not with peach blooms compare;
The best jade is sneered at by the fish eyes.
The priceless jade disc is left to shame bear;

In the State of Ch'u how many fruit flies!
Atop Mt. Chaste Ho Pian cried his heart out,
Feet cut off, though a man loyal and stout.
Ch'i Ning was known, singing a croon;
He was used soon beside the throne.
With five sheep skins Solemn did save
Him from Ch'u, called Hundredmile Slave.
Ascend to the blue sky one may,
Though he might be as low as clay.
From Mornsong the slaughterer old,
At Pan Stream his strategies sold.
At one time, he fished all around;
He built in Yingknoll his firm ground.
When he abode by the Wei there,
Who could know him with gray hair?
What a pity, people today
Just see the wild geese fly away.

* football: a game with a leather ball played by kicking between two parties, which originated in the age of Lord Yellow (2717 B.C.- 2599 B.C.), formally recorded in the Han dynasty and became popular in the T'ang and Sung dynasties.
* fish eye: It is said that a man bought a big pearl and his neighbor was jealous. On one occasion, the neighbor found a big fish eye and trumpeted he had a pearl. Hence, fish eyes have been used to indicate fake items.
* jade discs: jewels worn by royal families and nobles. Jade is exclusive to the upper echelon of the society, but gold and silver are not, as a saying goes, "Gold is priced while jade is priceless."
* the State of Ch'u: a vassal state of Chough, one of the powers in the Warring States period, conquered and annexed by Ch'in in 223 B.C.
* Mt. Chaste: a mountain in Hupei Province, located on the west bank of the River Han. It's said to be the mountain where Ho Pian found the jade.
* Ho Pian: a precious stone finder from the State of Ch'u. Ho found a piece of crude jade and presented it to two monarchs of Ch'u, but they misjudged it as ordinary stone and

had his legs cut for punishment. After Lord Civil of Ch'u was enthroned, Ho, holding the jade stone, cried bitterly for the misjudgment. Up to this point, the precious jade was finally appreciated by the new lord.
* Ch'i Ning: Ch'i's talent was unrecognized when he was young. When the lord was on his way out, Ch'i sang his frustration out as he beat an ox horn. His song successfully drew the lord's attention, and Ch'i was appointed as a senior official.
* Hundredmile Slave: Hundredmile was exiled to Ch'u after his motherland was subjugated. King Solemn of Ch'in saved him with five sheep skins and appointed him as a senior official.
* Mornsong: the capital of Shang.
* Pan Stream: Great Grand's alias and an allusion to the story of Great Grand, an influential strategist and statesman. He was once a slaughterer at his early age and remained diligent in hardship, expecting to display his ability for the country one day, but did not make any achievements until he was 70 years old. He went west at the age of 72. While fishing, he waited for King Civil so that he could sell his strategies, which finally won the king's appreciation. After Great Grand helped King Civil win his reign, Yingknoll was given him as his fief owing to his contribution.
* Yingknoll: the place King Civil granted Great Grand as his fief owing to his contribution, which is today's Lintzu, Shantung Province.
* the Wei: the River Wei, the biggest tributary of the Yellow River.

幽 涧 泉

拂彼白石，
弹吾素琴。
幽涧愀兮流泉深，
善手明徽，
高张清心；
寂历似千古松，
飕飗兮万寻。
中见愁猿吊影而危处兮，
叫秋木而长吟。
客有哀时失职而听者，
泪淋浪以沾襟。
乃缉商缀羽，
潺湲成音。
吾但写声发情于妙指，
殊不知此曲之古今。
幽涧泉，
鸣深林。

A Creek Flows

I stroke the boulder white;
And play my zither light.
The creek gurgling, the fountain is profound;
An expert fixes the strings for clear sound.
A calm heart goes through past and now;
While high above blows a pine sough.

Therein monkeys jump dangerously thru the moon gleam

And alight on rotten trees to scream.

Someone laments the time while the monkeys' cries he hears,

His clothes so wet with his tears.

So I adjust notes DO, RE, MI,

As serene as can be.

Feelings just flow from my dexterous fingers while I play;

I don't know how the melody has evolved till today.

The creek as e'er flows;

A wind thru trees blows.

* zither: a simple form of a stringed instrument, having a flat sounding board and from thirty to forty strings that are played by plucking with a plectrum. Zither, together with chess, calligraphy and painting are four skills that a traditional litterateur is expected to master.
* monkey: any of a group of primates having elongate limbs, hands and feet adapted for grasping, and a highly developed nervous system, including marmosets, baboons, and macaques, but not the anthropoid apes, though monkeys and apes are used alternatively in Chinese.

王昭君二首
Lady Glare, Two Poems

其 一

汉家秦地月，
流影照明妃。
一上玉关道，
天涯去不归。
汉月还从东海出，
明妃西嫁无来日。
燕支长寒雪作花，
蛾眉憔悴没胡沙。
生乏黄金枉图画，
死留青冢使人嗟。

No. 1

O'er the capital the moon fair
Sheds flowing light to Lady Glare.
Since she went out of Jade Gate Pass,
She has never come back, alas.
The moon rises as ever from East Shore;
Lady Glare married west is seen no more.
In the Rouge Mountains so cold snowflakes fly;
Lady Glare fades on Huns' sand, sigh on sigh.
Not having bribed, she was painted awry;
Today, by her desolate tomb we sigh.

* the moon: the celestial body that revolves around the earth from west to east as a satellite, which appears at night and gives off shining silvery light, an image of purity and solitude, and a good companion with one who is lonely and alone.
* Lady Glare: Lady Glare (cir. 52 B.C.- cir. A.D. 8), Chaochün Wang if transliterated, a lady in the seraglio of the emperor of the Han dynasty, one of the Four Belles in China. A maid of honour in the beginning, she was selected in 33 B.C. to marry the Hun chieftain who had proposed a royal marriage to consolidate mutual peace between two parties. She was one of the earliest victims of the political marriages, called Peace by Marriage, which the ruling house of China was compelled to make from time to time with the chieftains of the barbarian tribes in order to avoid their savage incursions into China, the Middle Kingdom.
* Jade Gate Pass: an important military fort and passage on the Silk Road, built in the Han dynasty. It was named because of the jade business between Han and the western regions.
* the Rouge Mountains: also known as the Rhubarb Mountains in modern times, so named because of the rhubarb growing there, and sometimes called Mt. Green Pines because of green pines there. It is a range of mountains in today's Ope-arms (Changyeh), Kansu Province, lush with pines and cypresses and various kinds of plants and grass such as rhubarb.
* Hun: one of barbaric nomadic Asian peoples who frequently invaded China, a general term referring to all northern or western aliens.

其 二

昭君拂玉鞍，
上马啼红颊。
今日汉宫人，
明朝胡地妾。

No. 2

She strokes the saddle, Lady Glare;
On the horse she cries in despair.
Now in Han Harem she blooms fair;
Morrow, she'll be a Hun wife there.

* Lady Glare (cir. 52 B.C.- cir. A.D. 8), one of the four most beautiful ladies in Chinese history. She was married to Uhaanyehe, the Hun chieftain in 33 B.C. as the latter had proposed royal marriage to Han as a means of armistice.
* Han Harem: In the harem in the age of Emperor Martial (156 B.C.- 87 B.C.) or Emperor Vital (74 B.C.- 33 B.C.), there were 3,000 concubines in a hierarchical structure of fourteen ranks.
* Hun: one of barbaric nomadic Asian peoples who frequently invaded China, a general term referring to all northern or western invaders.

中山孺子妾歌

中山孺子妾，
特以色见珍。
虽然不如延年妹，
亦是当时绝世人。
桃李出深井，
花艳惊上春。
一贵复一贱，
关天岂由身。
芙蓉老秋霜，
团扇羞网尘。
戚姬髡发入春市，
万古共悲辛。

King of Hilltown's Concubine

The king of Hilltown's concubine
Was favored because of her shine.
Although unlike Yannian's sister in prime,
She was the most beautiful of all time.
Peaches and plums in a deep court,
The most dazzling blooms of the sort.
Low or high, who can it decide?
It is for Heaven to preside.
The hibiscus touched with hoarfrost,
The round fan is now in dust lost.
Lady Ch'i, so shorn, so maimed, what a shame,

All deserted ones will end up the same.

* Hilltown: the Kingdom of Hilltown(Chungshan)(414 B.C.- 296 B.C.) established by a Hun group called White Plume, so named because there was a mountain in the capital.
* concubine: a cohabitant or secondary wife. China was a polygamous society from prehistoric years till the first half of the twentieth century. An ordinary man could have three wives and four concubines and a concubine could be bartered or sold or given as a gift in ancient China. An emperor might have thousands of concubines, for example, Emperor Deepsire had 40,000.
* Jade Pass: built in the Han dynasty, an important military fort and passage on the Silk Road. It was so named because of the jade business between Han and the western regions.
* Yannian: a musician of Western Han, whose sister was a shining beauty, a consort of Emperor Martial of Han.
* plums and peaches: a metonymy for plants in general; a metaphor for disciples or students, and sometimes symbolizing a flashy life.
* the hibiscus: a metaphor for Lady Ch'i, meaning she was once as beautiful as a hibiscus flower in full bloom.
* Lady Ch'i: a favoured concubine of Pang Liu, the founding emperor of Han. After the emperor's death, the queen became queen mother. The evil empress threw Lady Ch'i into captivity, having her hair cut and her neck bundled with an iron ring, and ordered her to husk rice. At last, Lady Ch'i was dismembered, eyes gouged out, ears stuffed with copper, tongue cut off, throat silenced with medicine, so she was made what is called "human swine", and was thrown into a lavatory to die in pain.

荆 州 歌

白帝城边足风波，
瞿塘五月谁敢过。
荆州麦熟茧成蛾，
缫丝忆君头绪多。
拨谷飞鸣奈妾何。

A Song of Chaste

By Whitegod, in the River giant waves rise;
In the fifth moon, Big Pond Gorge who dare pass?
In Chaste, wheat ripe, cocoons become butterflies;
Reeling off silk, I miss you, asking whys;
The cuckoos coo:"What can I do, alas?"

* Whitegod: an ancient city built by Shu Lordson (?–A.D. 36) in the Western Han dynasty, located near present-day Double Gain (Ch'ungch'ing). It is famous in history as the place where Pei Liu, the Emperor of Shu, died in the Three Kingdoms Period (220 A.D.–280 A.D.).
* Big Pond Gorge: one of the three most important gorges of the Long River.
* Chaste: Chaston or Chaste Town, a geographical region including areas of present-day Hupei and Hunan.
* silk: the fine, soft, shiny fiber produced by silk worms to form their cocoons, and the thread or fabric made from this fibre is used as material for clothing.
* cuckoo: any of a family of birds with a long, slender body, grayish-brown on top and white below, a symbol of sadness in Chinese culture. It is said that during the Shang dynasty, Cuckoo (Yü Tu), a caring king of Shu, abdicated the throne due to a flood and lived in reclusion. After his death, he, the human Cuckoo, turned into a bird cuckoo, wailing day and night, shedding tears and blood.

设辟邪伎鼓吹雉子斑曲辞

辟邪伎作鼓吹惊，
雉子斑之奏曲成，
喔咿振迅欲飞鸣。
扇锦翼，
雄风生，
双雌同饮啄，
趫悍谁能争。
乍向草中耿介死，
不求黄金笼下生。
天地至广大，
何惜遂物情。
卷善让天子，
务光亦逃名。
所贵旷士怀，
朗然合太清。

Exorcising Priests Play Pheasants Bright

The exorcising priests blow a flute song;
Pheasants Bright has been made to frighten the throng;
The chicks flutter their wings, cooing along.
Fanning their plumes hued,
Fanning as if wooed,
Two female pheasants pecking food;
Compete with the male one who could?
They would die upright in grass, their life stage

Rather than seek life in a golden cage.
How vast expand Heaven and earth!
Why chase a world without your worth?
Good Roll declined the demised throne;
Light Seeker fled, not to be known.
How noble they were, how well done!
Happily, they merged with the One.

* *Pheasants Bright*: an ancient song of a pheasant's love for her chicks and the pains of their parting.
* pheasant: a long-tailed gallinaceous bird noted for the gorgeous plumage of the male.
* Good Roll: a hermit in Hibiscus' times. Hibiscus intended to abdicate his throne to Good Roll, but he declined and lived in seclusion.
* Light Seeker: Wukuang if transliterated, a hermit in Hotspring's times, who escaped the throne given by Hotspring by drowning himself. Chinese hermits would always flee from world power, as is told in *Sir Lush*, "Mound would demise the throne to Freedom, who fled; Hot Spring would offer his state to Light Seeker, who burst into anger."
* the One: a philosophical concept of Wordism, the beginning of all things, as is defined in *Sir Lush*, "In the beginning was the None, having nothing, having no name. Then there arose the One, and nothing was formed yet." And in Laocius's *The Word and the World*: "The sky has gotten the One, hence blue and clear; the earth has gotten the One, hence staid and still."

相 逢 行

相逢红尘内，
高挥黄金鞭。
万户垂杨里，
君家阿那边。

An Encounter

Through hustle and bustle we meet;
Whip in hand, we each other greet.
All households lurch in willow trees;
Where is yours, wooing a brisk breeze?

古 有 所 思

我思仙人，
乃在碧海之东隅。
海寒多天风，
白波连山倒蓬壶。
长鲸喷涌不可涉，
抚心茫茫泪如珠。
西来青鸟东飞去，
愿寄一书谢麻姑。

Missing Her

My lady, lady fair,
Is east of the blue sea, is over there;
It's so windy and so cold;
White waves like mountains Fairyland enfold.
I can't go there, the giant whale huge waves hurls;
Heart-stricken and blank, my tears drip like pearls.
May the blue bird from west fly to the east,
To send Hemp Maid my word, hence we're appeased.

* Fairyland: P'englai Isles beyond East Sea, a fairyland supported by giant turtles underneath and enclosed by a dark sea according to legend.
* pearl: a lustrous, calcareous concretion deposited in layers around a central nucleus in the shells of various mollusks, and largely used as a gem.
* whale: a cetaceous mammal of fish-like form, as distinguished from dolphins and porpoises. It is a symbol of great ambition, fortitude and uniqueness, and sometimes of an impending threat.

* the blue bird: the messenger bird of Queen Mother's on Mt. Queen in the West.
* Hemp Maid: also called Lady Immortal or Void-quiet True, a Wordist goddess worshipped by Chinese folks. As is said, when a nineteen-year-old blooming girl, she had seen East Sea dried for three time. So when a girl's birthday is celebrated, a Hemp Maid figure is given to the girl for her health and longevity.

久 别 离

别来几春未还家,
玉窗五见樱桃花。
况有锦字书,
开缄使人嗟。
至此肠断彼心绝,
云鬟绿鬓罢梳结,
愁如回飚乱白雪。
去年寄书报阳台,
今年寄书重相摧。
东风兮东风,
为我吹行云使西来。
待来竟不来,
落花寂寂委青苔。

Apart for Long

It's a few years since I bade him good-bye;
Five times I've seen cherries by the sill die.
His letters betimes may come by;
Opening them, I can but sigh.
I bleed, but my sadness he does not care;
Listless, I don't take pains to comb my hair;
Worry like flurry, snow is whirled to the air.
Last year I sent a letter to Sun Mound;
This year I sent a letter, in tears drowned.
East wind, o east wind, I do pray,

Can you blow him like a cloud to me at all?

I wait and wait in vain, o nay,

To the green moss the lonely blossoms fall.

* Sun Mound: where Goddess of Mt. Witch stays, implying a place where lovers date for romance. In the preface to High T'ang, Jade Sung mentioned his trip with King Hsiang of Ch'u to High T'ang. The king dreamed of a woman and had sex with her. When leaving, the woman told him that she was a nymph living at Sun Mound on the south side of Mt. Witch.
* moss: a tiny, delicate green bryophytic plant growing on damp decaying wood, wet ground, humid rocks or trees, producing capsules which open by an operculum and contain spores. Under a poet's writing brush, it may arouse a poetic feeling or imagination.

白头吟二首
Ode to Gray Hair, Two Poems

其 一

锦水东北流，
波荡双鸳鸯。
雄巢汉宫树，
雌弄秦草芳。
宁同万死碎绮翼，
不忍云间两分张。
此时阿娇正娇妒，
独坐长门愁日暮。
但愿君恩顾妾深，
岂惜黄金买词赋。
相如作赋得黄金，
丈夫好新多异心。
一朝将聘茂陵女，
文君因赠白头吟。
东流不作西归水，
落花辞条归故林。
兔丝固无情，
随风任颠倒。
谁使女萝枝，
而来强萦抱。
两草犹一心，
人心不如草。
莫卷龙须席，
从他生网丝。

且留琥珀枕，
或有梦来时。
覆水再收岂满杯，
弃妾已去难重回。
古时得意不相负，
只今惟见青陵台。

No. 1

The Silk River there northeast flows;
Two mandarin ducks play waves blue.
The male builds a nest, Han's court close;
The wife on Ch'in's meadow does coo.
They'd die together, broken wing and heart
Rather than, astray in clouds, fly apart.
In Longgate Palace, Petite's envied now;
Alone, sitting there, she has a sad brow.
If His Majesty's eyes looked into hers,
She would spend plenty of gold on a verse.
Having sold a verse, Ssuma gained much gold;
One's fond of the new and tired of the old!
From Lushridge, he would marry a girl fair,
So Wenchün composed him *Ode to Gray Hair*.
The water flowing west will not east flow;
The petals dropped from twigs will not back go.
Dodder, senseless fodder,
Is blown by wind to totter.
To trailers it does cling,
What an intertwined thing.
Dodder and trailer combine;
Human hearts don't entwine.

Don't roll the dragon spread,

Strewn with all spider's thread.

Keep that amber pillow,

Free your dream of sorrow.

How can the water spilled refill the cup?

How can a wife deserted be cheered up?

Those whose love has remained fast and profound

Are but the Hans who died on Greenridge Mound.

* the Silk River: the river flowing through Silkton, that is, Ch'engtu, the capital of today's Ssuch'uan Province.
* mandarin ducks: web-footed, short-legged, broad-billed water birds that always appear in loving pairs; once one of a couple is caught, the other will die for having lost its mate. It is an entrenched metaphor for couples in Chinese culture.
* Ch'in: the Ch'in State or the State of Ch'in (905 B.C.- 206 B.C.), one of the most powerful vassal states in the Chough dynasty, which developed into the first unified regime of China, i.e. the Ch'in Empire.
* Petite: Empress Ch'en of Han. She moved to Longgate Palace after being deposed. Since then, Longgate Palace has become a symbol of an estranged queen. Being disgraced in Longgate Palace, Petite spent a thousand pieces of gold asking Hsiangju Ssuma for a verse. With the verse, Petite once more won Emperor Martial's favor.
* Hsiangju Ssuma: a famous litterateur and poet living between 179 B.C. and 118 B.C., Wenchün's husband. His *Sir Nothing* is a masterpiece, a literary genre between verse and prose, which can be termed as euph (a coinage based on euphuism and euphemism); it has exerted great influence upon later generations of scholars.
* Lushridge: Lush Township; one of Five Mausoleums of Western Han, the tomb of Emperor Martial of Han, the largest of all Han mausoleums, located in Lush Township, hence the name.
* Wenchün: a brilliant woman poet in Western Han. Hsiangju Ssuma and Wenchün were an affectionate couple. However, Ssuma wanted to have a concubine as his career was getting better in the capital. So Wenchün wrote him *Ode to Gray Hair* to remind him of their love. Being touched by the firmness of Wenchün's thought, Ssuma felt ashamed and gave up the idea of having a concubine.
* spider: a wingless arachnid having an unsegmented abdomen and capable of spinning silk in the construction of webs for the capture of prey such as flies and insects, usually

regarded as a mascot in China, a symbol of good luck or good news to come, sometimes also bespeaking desolation, especially in a deserted room.

* Greenridge Mound: In the Warring States period, King of Sung was fond of P'ing Han's wife. In order to have the lady, the king sent Han to build Greenridge Mound, and the couple could only commit suicide. Hearing this, the king was furious and gave an order that the couple not be buried together. Later on, it was said that two trees grew from their tomb, with their branches and roots entwined. And a pair of mandarin ducks perched on the tree, crying all day long.

其 二

锦水东流碧，
波荡双鸳鸯。
雄巢汉宫树，
雌弄秦草芳。
相如去蜀谒武帝，
赤车驷马生辉光。
一朝再览大人作，
万乘忽欲凌云翔。
闻道阿娇失恩宠，
千金买赋要君王。
相如不忆贫贱日，
官高金多聘私室。
茂陵姝子皆见求，
文君欢爱从此毕。
泪如双泉水，
行堕紫罗襟。
五起鸡三唱，
清晨白头吟。
长吁不整绿云鬓，
仰诉青天哀怨深。
城崩杞梁妻，
谁道土无心。
东流不作西归水，
落花辞枝羞故林。
头上玉燕钗，
是妾嫁时物，
赠君表相思，
罗袖幸时拂。

莫卷龙须席，
从他生网丝，
且留琥珀枕，
或有梦来时。
鹧鹋裘在锦屏上，
自君一挂无由披。
妾有秦楼镜，
照心胜照井。
愿持照新人，
双对可怜影。
覆水却收不满杯，
相如还谢文君回。
古时得意不相负，
只今惟见青陵台。

No. 2

The Silk River there northeast flows;
Two mandarin ducks play waves blue.
The male builds a nest, Han's court close;
The wife on Ch'in's meadow does coo.
Ssuma left Shu to worship Lord Martial, lo;
The four-steed drawn red cart he won did glow.
Reading Ssuma's *Great*, He was struck with awe;
He would take flight and up to the sky soar.
As is said, once Petite lost his favor;
So she bought a verse to win him over.
Ssuma forgot the love of his brilliant wife
And would live with concubines a new life.
All beauties in Lushridge would him entrance;
Hence tired of Wenchün he lost all romance.

Like from two wells her tears dripped down,
And in two lines stained her purple silk gown.
Roosters crowed three times before dawn;
She finished *Gray Hair* on the morn.
She released long long sighs, with unkempt hair;
Complaining much to Heaven in despair.
Ch'iliang's wife cried, so fell the wall;
Who says bricks have no heart at all?
The water flowing west will not east flow;
The petals dropped from twigs will not back go.
In hair the jade sparrow hairpin
Is the dowry that I brought in.
It's for you, a token to keep,
Which you should with a sleeve oft sweep.
Don't roll the dragon spread,
Strewn with all spider's thread.
Keep that amber pillow;
Free your dream of sorrow.
My fur coat's hung on the embroidered screen;
Since you went away, useless it has been.
I've a mirror from Tower of Ch'in
To reflect your heart out and in.
I would keep it for someone new,
To give his shadow a bright hue.
The water spilled cannot refill the cup;
Wenchün, the ignored wife, cannot cheer up!
Those whose love has remained fast and profound
Are but the Hans who died on Greenridge Mound.

* the Silk River: a river cutting across Silkton, the political and cultural center of Shu.
* mandarin ducks: duck-like love birds that always appear in pairs, a metaphor for

couples in Chinese culture.
* Lord Martial: Emperor Martial of Han, one of the greatest emperors in Chinese history.
* The four-steed drawn red cart: designated for officials in the Han dynasty.
* *Great*: an ode composed by Ssuma to please Lord Martial.
* concubine: a cohabitant or secondary wife. China was a polygamous society from prehistoric years till the first half of the twentieth century.
* Lushridge: Lush Township; one of Five Mausoleums of Western Han, the tomb of Emperor Martial of Han, the largest of all Han mausoleums, located in Lush Township, hence the name.
* Ch'iliang: a senior official of the State of Ch'u, who died in defence against Ch'i. His wife wailed so bitterly that the walls of the city broke down for her loss.
* a mirror from Tower of Ch'in: As said, there was a mirror in Ch'in's palace. If one stood in front of it with his hand covering his heart, it could reflect the inside organs and show if there was any illness; if a woman was disloyal, then it would be reflected on the mirror as well.
* Greenridge Mound: a height built by King Health of Sung in 290 B.C. There was an imperial palace built upon it and a park behind it.

采 莲 曲

若耶溪傍采莲女,
笑隔荷花共人语。
日照新妆水底明,
风飘香袂空中举。
岸上谁家游冶郎,
三三五五映垂杨。
紫骝嘶入落花去,
见此踟蹰空断肠。

Lotus Picking

Lotus picking girls in the Joyeh Stream
With lotus blooms between, laugh, talk and beam.
Their new clothes e'en cause the water to glare;
Their sleeves blown with fragrance wave in the air.
Who are those lads who loaf around and play?
Three or five of them sway while willows sway.
The brown horse chasing blown flowers loudly neigh;
At this, young dudes may wonder in dismay.

* lotus: any of various waterlilies, especially the white or pink Asian lotus, used as a religious symbol in Hinduism and Buddhism. The lotus is a common image in Chinese literature, as two lines of a lyric by Hsiu Ouyang (1007 – 1072) read: "A thunder brings rain to the wood and pool, / The rain hushes the lotus, drips cool."
* the Joyeh Stream: a stream in the south of present-day Shaohsing, flowing into Lake Mirror. It's said that West Maid did her laundry here.
* willow: any of a large genus (*Salix*) of shrubs and trees related to the poplars, having

generally smooth branches, and often long, slender, pliant, and sometimes pendent branchlets, a symbol of farewell or nostalgia in Chinese culture. The best image is in *Vetch We Pick*, a verse in *The Book of Songs*, which is like this: When we left long ago, / The willows waved adieu. / Now back to our home town, / We meet snow falling down.

临江王节士歌

洞庭白波木叶稀，
燕鸿始入吴云飞。
吴云寒，
燕鸿苦。
风号沙宿潇湘浦，
节士悲秋泪如雨。
白日当天心，
照之可以事明主。
壮士愤，
雄风生。
安得倚天剑，
跨海斩长鲸。

The Song of Wang, the Worthy, from Riverside

At Lake Cavehall trees whirl leaves to waves white;
Wild geese start to southern Wu Kingdom flight.
Wu's clouds float so chill,
The wild geese cry shrill.
The geese perch on the Hsiang Shoal while wind sighs;
Wang, the worthy, to the sad autumn cries.
High in the blue sky is the sun;
To the sagacious lord your heart shines on.
The gallant man growls;
The whirling wind howls.

Where to get a Sky Sword and sail
To surf the sea and kill the whale?

* Lake Cavehall: a lake in present-day Hunan Province, with an area of 3,879.2 square kilometers and 803.2 kilometers in circumference.
* Wu Kingdom: Kingdom of Wu or East Wu, one of the three kingdoms in the Three Kingdoms period, established by Ch'üan Sun.
* wild goose: an undomesticated goose that is caring and responsible, taken as a symbol of benevolence, righteousness, good manner, wisdom, and faith in Chinese culture.
* Sky Sword: a long sword, alluding to a verse, which reads like this: With a long sword, he leans against the sky.

司马将军歌

狂风吹古月，
窃弄章华台。
北落明星动光彩，
南征猛将如云雷。
手中电曳倚天剑，
直斩长鲸海水开。
我见楼船壮心目，
颇似龙骧下三蜀。
扬兵习战张虎旗，
江中白浪如银屋。
身后玉帐临河魁，
紫髯若戟冠崔嵬。
细柳开营揖天子，
始知霸上为婴孩。
羌笛横吹阿亸回，
向月楼中吹落梅。
将军自起舞长剑，
壮士呼声动九垓。
功成献凯见明主，
丹青画像麒麟台。

The Song of General Ssuma

A mad wind whirls to the Hun moon
While stealing across Flora Mound.
The star in the northern sky twinkles bright.

The troops for the southern land quake the ground.
The sky swords in hand flash like lightning on,
Cutting the long whale that splashes the blue.
The tower ships awaken all eyes and hearts,
Like Rui Wang's dragon warships up to Shu.
The manoeuvre flags flutter up and down;
The blue waves with white foams rush, forward bound.
The commander in the tent eyes the moon,
His whiskers like halberds on a high mound.
Like Chou at Willow Tent bowing to Lord,
He comes to know the soldiers like babes cower.
The Ch'iang flute tune *O Chubby* is now played,
And *Plums Falling* comes down from Moon Tower.
The general stands up for a sword play,
His shouts shaking the sky, quaking the ground.
When he has won the war and seen the crown,
His portrait would be on Unicorn Mound.

* Flora Mound: built in the Spring and Autumn period, referring to the land conquered by Huns.
* the star in the northern sky: In Chinese astrology, as is believed, it is time to send troops when the star in the northern sky twinkles bright.
* Rui Wang: In the Chin dynasty, Rui Wang built a giant warship that could hold 2,000 troops to attack Shu.
* Chou at Willow Tent: General Yafu Chou quartered his troops at Willow Tent. Under his command, the troops ran in a rigorous order, and even Emperor Civil had to follow the rules in the tent when he came to visit.
* Ch'iang: a nationality having a long history, and Ch'iangs today mainly live in modern-day Ssuch'uan.
* *O Chubby*: a song from West China.
* *Plums Falling*: an old flute tune.
* Unicorn Mound: The unicorn is an auspicious creature in Chinese tradition, which is

occasionally used to indicate a man of prominent talent and nobility. Unicorn Mound was built in the Han dynasty to memorize those who had made great contributions to the empire.

君 道 曲

大君若天覆，
广运无不至。
轩后爪牙常先太山稽，
如心之使臂。
小白鸿翼于夷吾，
刘葛鱼水本无二。
土扶可成墙，
积德为厚地。

Lord's Worth

Behold, His Majesty's great worth
Does cover all, Heaven and earth.
Lord Yellow's man used to govern Mt. Arch,
Like a heart commanding an arm.
Prince White regarded Kuanchung as his hand;
Pei Liu and Ch'uke side by side did stand.
Earth piled up can be a high wall;
Worth gathered can spread over all.

* Heaven: the space surrounding or seeming to overarch the earth, in which the sun, the moon, and stars appear, popularly the abode of God, his angels and the blessed, and in most cases suggesting supernatural power or sometimes signifying a monarch.
* Lord Yellow: alias Cartshaft, the first of the five heavenly gods in myth and the earliest ancestor of Chinese people.
* Mt. Arch: one of the Five Mountains in China, located in Shantung Province, along with Mt. Ever in Shanhsi, Mt. Scale in Hunan, Mt. Flora in Sha'anhsi, and Mt. Tower

in Honan. Mt. Arch is the most sacred of the five, because 72 sovereigns in prehistoric China made sacrifices to the god of the mountain and 12 emperors made sacrifices from the Ch'in dynasty to the Ch'ing dynasty, clearly recorded in history books.
* Prince White: Lord Pillar of Ch'i, with Kuanchung as his minister. They introduced reforms and implemented the policies to unite military with policy, army with people, and institute official prostitution. Gradually Ch'i grew stronger and became the most powerful state of Five Hegemons in the Spring and Autumn period.
* Kuanchung: a descendant of King Solemn of Chough, a famous economist, philosopher, politician, and militarist, praised as Precedent of Legalism, Teacher of Saints, the First Premier of China, and the Protector of Chinese Civilization.
* Pei Liu: a descendant of the royal family of Han (A.D. 161 – A.D. 223), the founding lord of Shu in the Three Kingdoms period.
* Ch'uke: Liang Ch'uke (A.D. 181 – A.D. 234), premier of the Kingdom of Shu, a prominent statesman, military strategist, prose writer, and inventor in Chinese history.

结 袜 子

燕南壮士吴门豪，
筑中置铅鱼隐刀。
感君恩重许君命，
太山一掷轻鸿毛。

Knitting Socks

The bold was from Yan and the brave from Wu,
Lead cast in the ball, fish hiding the knife.
To pay their lords a debt of gratitude,
All they could throw away, even their life.

* the bold from Yan: referring to the knight from Yan by the name of Chienli Kao, a patriot who was good at playing the 13-stringed zither. After Ch'in subjugated the seven states, Emperor First asked Kao to play music, but gouged out his eyes because of his failed assassination. As was recorded, Kao hid lead in his instrument and cast it at the emperor. Being cautious, the emperor shunned the hit.
* the brave from Wu: referring to Chuan Chu. He took his lord's order to assassinate King of Wu. He hid his knife in a fish and killed the king while he was serving him fish.

结客少年场行

紫燕黄金瞳,
啾啾摇绿骏。
平明相驰逐,
结客洛门东。
少年学剑术,
凌轹白猿公。
珠袍曳锦带,
匕首插吴鸿。
由来万夫勇,
挟此生雄风。
托交从剧孟,
买醉入新丰。
笑尽一杯酒,
杀人都市中。
羞道易水寒,
从令日贯虹。
燕丹事不立,
虚没秦帝宫。
舞阳死灰人,
安可与成功?

The Gallants Gather at East Gate

The horse Purple Swallow's gold eyes
Shine while waving its mane to neigh.
The gallants gallop at daybreak

And gather at East Gate to play.
The boys are good at playing swords;
Even White Ape would feel abased.
In a pearled gown with a silk belt,
Wearing a dagger on the waist.
One may brave ten thousand troops strong
And he's now armed with spirits true.
They make friends like heroic Chümeng
Cup by cup drinking Newrich brew.
Having drunk some wine with a laugh,
They dare kill on the thoroughfare.
To learn from Chingk'e they're not fain;
With his valor they won't compare.
Because he failed in his mission
And in Ch'in's palace lost his life.
With a coward such as Wuyang,
How can one succeed in a strife?

* Purple Swallow: name of a fine horse in ancient China and a metonymy for fine horses.
* White Ape: As is said, in the State of Yüeh, there was a girl good at swordplay. She once met an old man who called himself White Ape and asked for a competition in swordplay. As they finished the fight, the old man turned into an ape and went away.
* Chümeng: a gallant in the Fore-Ch'in period, who often saved people from danger.
* Newrich: located in the northeast of Lintung, celebrated for fine wine.
* Chingk'e: an assassin from Yan, who attempted to kill Emperor First of Ch'in but failed.
* Ch'in: the Ch'in State or the State of Ch'in (905 B.C.- 206 B.C.), one of the most powerful vassal states in the Chough dynasty, which developed into the first unified regime of China, i.e. the Ch'in Empire.
* Wuyang: Wuyang Ch'in, who went on the mission of assassination with Chingk'e, but looked extremely frightened, which made Chingk'e more cautious.

长干行二首
Long Vale Lane, Two Poems

其 一

妾发初覆额,
折花门前剧。
郎骑竹马来,
绕床弄青梅。
同居长干里,
两小无嫌猜。
十四为君妇,
羞颜未尝开。
低头向暗壁,
千唤不一回。
十五始展眉,
愿同尘与灰。
常存抱柱信,
岂上望夫台。
十六君远行,
瞿塘滟滪堆。
五月不可触,
猿声天上哀。
门前迟行迹,
一一生绿苔。
苔深不能扫,
落叶秋风早。
八月蝴蝶黄,
双飞西园草。

感此伤妾心，
坐愁红颜老。
早晚下三巴，
预将书报家。
相迎不道远，
直至长风沙。

No. 1

New fringe covering my forehead,
I plucked a flower for a child's play.
You galloped a bamboo horse here
Around the well with a plum spray.
We lived in the same Long Vale Lane,
Both naive, free of craft and guile.
At fourteen I became your wife,
Too abashed to put on a smile.
I lowered my head to the corner,
Not turning back for all your call.
At fifteen, I could raise my brows
And would live with you, sharing all.
I oft believed in pillar faith,
And Mt. O-hubby would climb ne'er.
At sixteen, I saw you off then
To sail for Big Pond Boulder there!
Fifth moon, the reef should be kept off;
The monkeys scream toward the sky.
The trace you left on the doorway
Has been tinged with moss by and by.
The moss is too deep to sweep off,
And leaves fall with a sough, alas.

Eighth moon, butterflies turn yellow;
Two fly to West Park, o'er the grass.
At this I cannot but feel sad,
Sitting there, old, older I grow.
Whene'er you come back home to Pa,
Send me a letter, let me know.
The long long way I can well stand;
I will meet you at Long Wind Sand.

* Long Vale Lane: a settlement of boatmen, located in Gold Hill, present-day Nanking. Most works with the title of *Long Vale Lane* are about the affection of ferry girls.
* pillar faith: devout faith or love. According to *Sir Lush*, "Rear Born had a date with a girl under a bridge but the girl did not come on time. When water rose, he did not leave, and was drowned, hugging a pier." This kind of faith or love has been eulogized as pier faith or pillar faith.
* Mt. O-hubby: also called Mt. O-Come-hubby. More than one hill in China has taken this name because of a similar tradition of a wife who climbed the height to watch for the return of her husband.
* Big Pond: a gorge with rapids and in steep hills, located in modern-day Ssuch'uan Province.
* Big Pond Boulder: also called Bird Nest Boulder and called Waver Boulder in ancient times, located in the mouth of Big Pond Gorge under the city of Whitegod, about 30 meters long, 20 meters wide and 40 meters tall, removed as a blockade in 1958.
* moss: a tiny, delicate bryophytic plant growing on damp decaying wood, wet ground, humid rocks or trees, producing capsules which open by an operculum and contain spores. Under a poet's writing brush, it may stir up a poetic feeling or imagination.
* Pa: an ancient state referring to an area covering present-day Double Gain (Ch'ungch'ing), the east of Ssuch'uan, the west of Hupei, and north of Kuichow and the northwest of Hunan.
* Long Wind Sand: a shoal in the Long River, located in present-day Anch'ing, Anhui Province.

其 二

忆妾深闺里,
烟尘不曾识。
嫁与长干人,
沙头候风色。
五月南风兴,
思君下巴陵。
八月西风起,
想君发扬子。
去来悲如何,
见少别离多。
湘潭几日到,
妾梦越风波。
昨夜狂风度,
吹折江头树。
淼淼暗无边,
行人在何处。
好乘浮云骢,
佳期兰渚东。
鸳鸯绿浦上,
翡翠锦屏中。
自怜十五馀,
颜色桃李红。
那作商人妇,
愁水复愁风。

No. 2

When I was in my boudoir then,

I knew not any dust or stain.
When I got married to this man,
On the bank I met wind and rain.
In the fifth moon, south wind arose;
To the Pa Hills you would depart.
In the eighth moon, west wind blew up,
From the Yangtze, you were to start.
Leaving or coming, glad or sad,
Union less and disunion more.
When will you arrive at Hsiangt'an?
In my dream, wind and waves did roar.
Last night a high wind raged like mad;
It blew to the bank and broke a tree.
The waves expand afar, so dark;
Where are you and where can you be?
To meet you east of Orchid Shoal,
A cloudy piebald I would ride.
Kingfishers sewn on the silk green,
Mandarin ducks playing riverside.
How loving, fifteen years old,
Like peaches and plums I did burst.
When I became a merchant's wife,
With ill water and wind I was cursed.

* the Pa Hills: what is today's Hillshine (Yüehyang), located south of Mt. Mufu and near Lake Cavehall, first built in 505 B.C. in present-day Yüehyang, Hunan Province.
* the Yangtze: the Yangtze River, a part of the Long River, the part from today's Nanking to Shanghai.
* Hsiangt'an: what is today's Hsiangt'an, Hunan Province.
* Orchid Shoal: name of a shoal, in today's Shaohsing, Chechiang Province.
* silk: the fine, soft, shiny fiber produced by silk worms to form their cocoons, and the

thread or fabric made from this fibre is used as material for clothing.
* mandarin ducks: duck-like love birds that always appear in pairs, a metaphor for couples in Chinese culture.
* peaches and plums: a metonymy for plants in general; a metaphor for disciples or students, and sometimes symbolizing a flashy life.

古朗月行

小时不识月，
呼作白玉盘。
又疑瑶台镜，
飞在青云端。
仙人垂两足，
桂树何团团。
白兔捣药成，
问言与谁餐？
蟾蜍蚀圆影，
大明夜已残。
羿昔落九乌，
天人清且安。
阴精此沦惑，
去去不足观。
忧来其如何？
凄怆摧心肝。

The Bright Moon

When small I did not know the moon;
I called it a plate of white jade.
And a fay's mirror it might be
That flew to the clouds and there stayed.
An immortal spread its legs there,
And a laurel tree looked so fine.
White Hare pestled herb medicine;

"May I ask who will come to dine?"
Then a toad came to eat the moon;
Which waned bit by bit, day by day.
Once King Archer shot off nine suns
So that Heaven and men could stay.
Shade Spirit stole the shine of moon
So Luna's not good to look at.
How worried a person can be?
I am saddened and grieved like that.

* the bright moon: In Chinese myths, E'erfair (Ch'ang'o) took elixir of longevity and flew to the moon. On the moon, there are a laurel tree, a three-legged toad and a hare making elixir.
* laurel: laurus nobilis, an evergreen shrub with aromatic, lance-shaped leaves, yellowish flowers, and succulent, cherry-like fruit. In Chinese mythology, there is a colossal laurel tree that is more than 1,500 meters tall on the moon, and it would never fall even though Kang Wu, a banished immortal, has kept cutting it.
* White Hare: also known as Jade Hare that makes elixir on the moon according to legend.
* King Archer: a legendary figure in Chinese myths. In Mound's age, there were ten suns in the sky, making everything hard to survive. To save the people, King Archer shot off nine of them.
* Heaven: the space surrounding or seeming to overarch the earth, in which the sun, the moon, and stars appear, popularly the abode of God, his angels and the blessed, and in most cases suggesting supernatural power or sometimes signifying a monarch.
* Shade Spirit: In Chinese tradition, the moon is the shade of Heaven and earth, and spirit of metal.
* Luna: the moon, which has an important position in Chinese literature, the most frequent image of coolness, loneliness, and hope for a happy reunion.

上 之 回

三十六离宫,
楼台与天通。
阁道步行月,
美人愁烟空。
恩疏宠不及,
桃李伤春风。
淫乐意何极,
金舆向回中。
万乘出黄道,
千旗扬彩虹。
前军细柳北,
后骑甘泉东。
岂问渭川老,
宁邀襄野童。
但慕瑶池宴,
归来乐未穷。

Coming Back

Thirty-six detached palaces
Tower high all the way to the sky.
Thru the corridor walks the moon
And a beauty in mist does sigh.
When having lost favor and grace,
Even peaches feel sad, alack.
When will His fun come to an end

So that His gold cart may come back.
His cart runs on the Ecliptic,
With a thousand flags flowing at least.
The vanguard's north of Thin Willows;
The rear's still at Spring in the east.
Will He ask the old man ashore
Or the shepherd in Hsiang invite?
How I admire a Jade Pool feast
Where I could have so much delight!

* the moon: the planet of the earth, which appears at night and gives off shining silvery light, an image of purity and solitude in Chinese culture.
* the old man ashore: referring to Great Grand, an influential strategist and statesman. Though he was a butcher at his young age, Great Grand remained diligent in hardship, expecting to display his ability for the country one day, but he did not make any achievement before he was 70 years old. He went west at the age of 72, fishing as he waited for King Civil, and finally won his appreciation.
* Thin Willows: the place where General Yafu Chou's troops were stationed. In 158 B.C., the Hun chieftain renounced the policy of peace through royal marriage and waged a war against Han. As Yafu Chou finally won the war, his troops were also called Thin Wallows.
* the shepherd in Hsiang: a boy from whom Lord Yellow quested for enlightenment.
* Jade Pool: a fairy pool on Mt. Queen, by which Mother West holds banquets.

独 不 见

白马谁家子，
黄龙边塞儿。
天山三丈雪，
岂是远行时。
春蕙忽秋草，
莎鸡鸣西池。
风摧寒棕响，
月入霜闺悲。
忆与君别年，
种桃齐蛾眉。
桃今百馀尺，
花落成枯枝。
终然独不见，
流泪空自知。

He's Away

Who's that on a white horse astride?
A lad guarding the border town.
How can one go afar outside,
When does Mt. Heaven vast snow drown?
Cymbidium turns into dry grass;
Crickets by the Western Pool shrill.
A wind blows the cold palm so loud;
Her boudoir's hoary, moonlight chill.
When her husband set out that year,

The peach was as tall as her ear.
It's grown more than thirty feet now;
Its blossoms have dropped to decay.
But he is away, ne'er seen again,
Her tears dripping down, all in vain.

* Mt. Heaven: one of the seven mountain chains in the world, 2,500 kilometers long, 250 to 350 kilometers wide on average.
* cymbidium: commonly known as King of Orchids, native to the cool highlands of China and northern Asia, prized for large stems of fragrant flowers in multitudes of colors which can remain in bloom for up to 3 months.
* cricket: a leaping orthopterous insect, with long antennae and three segments in each tarsus, the male of which makes a chirping sound by friction of forewings, a common image of a quiet night in Chinese literature.
* peach: any of the plant (*Prunus Percica*), bearing a fleshy, juicy, edible drupe, cultivated in many varieties in temperate zones considered sacred in China, often used as a metaphor for a young woman, as a section of a poem in *The Book of Songs* reads: The peach twigs sway, / Ablaze the flower; / Now she's married away, / Befitting her new bower."

白纻辞三首

White Hemp, Three Poems

其 一

扬清歌，发皓齿，
北方佳人东邻子。
且吟白纻停绿水，
长袖拂面为君起。
寒云夜卷霜海空，
胡风吹天飘塞鸿。
玉颜满堂乐未终，
馆娃日落歌吹濛。

No. 1

Her pure song so clear, her crystal teeth glare;
Like the north belle and the east girl so fair.
The white hemp sways by the river, she sings;
Her long sleeve 'cross her face at you she flings.
Cold clouds are hurled over the sea at night;
A northern wind blows the wild geese to flight.
A full hall of girls play, the music on;
A moving song flows thru the setting sun.

* The north belle and the east girl: the former referring to the wife of Yannian Li and the latter a figure in Ssuma's verse, implying beautiful ladies in ancient poems.
* hemp: a tall annual Asian herb (Gannabis sativa) of the mulberry family, with small green flowers and a tough bark, the fibers from which are used for cloth and cordage.
* wild goose: an undomesticated goose that is caring and responsible, taken as a symbol of benevolence, righteousness, good manner, wisdom and faith in Chinese culture.

其 二

月寒江清夜沉沉，
美人一笑千黄金。
垂罗舞縠扬哀音，
郢中白雪且莫吟，
子夜吴歌动君心。
动君心，冀君赏。
愿作天池双鸳鸯，
一朝飞去青云上。

No. 2

The night deep, the moon chill, the river cold,
The belle's smile worth a thousand taels of gold.
Her dancing sleeves wave up an air of woe,
She would not sing Ch'u capital's *White Snow*,
But *Wu Song at Night* wherewith to move you.
At night to move you, to have your love true.
May you be two mandarin ducks to love,
And one day fly to the clouds high above.

* the moon: the celestial body that revolves around the earth from west to east as a satellite, which appears at night and gives off shining silvery light, an image of purity and solitude in Chinese culture.
* Ch'u: the State of Ch'u, a vassal state of Chough, one of the powers in the Warring States period, conquered and annexed by Ch'in in 223 B.C.
* *White Snow*: a song regarded as a highbrow work.
* *Wu Song at Night*: a song for common amusement.
* mandarin ducks: web-footed, short-legged, broad-billed water birds that always appear in loving pairs, a metaphor for couples in Chinese culture.

其 三

吴刀剪彩缝舞衣，
明妆丽服夺春晖。
扬眉转袖若雪飞，
倾城独立世所稀。
激楚结风醉忘归，
高堂月落烛已微，
玉钗挂缨君莫违。

No. 3

Her dance dress tailored with Wu scissors, lo,
So brilliant, so bright, outshines the spring hue.
Raising her brows, she swirls, like flying snow;
In this world such ladies are very few.
She forgets to go back, in pathos drowned,
The moon sinks, candles taper, dim around.
May you stay for the night, her love profound.

* Wu scissors: iron weapons and tools from Wu were the sharpest in ancient China.
* the moon: an important image in Chinese literature or culture as it can give rise to many associations such as solitude and nostalgia on the one hand, and purity, brightness and happy reunions on the other. Philosophically, it is the very germ or source of *Shade*, and the sun is its *Shine* counterpart. The moon is celebrated with mooncakes in China on Mid-autumn Day when the moon is at its full glory.
* candle: a cylinder of tallow, wax, or other solid fat, containing a wick, to give light when burning, first seen in literature in the Eastern Han dynasty. The most famous lines about candles are from a poem by a T'ang poet named Shangyin Li, "Silkworms stop offering silk when they die; / Candles become ash as their tears run dry."

鸣 雁 行

胡雁鸣，
辞燕山，
昨发委羽朝度关。
衔芦枝，
南飞散落天地间，
连行接翼往复还。
客居烟波寄湘吴，
凌霜触雪毛体枯。
畏逢矰缴惊相呼，
闻弦虚坠良可吁。
君更弹射何为乎？

Wild Geese in Flight

The Hun wild geese cry,
Leaving Mt. Yan high.
From Plumes now o'er the dawn-lit pass they fly.
A reed in their bills,
Their downs drifting, drifting twixt earth and sky,
Wing upon wing, along the route they hie.
Between Hsiang and Wu, in mist they abide;
Thru frost and snow they grow weak, feathers dried.
All hunters' shouts or shots will them scare;
Even stray arrows make them fully aware.
Why do we shoot them, why not these birds spare?

* Hun: referring to the northern area where Huns lived.
* wild goose: an undomesticated goose that is caring and responsible, taken as a symbol of benevolence, righteousness, good manner, wisdom and faith in Chinese culture.
* Mt. Yan: one of the most famous mountains in Northern China, rolling from Changchiak'ou to Mountain-sea Pass, 420 kilometers long, 200 kilometers wide at most.
* Plumes: an extreme northern land in myths.
* a reed in their bills: Wild geese often hold a reed in their beak to avoid being entwined by a string tied to an arrow.
* Hsiang and Wu: referring to southern lands.

妾　薄　命

汉帝重阿娇，
贮之黄金屋。
咳唾落九天，
随风生珠玉。
宠极爱还歇，
妒深情却疏。
长门一步地，
不肯暂回车。
雨落不上天，
水覆难再收。
君情与妾意，
各自东西流。
昔日芙蓉花，
今成断根草。
以色事他人，
能得几时好。

Me Alone

Lord Martial loving Petite much
Kept her in a gold house as such.
Her saliva falling like from the sky
Was seen as pearls a wind blew by.
But when their love reached the top,
His favor soon came to a stop.
In Longgate she was kept apart;

To her He would not turn His cart.
Rain fallen down will not go up;
Tea spilled can't be put in a cup.
His romance and her affection
Flow to a different direction.
The lotus flowers of yesterday
Have fallen aground to decay.
Serving with beauty that's skin deep,
Who on earth can good results reap?

* Lord Martial: Lord Martial (156 B.C.- 87 B.C.), the seventh emperor of the Han dynasty, a prominent statesman, strategist and poet, who made the empire prosperous in all aspects.
* Petite: referring to Empress Ch'en of Han. Lord Martial once loved Petite and promised her a gold house when they were young. But Petite lost his love and moved to Long Gate Palace after being deposed.
* pearl: a smooth, lustrous, white or bluish-gray calcareous concretion deposited in layers around a central nucleus in the shells of various mollusks, and largely used as a gem.
* Long Gate: referring to Long Gate Palace, where Petite moved after being deposed. Since then, Long Gate Palace has become a symbol of an estranged queen.
* lotus: any of various waterlilies, especially the white or pink Asian lotus, used as a religious symbol in Hinduism and Buddhism. The lotus is a common image in Chinese literature, as two lines of a lyric by Hsiu Ouyang (A.D. 1007 - A.D. 1072) read: "A thunder brings rain to the wood and pool, / The rain hushes the lotus, drips cool."

幽州胡马客歌

幽州胡马客,
绿眼虎皮冠。
笑拂两只箭,
万人不可干。
弯弓若转月,
白雁落云端。
双双掉鞭行,
游猎向楼兰。
出门不顾后,
报国死何难?
天骄五单于,
狼戾好凶残。
牛马散北海,
割鲜若虎餐。
虽居燕支山,
不道朔雪寒。
妇女马上笑,
颜如赪玉盘。
翻飞射野兽,
花月醉雕鞍。
旄头四光芒,
争战若蜂攒。
白刃洒赤血,
流沙为之丹。
名将古是谁,
疲兵良可叹。
何时天狼灭?

父子得闲安。

The Hun Man on His Horse Astride

The Hun man on his horse astride,
In tiger skin hat, and blue-eyed!
He holds two arrows with a smile,
Ten thousand troops scared off a mile.
He bends his bow up to the moon,
A wild goose falls down all too soon.
With his mates he gallops away
To Lowland for a hunting play.
With no worries they go all out,
To die for their state with no doubt.
The five chieftains beaming with pride
Are given to cruel homicide.
Around North Sea their herds dispersed,
Like tigers for blood they all thirst.
They do not fear hard ice or snow,
Living in the Rouge Mountains though.
Their women on the horses smile;
Beaming red, they can all beguile.
On horseback they shoot birds down;
In moonlight and blooms they may drown.
Their yak-tail flags shine all around;
Their troops swarm on the battleground.
On their sharpened blades blood is spread;
The desert's soaked with gore so red.
Who's the famous general of yore?
His fatigued soldiers we deplore.

When will he go and Dog Star slay
So that all folks can have their day?

* Hun: one of barbaric nomadic Asian peoples who frequently invaded China, a general term referring to all northern or western invaders.
* the moon: the celestial body that revolves around the earth from west to east as a satellite, which appears at night and gives off shining silvery light, an image of purity and solitude in Chinese culture.
* wild goose: an undomesticated goose that is caring and responsible, taken as a symbol of benevolence, righteousness, good manner, wisdom and faith in Chinese culture.
* Lowland: Kroraina, an ancient small city-state in the western regions, specifically in the west of Lop Nor, having an important position on the Silk Road, which was founded in 176 B.C. and mysteriously disappeared in A.D. 630.
* North Sea: what is modern-day Lake Baikal, the deepest lake in the world, today's Siberia, Russia.
* tiger: a large carnivorous feline mammal of Asia, with vertical black wavy stripes on a tawny body and black bars or rings on the limbs and tail, praised as king of all animals.
* the Rouge Mountains: a mountain range once inhabited by Huns, in modern-day Opearms (Changyeh), Kansu Province.
* Dog Star: indicating aggression and invasion in Chinese astrology.